Allan Massie is a novelist, historian and journalist. He was brought up in Aberdeenshire and educated in Glenalmond and at Cambridge, but it was while living in Rome for some years that he developed the interest in Roman history which led to the writing of his series of novels set in the Rome of the emperors: *Augustus, Tiberius, Caesar, Antony* and now *Nero's Heirs*. His other novels include *A Question of Loyalties* and *Shadows of Empire*. He is married and lives in the Scottish Borders.

ALLAN MASSIE
NERO'S
HEIRS

Allan Massie

SCEPTRE

First published in 1999 by Hodder and Stoughton
A division of Hodder Headline
A Sceptre paperback

10 9 8 7 6 5 4 3 2 1

A CIP catalogue record for this title is available from the British Library

ISBN 0 340 71877 3

Typeset by Palimpsest Book Production Limited,
Polmont, Stirlingshire
Printed and bound in Great Britain by
Clays Ltd, St Ives plc

Hodder and Stoughton
A division of Hodder Headline
338 Euston Road
London NW1 3BH

For Alison, as ever.

I

To C. Cornelius Tacitus, Senator:

I confess that I do not know whether I am more honoured or more amazed: that you, the distinguished author of the *Dialogue on Oratory*, and of the ever to be admired Life of your father-in-law, the Imperator C. Julius Agricola, should turn to me and request my help in preparing the materials for the History of our own terrible times, on which you tell me you have audaciously embarked.

What can I say? I cannot deny you, all the less because I am persuaded that your History will be immortal, and this makes me all the more anxious that my name should be, however vestigially, associated with it. And yet I shrink from the task you set me, in part because I am conscious of my own inadequacy, in part because the thought of venturing into the gloomy cave of memory fills me with fear, foreboding, and self-hatred. I, like all our generation, have waded deep in innocent blood. The cries of those dragged to prison and execution still ring in my disturbed and fearful nights. And I do not know if I can summon the fortitude to set down for you what I recall – still less what I was guilty of – in the time of terror.

You know this yourself, being, as I remember, a man of lively and sympathetic imagination – the source which feeds your genius. Yet you ask this of me, and such is my respect for you that, as I say, I cannot deny you, though every fibre of my nervous being cries out to me to do so.

Even the particular reason why you seek my help makes me shudder. You do not state this reason, but I know it is in your mind.

I was indeed the schoolfellow, and for some years the dearest friend,

1

perhaps the only friend, of the tyrant Domitian. I knew, if any did, the innermost thoughts of that dark and secret man. We were brought up together, my own (reputed) father having been killed at the side of his father Vespasian in some scuffle with barbarians in the British campaign. Vespasian himself often spoke warmly of my father, and even let me understand that he owed his life to him. Perhaps he did; why say so otherwise? Then I was with Domitian throughout that terrible year when Rome stumbled and seemed about to be engulfed in civil disaster.

Oh, yes, I know it well. I know too much. I learned, when too young for such knowledge, that the gods take no thought for our happiness, but only for our punishment.

You tell me it is now safe for me to return to Rome, the tyrant being no more. I knew it already. It is not fear that keeps me here, in this distant town on the edge of barbarian lands, far from where the lemon trees bloom. It is rather a species of lassitude. Why should I move? I have made a sort of life for myself. The wine is thin and often sour, but there is no shortage of it. I confess I often go drunk to bed; drunkenness wards off evil dreams. And I have a woman, part-Greek, part-Scythian, who loves me, or says she loves me, and at any rate acts often as if she did. We have children, too, four curly-headed brats. What would the like of them do in Rome? What could Rome do for them? Here they will grow to be farmers or traders, useful creatures.

Tacitus, you who have survived and continued to inhabit the Great World, and engage in public affairs, will no doubt despise me and my way of life. But you have survived by grace of qualities which I lack, perhaps by grace of virtue also (though in our time virtue has too often invited punishment) and, it may be, by a touch of Fortune also. It occurs to me that you are a favourite of the gods, if such a thing is possible. But I have too much with which to reproach myself. I have acquiesced in murder and, for a time, profited by my weakness. I was ambitious, and, to further my ambition, stood by while evil was done.

You ask me to revisit scenes of bloodshed, to re-enter a world of treachery and malice, to confront the stuff of nightmare. You do not know what you ask of me; it is to explore memory to destroy such peace as I now possess.

Nevertheless I shall do as you ask. There will be at least one former friend whom I have served well.

II

You ask me, my dear Cornelius Tacitus, for my first memories of
Domitian. Your request is impossible to satisfy, for this reason: that
I cannot recall any period of my life from which Domitian was
absent.

As you know, his father, the now-glorious-in-memory Emperor
Vespasian, was a man of no particular birth or early renown. He
was born, when the Divine Augustus was still Princeps, at Reiti in
the Sabine Hills, and was brought up by his grandmother who had
a small farm at Cosa. I think his father was a tax-collector employed
in Asia, but I may be mistaken here. Of course, when Domitian, or
indeed his brother Titus, still lived, it would have been unwise to
expatiate on Vespasian's humble origins, though the man himself
never troubled to hide them. Now, since you are writing a truthful
history, it is as well to be clear on the matter: the family was of no
significance.

I can say this because as you know it was not so in my case. Or
rather, as you think you know. My own birth was as distinguished
as could be. My mother belonged to the Claudian *gens*, and so was
connected by cousinship with the imperial family itself. My father
could boast numerous consuls among his Aemilian ancestors. I
belonged by birth to the highest aristocracy of Rome. It seems
amusing to me now, in my present circumstances.

But now, since nothing matters to me any more, I can confess to
you what pride has throughout my life compelled me to conceal:
that M. Aemilius Scaurus, himself son of that Scaurus who held
a consulship under Tiberius, was my father only in law and not

3

in actuality. A peevish effeminate man, whose lust for wealth and office far surpassed his ability, he acquiesced with a contemptible complacency in the seduction of his wife, my noble mother, by Narcissus. Do I need to remind you that he was the freedman who swayed the judgement of the feeble Emperor Claudius, was said, indeed, to have controlled him; he also commanded the detachment of the Praetorian Guard which arrested and put to death the Emperor's third wife Messalina, notorious (as you will recall) for her flagrant immorality.

I have no doubt, my friend, that you, with your stern, if antique, ideas of Republican virtue, both deplore and despise Narcissus and all that he represented. I shall take no issue with you there; beyond remarking that he was evidently a man of some capacity. Now that, in exile, I care nothing for lineage, I can say what I would once have been ashamed to utter: that I find more satisfaction in being in reality the son of the capable, though ruthless and corrupt, Narcissus than of the feeble Scaurus whose name I bear and of whose ancestors I used to boast.

Of course I didn't for years know my true paternity. My mother – a woman of strong character – burst out with it in one of our many quarrels. I have no doubt that she spoke the truth, if only because Narcissus was long dead by then, and rumours of her association with him could have brought her nothing but disgrace. Her admission gave me a weapon, which subsequently I did not scruple to use against her. She was stern, harsh-judging woman. Yet I adored her in youth when her beauty seemed to me to rival that of Venus herself.

You will understand the relevance of my confession to your inquiry, for you must know that it was by the patronage of Narcissus that Vespasian rose from obscurity, obtaining first the command of a legion, then sharing the glory of the conquest of Britain, where he subdued the whole Island of Wight, subsequently being rewarded with triumphal decorations and a consulship. Without Narcissus, Vespasian would, in his middle forties, have been a retired officer of no consequence, subsisting on half-pay, and farming on a con-temptibly small scale. It is indeed not by merit alone that men rise in our degenerate world!

One consequence of my father's patronage was that Vespasian's elder son Titus was brought up in court circles where he became the companion and closest friend of Tiberius Claudius, later known as Britannicus, the son of the Emperor and the dissolute Messalina. Britannicus and Titus were some five or six years older than I was myself, and I was six months older than Domitian. I may say that, though Domitian was designated my playmate, he was as a very small boy, shy, surly, and disinclined for any company, even mine. Titus and Britannicus, in contrast, were dazzling and alluring. Soon however both were to be cast into the shade by Nero, when he succeeded his (murdered?) stepfather as Emperor.

Posterity will, rightly, recall Nero as a monster of depravity, and as an Emperor who disgraced the purple he wore. History will judge him severely. You, my dear Tacitus, will make sure of that. I can't blame you. I don't even wish to blame you. After all, I suffered at the beast's hands myself. Not only did he have my natural father Narcissus put to death, but once when I was a boy of eleven he seized me in the gymnasium, and crying, 'The wolf is ready to ravish you', attempted precisely that.

Before Narcissus was dislodged, he had had Vespasian appointed Governor of Africa, where, though no great success, and once pelted with pumpkins by riotous provincials, he was at least at a safe distance from Nero. Actually, Nero had no dislike of him, since he neither feared nor envied him. He saw him as a butt. Vespasian's wooden countenance inspired him to all sorts of childish and malicious jests. So Vespasian was more fortunate than those who provoked Nero's jealousy.

Yet Nero had charm. I hope you will make that clear. Even Petronius, whom he called his Arbiter of Elegance, and who despised him as only a clever and unhappy man can despise a boisterous clown, testified to that. Petronius was a friend of my mother. When I was fourteen he sought to make me his catamite, but I would not have it. I directed him to Domitian instead. He shuddered and said, 'That scrofulous boy? You can't be serious.' 'Well,' I said, 'I assure you he would be willing, as I am not.' He laughed. I admired Petronius but he smelled of rotten apples. It was some sort of disease, I suppose. He used to read his novel, *The Satyricon*, to me. I think he hoped that its obscenity would excite me to grant him his desire. But I was then in a virtuous mood. A boy of fourteen can be very priggish.

This is not what you want to hear. You want to know about Domitian's boyhood.

But I'm a little drunk, as I usually am by evening. I'll close this letter, and continue tomorrow.

III

My father divorced my mother as soon as Narcissus was disgraced. He hadn't dared do so before. Then he withdrew to sulk on his estates in the hills beyond Velletri, to write lame verses (his *Tristia*) in feeble imitation of Ovid. I never saw him again.

My beautiful mother, whose own parents were dead and whose elder brother for some years refused to receive her or even provide for her, as was his duty, now found herself poor and almost friendless. She carried me off to a third-floor apartment in an *insula*, in the fourteenth region of the city on the other bank of the Tiber. It was all she could afford and was a miserable place, damp and cold in winter and, on account of the low ceilings and the fact that it looked onto an airless inner courtyard, intolerably hot in the summer which we could not escape, as people of our class were accustomed to, by retreating to the hills or the seaside. Our neighbours were the lowest sort of people, some of whom on winter nights used the common staircase to relieve themselves rather than venture forth to the icy public latrines. My own chamber was a mere cupboard, without ventilation, and on sleepless nights I lay there planning my future and the revenge I would take on the world for the misfortune which had so early engulfed me.

My mother bore her far greater ill-fortune stoically. She spent long days polishing her jewellery and her memories. In time, to pay for my education, she sold her jewels, piece by piece. She lived, I see now, only for me, and denied herself luxuries, even on occasion necessities, in order that I might make a show in the world. At the time I understood nothing of her self-denial, and resented the demands she made on me, and her refusal to allow me to play with the ragged and often criminal boys of our wretched quarter.

So we had few friends. That is how I came to pass so much of my childhood with Domitian. His circumstances resembled mine. He was boarded with an aunt – a sister of his father – in the Street of the Pomegranates in the sixth region, a neighbourhood little more salubrious or respectable than ours. You may think the distance between our homes makes our companionship surprising, since half the city lay between us. But the explanation is simple. His aunt revered my mother, who had been kind to her (she frequently said) in her days of prosperity. This aunt had buck teeth, stammered, and was nervous of strangers. So she would lead the young Domitian all the way over to Trastevere to pay her respects to my mother. For her part, my mother found the aunt useful. She had few domestic skills herself (how should she have had?), was reluctant to leave our apartment, despised our neighbours, or at least kept her distance from them, which incidentally increased the respect they held her in. Two lonely women, resenting the world, fearing it in the aunt's case, despising it in my mother's, they formed an alliance of convenience.

The child, they say, is father of the man. True, I suppose, though I have known those, myself among them indeed, who react so fiercely against the constraints of their childhood that, in retrospect, it is hard to believe that the adult man grew out of the child.

I could say more on this matter. But you do not wish my autobiography and, indeed, in bitter exile I have no taste to write it.

Domitian then: as a child, he was silent, brooding, resentful. You know how in his time as Emperor he was said to amuse himself by stabbing flies with his pen, so that the joke went round that 'No one was with the Princeps, not even a fly.' The jest was not without substance; he was the kind of little boy who delights in pulling the wings off insects, legs off spiders, and so on. Once, I recall, he brought a live frog to our apartment and proceeded to dismember it. When I begged him to refrain from torturing the beast, and at least to kill it before he anatomised the wretched creature, he muttered, without lifting his shaggy head – you remember how he could never look one in the eye – that he learned more by dissecting what was still alive. He had, he said, a keen interest in the nervous system. I think he was ten at the time.

His shaggy head was then sometimes infested with lice, for his aunt was short-sighted, and indifferent to such matters in any case. He went bald early, as you know; more cause for resentment.

In those days he didn't care for me. I put that wrongly. He disliked me. The reason was simple: my excellence rebuked his incapacity. I learned easily what he struggled to retain. For some years we attended the same schoolmaster, a Greek *grammaticus*, by name Democritos. He was a rough brutal man, fond of the rod. I believe his chief pleasure lay in chastising his unfortunate pupils. Domitian, being slow and of little account socially, was a choice victim. I have often seen his legs run with blood. Furthermore, the terror he displayed when condemned to a beating merely incited our master's ardour. The more Domitian howled for mercy, the harder the strokes fell. Once, at least, the wretched boy pissed himself in his abject fear. This naturally made him an object of mockery to his fellows. You will not be surprised to learn that after he became Emperor he had his agents seek out the now aged Democritos, drag him from the dingy apartment where he lingered, and bring the wretch before his former pupil who, spurning him with his toe, ordered him to be whipped to death. 'For,' he said, 'this man is so fond of the rod that it is only fitting that the rod should be the last thing he experiences in life.'

Curiously, it was this brutal wretch who first awoke in Domitian a warm feeling for myself. One day, when Democritos had been more than usually cruel to him, exceeding even his habitual measure of strokes, and had commanded two of our fellow-pupils to hold the boy up so that he might strike him again, something in me revolted against his barbarity. Perhaps – who knows? – I had long reproached myself for the timidity which I had displayed in tolerating the beast. Be that as it may, I now rose from my desk, ran towards him and, seizing the rod (then at the top of the backstroke) from his hand, turned it on our master, belabouring him about the neck and shoulders. 'See how you relish your own medicine,' I cried. 'Take that, you brute, and this, and learn to respect free-born Romans, you base Greek slave.' It was a moment of the purest exhilaration I have ever known. It could not last, of course. The brute was stronger than I and, swinging round, felled me with one blow of his fist. Then, calling on his assistant and one of our fellow-pupils to help him, he regained his rod and, when he saw I was held fast over the block, thrashed me with all his infuriated strength. He thrashed me, indeed, till I fainted, and when I recovered my senses it was to find myself alone with Domitian who was sponging my face and muttering his perplexed gratitude for my intervention. We agreed to inform my mother and his aunt of what had happened, and from that day we did not return to the torments of Democritos. From that day also, for two years or more, Domitian gave every sign of being devoted to me. I mention this because you have often observed that nothing is more common than a man's resentment of his benefactor. It wasn't like this in our case. I may say, modestly, that Domitian regarded me as his hero.

The harmony of our relationship was however to be broken. Titus returned to Rome from Africa, where he had been serving as his father's legate. He called, from courtesy, to see my mother.

'My father,' he said, 'sends you – has asked me to convey to you – the assurance of his high regard. He is fully sensible of the debt he owes you for his advancement. He has asked me to say that he is anxious to do whatever is in his power to – oh . . .' He broke off, and, with a sudden smile that seemed to light up our mean apartment, extended his hands in a vaguely helpless gesture and, abandoning his tone of formality, resumed: 'I'm no good at this kind of thing, my lady, though I have been trained in rhetoric. So let me put it in my own words, however loose and lacking in proper formality they may be. He's distressed to have learned of the condition in which you are obliged to live and now I see it for myself, well, I'm horrified, that a lady like you, of your birth, one who has been so kind to us, to me as a child, should be living like this. I remember that when poor Britannicus, my dearest friend, was so cruelly murdered – I can call it murder here, I suppose, though it would be as much as my life is worth to speak the word in other quarters – I remember then that when I wept, you dried my tears and comforted me, and that in the terrible days after, when I became like a little boy again, it was with your help and thanks to your sympathy and wise words that I was able to recover and resume my life. So, to see you confined in this miserable apartment makes me sad. More than that, it disgusts me. So, if there's anything I can do, anything my father can do – not that he can do much because, in my opinion, he clings to office, to his own position and perhaps even to his life by bare fingernails and fortune – well, just let me know. I really am devoted to you and your interest.'

He spoke beautifully, if a little incoherently, but that, it seemed, was evidence of his sincerity. The words tumbled forth, unbidden, straight from the heart, I couldn't doubt. My mother, of course, received them with gracious reserve, as her due. Whatever our circumstances, she was a great lady, a Claudian, while Vespasian and his family were *parvenus* – *parvenus* moreover who had not actually succeeded in arriving. But she was charmed by Titus nevertheless.

Who wasn't in those days?

I have only to close my eyes to see him clearly: tall, long-legged, blond, his hair worn rather long and waved, his skin translucent, despite the African sun, nose short and straight, eyes cornflower blue, lips a little loose, the upper very slightly overhanging the lower, as if stung by a bee. And I can hear him, too: a beautiful voice, rather light, almost girlish in its upper notes, but saved from effeminacy by a few residual long Sabine vowels, caught from his father, or perhaps a childhood nurse. Then, just as his voice was rescued from the suspicion of affectation by this underlying strength, so too his manner, which might have seemed that of the self-consciously elegant dandy, was saved by a certain clumsiness – his feet were too large and he was inclined to knock things over with sudden movement.

I have given myself away, haven't I? Yes, while I listened to him and then poured him wine with a hand that I could not prevent from shaking, I fell headlong in love, as only a fourteen-year-old boy can fall in love, with an intensity in which hero-worship quite superseded any physical desire. I simply wanted to be with him, all the time from then on, to be noticed by him, cherished by him, and permitted to serve him.

I was not disappointed. Titus, though naturally I was ignorant of this, already deserved the reputation that clung to him in later years, of a great *coureur* – I use the Greek because we have no Latin term that so exactly fits – of both boys and women. And, if I may say so, I was in those days worth running after, and accustomed to being eyed and ogled and propositioned at the baths: I was athletic and slim; my face was framed by tumbling black curls, my skin was creamy, my eyes the darkest of browns and large, my nose straight, and my lips – as Titus was to say – were 'made for the madness of kisses'. In short, though I say it myself, in the knowledge that this passage will arouse your stern moralist's disapproval, I was what the pederasts who thronged the baths used to call in my day 'a peach'. I never allowed their admiration to go beyond flirtation, in which like so many pretty boys I excelled, taking a lively delight in fanning an ardour which I had no intention of satisfying. But it was different with Titus, though at first

I took care not to allow him to gain the easy victory that I anticipated with relish.

I dwell on this, because that visit of Titus to my mother would determine the course of my life. It would lead me to action in Judaea, to military renown, to joy and heartache, and I think now that it also aroused Domitian's jealousy – though there were to be other, perhaps more substantial, reasons for that.

But now, when Titus smiled on me and said, 'I've been out of the city for so long, I'm almost a stranger. Will you be my guide, kid?' what could I do but say yes, blushing with delight and hoping that neither my mother nor Titus himself fully comprehended why the colour should flood into my cheeks?

First love . . . no, it is too painful to dwell on now and, besides, my old friend, it is not what you want to hear. You are interested, are you not, in political history.

It was Titus, however, who aroused my interest in that, too. For him dalliance, flirtation, love-making were mere pastimes. Politics was his consuming interest, and it was not long before he began my political education, not without some disparaging remarks about his little brother Domitian, who would, he said, never amount to anything, and was not therefore worth the trouble of trying to enlighten, even on the dangers that threatened their family.

'I have to admit,' he said, 'that my father's position is precarious. He clings to office only because he has not distinguished himself in any way, and so is not seen as a threat by the buffoon on the Palatine' – this being his normal fashion of referring to the Emperor.

Nero, he told me, hated soldiers. He was not only jealous of any who had ever achieved military renown; he both feared and detested them. 'It can't last,' Titus said. 'Rome is its army first and foremost, and it is impossible that the Empire should be governed by a man that the legions have learned to despise.' He smiled and ran his hand through my curls to fondle my cheek, then let his fingers dance along the line of my lips. 'You won't talk of this, will you, now? It would be as much as my life is worth. In speaking to you in this manner I am indeed putting my life in your hands. But then where could it better be?' I nibbled his finger like a pet dog.

One day that summer Titus sought permission from my mother, to whom he was unfailingly courteous, that I might accompany him for a few days to a villa near Laurentum which belonged to his uncle Flavius Sabinus, who then held the post of Prefect of the City. My mother, who knew and approved of the passionate friendship between me and Titus, naturally consented, though she declined the suggestion that she, too, should accompany us.

'No,' she said, 'such a visit would recall happier days to me, and disturb the accommodation with misfortune which I have made.' My revered mother, for all her virtues, was inclined to take pleasure in her misery.

'Don't you think you should invite Domitian, too?' I said. 'He'll be awfully put out if you don't.'

'Not he. My little brother has already accepted an invitation from his admirer, Claudius Pollio, to join him for a few days hunting in the Alban Hills. It seems that my brother would rather kill wild animals than enjoy the beauties of the seaside and the pleasure it can offer.'

The villa was indeed beautiful. I need not describe it, for you know it well, my dear Tacitus, since it was later bought by our friend Pliny and you have often been a guest there yourself.

So you will recall – though with less immediate pleasure than I do – that portico beyond the garden, that looks out on to the sea which lies below it, separated by a sandy beach and a rocky hillside covered with juniper and thyme. On the terrace before the portico we lay one afternoon after bathing in an air fragrant with the scent of violets. We had lunched on prawns, caught that morning, cheese, olives and the first peaches of the season, and had drunk a flask of Falernian. Titus was in his most affectionate mood, and then we slept a little.

When we woke the sun had moved round and a cool breeze blew from the sea.

'I didn't bring you here only for pleasure,' Titus said, 'but because there is nowhere I know where I think more clearly than in this charming place, and I wish to share my thoughts with you. You are only a boy, but you will soon be a man and will enter on the world which I myself am only beginning to understand.

'I have said to you before that Nero's rule cannot last, any more than Caligula's did. One year? Two? Five? No more than that, surely. He is despised by the soldiers and the aristocracy alike. He spends his time in pursuits which, while they might be thought tolerable if indulged in by a private citizen, are quite ridiculous in an Emperor:

acting, singing, taking part in chariot-races. You can't wonder that I think him a buffoon.

'But he is a bloody-minded buffoon. He is a coward, and all cowards are dangerous. You, kid, belong by birth to the highest rank of the old aristocracy, as I don't. There is scarcely a single man of your birth who does not view Nero with contempt. They know how to get rid of Emperors. How many of those who have ruled the state have died natural deaths?'

'Augustus himself,' I replied. 'Tiberius perhaps.'

'Exactly. Pompey was murdered. Julius Caesar also, Gaius Caligula, and in my opinion Claudius. And none of them was as despised as Nero. So he can't last.'

I looked out to sea. It was calm, deep blue, untroubled. If I had been alone I might have fancied I could hear the Sirens sing. I nibbled a stem of grass. Titus ruffled my hair.

'Last week,' he said, 'I was made party to a conspiracy. At least I think I was. Hints were dropped. There were many "if onlys" and "do you thinks". I turned away. Why did I do that, kid?'

'Do you want an answer?' I said. 'Or is the question addressed to yourself? And why are you telling me this? Isn't it dangerous? Dangerous, I mean, to speak of these things.'

'Nero murdered my friend, Britannicus,' he said. 'Nero has no children, brothers or nephews. Do you realise what that means? It means that when he is . . . disposed of, as he will be, somehow, the Empire will be a prize to be won. The secret of Empire will be revealed: that Emperors can be made elsewhere than in Rome. Emperors will be made by the legions. That is why I turned away from an aristocratic conspiracy. It's the wrong way to go about things, if we seek stability. Don't look like that. None of this is over your head.'

I watched a lizard skim up the wall of the terrace.

'My mother's father,' I said, 'was cousin to the Emperor Tiberius. She always says he would have liked to restore the Republic.'

'If I crushed that lizard with a rock,' Titus said, 'could you restore it to life?'

'I shouldn't think so, except by magic, if such magic is to be found . . .'

'Even Tiberius discovered that the Republic was as dead as that lizard would be then.'

'If the Emperor is to be made elsewhere than in Rome,' I said, 'then whoever commands the best legions will wear the purple. How many legions has your father, Titus?'

'Very few. At present.'

'So there's not much chance of him becoming Emperor, and then you succeeding him,' I said. 'Rather a pity. You'd make a wonderful Emperor.'

'I'm glad you think so, too.'

'Well, naturally. And if you were Emperor, or even heir to the Empire, then I could hope to restore the fortunes of my family, couldn't I?'

'It would be my first concern,' Titus said. 'I think we should sleep on that.'

'Sleep?'

You may dismiss this conversation, Tacitus, as a sort of verbal love-making, to excite us both. As indeed it did, very pleasingly. I can understand why you should do so. I was only a boy, and Titus was scarcely a grown man, though older, as he reminded me, than Octavian Caesar was when he embarked on the great adventure that in time made him Augustus and Master of the World. But you would be mistaken. Oh, I admit that Titus was showing off, to impress me. But there was more to it than that. He had sniffed the wind, and I am certain now that during this visit to Rome, when he had talked at length with his uncle, the Prefect of the City, and been admitted to at least the fringes of a company of disaffected nobles, he had caught a glimpse of his future. He had seen – what I could not then have credited – that his father Vespasian, however lowly his birth and comparatively humble his present position, could not be excluded from the struggle for Empire which he foresaw. Vespasian was, after all, a general whom the soldiers trusted; and there were few such left. And before Titus left Rome, to return to his father, he had done two things: he had taken soundings and estimated the strength and purpose of the opposition to Nero; and he had commissioned me to send him reports of what I learned of happenings in the city. When I protested that I was still a boy and therefore unlikely to learn of great events anything more than was the gossip of the market-place, he smiled and said, 'I think better of you than that.' He even taught me a simple cipher in which to write to him. So you see he was serious.

IV

There are things I choose not to write to my friend Tacitus. I did not, for instance, send all that last letter, but only an edited version of the first part. Nor could I reveal the nature of my congress with Titus, which still returns to me in dreams wherein I cross the threshold of the perfection of all physical delights before clouds roll up and all is lost to memory.

Then there is at least one element in my relations with Domitian which I cannot decide whether I dare recount. That it is germane is certain. But the incident doing me so little credit is one which I am loth to unfold. More of it in this notebook, perhaps, subsequently. It relates to Domatilla, sister of Titus and Domitian, a year younger than the latter. If I was even to drop her name in this context into my narrative, Tacitus would quiver like a hunting-dog that has scented game. Why is it that puritans like Tacitus, and indeed Domitian too, are so excited by a whiff of sexual scandal, and take so prurient and inquisitive an interest in the sexual activities of others, especially when they are what is termed 'deviant'? In Tacitus' case, doubtless because he has enjoyed so little sex himself. Domitian too perhaps? He talked much of 'bed-wrestling'; how much was wishful talk I never knew. Tacitus can't believe that Domitian was a puritan like himself. But then, my friend, though a master of language, is deficient in the knowledge of men; he has no understanding of what Greeks call psychology.

I have so little now to occupy me it is no wonder that, gazing on this sullen wind-whipped sea, past scenes move in the stage-set of my memory.

Obedient to Titus, I now began to frequent the new baths on the

Campus Martius, which were given the name of Nero's, though everyone knew that they had actually been commissioned by his minister Burrus, since murdered by imperial command. I went there at the hour favoured by young nobles, among whom I belonged by birth if not fortune. Naturally, it wasn't long before I attracted attention.

(It amused me by the way to remind Tacitus in my last letter of my youthful beauty. He looked like a scraggy crowling himself.)

Among my admirers was the poet Lucan. He approached me one afternoon as I reclined on a bench in the palaestra after my bath, and at once launched himself into a long speech of which I cannot remember a word, though he was certainly voluble. But his eyes were more eloquent still. It was clear that he had concluded from my attitude that I was in search of an admirer.

'You're a dancer, aren't you?' he said. 'I've seen you at the theatre . . .'

I allowed him to continue some time in this fancy, neither confirming nor denying his words, and favouring him with a smile that was friendly rather than inviting.

At last, when he had exhausted his store of flattery – for the time being only, since I have rarely known anyone with such a flow of words – and had made it quite clear what he wanted of me, I told him my name, and was rewarded, as I had expected, with a flush of embarrassment. To mistake a Claudian for a professional catamite was, at least in those days, a social blunder of the first order.

But Lucan was resourceful. He collected himself quickly, changing his words, though still singing them to the same tune. I was impressed. Only the thought of Titus prevented me from responding with the ardour my new friend so clearly sought.

I parried his attack, knowing that nothing is so desirable as a boy who protects his virtue and yet shows no sign of being offended by attempts to undermine it.

Lucan, accustomed, on account of good looks, self-confidence and literary reputation, to easy conquests, was enthralled by my resistance and redoubled his efforts to seduce me.

Discovering that his physical charms were not sufficient for his purpose, and that not even his sublime eloquence could persuade me to share his bed, he rashly sought to win me over by admitting me to his secret world in order to excite me by making me aware of his importance.

So he dropped hints that he was engaged in a great and dangerous enterprise. I smiled and said he would be wiser to tell me nothing of it. I was only a boy, I reminded him, and had no concern with such matters. Wouldn't it be better if he recited to me some more of the great poem he was writing? I would appreciate that more; literature, I said, fluttering my eyelashes, was more interesting to me than poltiics. Besides, politics belonged to the Republic which he invoked so marvellously in his verse. There could be no politics now that we lived under the despotism of Empire.

My indifference spurred him on to ever greater imprudence. I might flatter him as a poet. That was not what he wanted. Or rather it was not enough for him. I daresay, if I had yielded, I would not have been enough either. He was, I see now, a man of that unhappy sort whose every success serves to sharpen their innate dissatisfaction. Such types are more common than you might suppose. I should know. It is, or was, my type also.

Lucan was eaten up with pride of birth. Yet he was actually more notable for the eminence of recent connections, such as his uncle Seneca, than for his more distant ancestors. He was after all, Spanish by birth, not a true Roman at all, a descendant of some younger son who had established himself in Spain – Cordoba, I believe – seeking in the provinces what was denied him in Rome. Perhaps it was simply because Lucan was what I then thought of, scornfully, as a colonial, that he was so eager to impress on me his sense of the greatness of his family.

I smiled, and removed his hand from my thigh.

'But,' I said, 'your poetry will make you immortal. In that case what do your ancestors matter?'

He didn't care for that response, which indicates that he was not a true poet perhaps, since almost every poet I have known – and in my time I have been plagued with whole tribes of the creatures – has thrilled at the thought of immortality, and been ready to swear that the taste of future generations must be markedly superior to that of today.

But Lucan, lacking self-knowledge, saw himself as a great aristocrat, who threw off poetry with a negligent ease. It was something he did with style, but it didn't matter to him, except in as much as he acquired repute by his verses. He did not – perhaps it is needless to say – seek to impress other poets and critics, for he despised with some justice what he called 'literary sewing-circles'. The audience he aimed at was composed of the politically restless and dissatisfied, great ladies, beautiful women, and at least one very pretty boy.

When he realised that I was prepared to admire his verses and yet not yield to his advances, he was seized with rashness. The hints he had already dropped concerning his engagement in a matter of great moment were now amplified. He was, he told me flatly, one of a conspiracy against the Emperor. Indeed he was one of its most ardent spirits. What did I think of that?

'I think you are unwise to tell me,' I said.

'I tell you,' he replied, 'to demonstrate that my love is such that I am ready to put my life in your hands.'

'Your life, and the life of others,' I replied. Yet, despite everything, I would not yield. His eyes, I have remembered, were small and too closely pressing on his nose.

I was however sufficiently touched by the candour he had displayed to me, even though I was in no doubt as to the motive, to draw on my conversation with Titus in order to convey some sort of warning to my admirer.

So I asked him what measures he and his friends had taken to secure the support of the legions.

'The army,' he said, 'will be obedient to the Republic which will speak through the Senate.'

Then, young though I was, I knew that he was lost in silly dreams.

Naturally I reported our conversations to Titus, employing, as I had promised, the cipher he had taught me.

Lucan was not, as I learned much later, central to the conspiracy. His suggestion to me that he was proved to be only another example of that vanity characteristic of literary men. The head of the conspiracy was a man of much higher birth, G. Calpurnius Piso. (He had a nephew whom I often saw with Lucan at the baths; perhaps it was through him that Lucan became involved.) Even Piso may only have been the nominal head. He certainly wasn't cut out for that sort of thing. For instance, when it was proposed that Nero should be invited to Piso's villa near Velletri and murdered there, after a banquet, Piso vetoed the plan. He said that to stain his hospitality in this manner would create a bad impression. Even Lucan, with his absurd admiration for that 'Republican virtue', belonging to an age which had vanished, found this ridiculous.

'Really,' he said, 'if you are murdering an emperor, it's an excess of delicacy to worry about the abuse of hospitality.'

That *bon mot* was often quoted, subsequently; 'excess of delicacy' became a sort of catch-phrase, as in, for example, 'It would be an excess of delicacy not to bugger that boy.'

Curiously, however, I believe that Lucan's admiration for Piso was enhanced rather than diminished by this evidence of his leader's scruples. I even once heard him compare Piso to Marcus Brutus, his Republican hero. Not that Brutus showed any 'excess of delicacy' when despatching Julius Caesar on the Ides of March.

The second plan was apparently to dispose of Nero in his box at the Games. One of the conspirators would approach him, and throw himself at his feet as if begging a favour. Then he would seize Nero's ankles and pull him to the ground to allow his fellow-conspirators to rush in with their daggers. No doubt the intention was that they should then all leap up crying that Liberty had been restored to Rome.

Even as a boy I could see that this imitation of the murder of Julius was grotesque. I could imagine Titus laughing aloud when he read my account of what was proposed, before inveighing against the folly of the times. Lucan on the other hand was offended when I told him that this scheme was ridiculous and could never succeed.

In short the whole thing was amateurish. It would have been discovered even if Lucan had never blabbed to me and if I had not recounted all he said in my letters to Titus. As it happens, I have never known whether Titus made any use of my information.

I can't recall now how many executions took place when discovery was finally made. The story circulated that the conspiracy was revealed by a freedman in the employment of Flavius Scaevinus, who had volunteered (as had others, including, by his own account, Lucan) to strike the first blow. It was said that in his excitement he had blabbed at his own dinner-table. Perhaps so. It was certainly convenient that a freedman should be held responsible.

What is certain is that investigations ordered by the Emperor were first conducted by Faenius Rufus, who shared command of the Praetorian Guard with Tigellinus, the most disgusting of Nero's creatures, and a colonel of the Guard called Subirius Flavus. Both men were actually privy to the conspiracy. Yet, in their degenerate panic, they did not hesitate to connive at the torture and subsequent execution of their comrades. I am not sure if Tacitus knows this; Faenius Rufus, who was connected in some way with my friend's revered father-in-law Agricola, was by way of being a hero of his. So he may not be ready to admit his depravity to his record of history. Even the most scrupulous works of history are deformed by personal affections, and personal prejudices.

Word went round that Nero asked Subirius Flavus, when his role in the conspiracy was at last uncovered, why he had broken his oath of loyalty, and that he had replied: 'Because I hate you. I remained as loyal as anyone while you deserved my loyalty. But I turned against you when you murdered your wife and mother, and became charioteer, actor and fire-raiser.'

Domitian was much impressed by the nobility of this reply.

'It sounds to me,' I said, 'like something invented by his friends.'

Lucan was ordered to kill himself, and obeyed. He would have described his act as an example of Republican virtue. I thought it contemptible, even then.

Now? Yes, it still seems contemptible, a piece of play-acting. But I despise it less than I did, because to abandon hope and yield to what appears to be necessity, is only too easily understandable.

V

My dear Cornelius Tacitus:

You reproach me for my tardiness, and also for the quality of the information I have sent you. You do not realise how painful it is for me, marooned in this frontier region, to cast my mind back to the days of my youth. Even the image of afternoon dying in the Gardens of Lucullus and the setting sun turning the pine trees of the Palatine a soft dusky purple-blue disables me for hours. And when in memory's ear I listen to the babble of the streets and the raucous cries of the stall-holders calling to customers, I am seized with so sharp a pang of nostalgia that I dissolve in tears or drown my sorrows in a flask of sour wine. And I have other distractions here, though I shall not weary you with an account of them.

You say – having first asked me for memories of Domitian's childhood – that this does not interest you now, and that what you wish to learn is what he did and how he conducted himself in the terrible months that followed the revolt of the legions against Nero.

But how can I tell a story without an introduction? And, even granting that all you seek from me is notes towards the making of your History, how can I be certain that you will use my notes aright, if I do not supply at least a sketch of the background – however familiar this may already appear to you?

I add that qualification for this reason, though it may irritate you: I do not believe there is, or ever can be, a fully accurate history. One man's impression of events runs counter to another's. Surely your experience of marriage has taught you that.

But I am quite happy to heed your request and skip over the years of my adolescence. I shall therefore spare you my memories of the Great Fire which raged through the city for six days and left so much of it in smouldering ruins. I could write of it vividly, for I climbed the Janiculum, along with many others who lived on the 'wrong' side of the river, to get a good view. Then, in the days that followed, I picked my way through the embers, amazed at the destruction and yet – I confess with some degree of shame – also elated. But you will have many other sources to draw on for your account of the disaster.

I wonder, however, whether you will hold Nero himself responsible, as so many did at the time – and not only because he took advantage of the devastation to create his ideal rural landscape within the city bounds and to start work on what was to be his masterpiece, the Golden House. People held him guilty before these plans were known, and it was said that he had chanted verses of his own composition celebrating Troy in flames as he watched the blaze.

Well, you will make up your own mind as to his guilt. You may even conclude, as he pretended to, that the real arsonists were the wretched sect of slaves and freedmen known as Christians, delinquent Jews whom he punished so severely.

But I shall not weary you with such speculations. It is of Domitian that you wish me to write.

He was always a difficult friend, more so as we grew older and approached the threshold of adult life. In Nero's last year, or perhaps a little earlier, he became more withdrawn, more bitter, more full of resentment. His sister Domatilla feared for his sanity, or said she did. His affair with the senator Claudius Pollio was over – if it was an affair, and not merely a friendship, as Domitian, blushing, swore. They had fallen out. He let me understand that this was because Pollio sought to leap the bounds of friendship, even assaulting his virtue. That may have been so. But many years later Pollio used to boast that he had a letter from the young Domitian promising to go to bed with him. In his cups he once promised to show it me, never did however. So who knows? Both men being liars, where is the truth? One can only guess.

In any case, there were other causes of Domitian's instability. There was matter close at hand. He was jealous of my friendship with his sister. She used to complain that he wanted to possess her entirely; but then I felt that he demanded the same of me.

'He's obsessed,' she said, 'with keeping me safe, and would make me a prisoner if he could.' No doubt this was the case. Yet he also sulked whenever I preferred another's company to his, and would question me severely as to my doings when we were not together.

Domatilla was fond of him, distressed by his evident unhappiness. She felt sorry for him because he lacked Titus' charm and, as she said, seemed in need of her protection himself.

'It's difficult,' she said. 'I seek to protect him while also wanting to enjoy myself, and he would deny me any enjoyment except in his company. It's not easy.'

Domitian also resented the fact that he had as yet no share in the improving fortunes of his family. Vespasian had been made Governor of the province of Judaea, where Jewish extremists had revolted against our Empire. The origins of the revolt are obscure, as indeed are most matters concerning that turbulent and disagreeable people. It began, apparently, with a dispute between Jews and Greeks in the city of Caesarea. The Greeks attacked the Jewish quarter, intending to drive them out of the city; the usual sort of ethnic violence you get when distinct communities live cheek by jowl. The Greeks' initial success stimulated a response, even though the respectable element among the Jews – the better-born and the religious leaders – tried to restrain the fanatics. They failed. Our garrison in Jerusalem was massacred. Then, when Cestius Gallus, Proconsul in Syria, marched against the city, he was alarmed by the strength of the Jewish resistance, lost his nerve, and ordered a retreat which turned into a shameful rout.

It was at this time that Vespasian was put in command, recalled from obscurity. Nero chose him for three reasons. The first was his low birth, which made Nero suppose that no success won by Vespasian could make him a rival, since he had no independent support among the nobility; Nero could not conceive that they would ever submit to one so low-born as Vespasian. Second, as I have mentioned, Nero had always made Vespasian the butt of his impertinent and indeed adolescent wit, and quite liked him for that reason. Finally, the choice was limited. He had ordered the greatest general of our time, Corbulo, to kill himself a few months previously.

Titus was delighted by his father's appointment. He was certain it would be the making of his own career. He wrote to me in a tone of great enthusiasm, then remarked that, while Domitian would be eager to join his father in Judaea, this was not a proposal to be encouraged. 'Domitian disturbs him,' he wrote, 'though I don't know exactly why.

Perhaps you have some inkling. You know my little brother better than I do, and I respect your opinion. But do what you can to soothe his feelings. Perhaps you could suggest that my father will rely on him to send reports of how things stand in the city. You will realise this suggestion is ridiculous. Father depends on the information his brother Flavius Sabinus sends him. But if you can pull this particular wool over Domitian's eyes, then you will be doing me a service – which is of course your greatest pleasure, isn't it? The fact is that Domitian is not ready for military life. He may never indeed be suited to command.'

Naturally I did as he asked, but I failed to convince Domitian. He saw that the reassurances I offered were the veriest nonsense, and guessed that I was his brother's mouthpiece.

'That's what Titus told you to tell me,' he said. 'He's determined to keep me in the shade. Well, he shan't succeed.'

All the same, despite this petulance, it was in the shade that he remained. He became more moody and more disagreeable, some-times going for days without speaking. 'I think he's forgotten how to smile,' Domatilla said.

Only my mother seemed to understand him. She said he was like a bird with a broken wing. She felt sorry for anyone who had set his heart on something beyond his reach. When he visited us, he relaxed in my mother's company. It may even be that he felt a disinterested affection for her.

I am weary and shall resume this letter later. But meanwhile the messenger has come to inform me that the boat is about to sail. So I shall send this now, as evidence of my willingness to help you – though I fear you will find it inadequate.

VI

Tacitus will be irritated that I sent him only an extract from Titus'
letter. There were sentences too intimate for me to wish to disclose
them to his disapproving scrutiny. But why I should wish Tacitus to
think better of me than I think of him, especially since we shall never
meet again, baffles me. Yet it is so.

He is so suspicious that he may even think I have concocted that
letter. But I have always hoarded correspondence and, though some
has gone missing, much remains. When I was condemned to exile, I
arranged to have several boxes of documents forwarded to me by way
of my bankers.

I do not know how much that is private and not public I can bring
myself to reveal to Tacitus.

I have no reason to protect Domitian's memory, and yet I am
reluctant to tell him all that I know about the late Emperor: for
instance, that he once, at least, sought to bed his sister Domatilla.
This happened later, when she was a married woman. I didn't hear
of it at the time – I was soldiering in the East. But it was soon after
my return that she told me – in her bed, as it happens. Since her
confession came *post-coitum*, after our own act of adultery, when her
hair lay on my damp shoulder, and her flesh was pressed against
mine, I did not doubt her. I could not then doubt either that she
had refused him, though, jealousy working in its crab-like fashion, I
was subsequently for months tormented by the suspicion that she had
not done so, but had lied to me, even while lying with me. And this
suspicion was magnified by the vivid memory of a dream or nightmare
I had had in the year of terror which Tacitus has asked me to recall.

Was that dream a premonition? The thought tormented me or, rather, I tormented myself by indulging it.

But, at the moment that she told me of her brother's criminal assault – with her soft lips mouthing my ear – I felt pity for Domitian rather than indignation. That he should have been so driven by incestuous lust, and yet denied what I had just enjoyed!

Will Tacitus, or rather would Tacitus, for I shall not tell him, believe that? I don't think so. Human nature is too complicated for the schematic ways of historians.

The truth is that Tacitus will present men and women as if they are capable of being understood. There is no other way of writing history perhaps. It is the historian's impulse to make sense of what happens. But can the sense they create be true to experience? I think not. Does any man really understand even himself? And if that is beyond us, how can one pretend to understand other people whom we know only by observation and intermittent congress?

Of course I did not think like this when I was young. In those days I had few doubts, and was confident of conquering the world, and winning love where I chose. I had been certain that Titus loved me. Now that I had, at the age of seventeen, assumed the *toga virilis* and had entered on adult life, that love properly fell away, or rather was transformed into, as I thought, the friendship between equals, formed of mutual respect and affection, which Roman noblemen have always valued as the foundation of social and political life. Or so I told myself, Titus being absent in the East.

Moreover, I was at that stage when the developing soul turns its most ardent and compelling desires from the immature passions of boyhood, characteristically addressed to others of one's own sex, to the other and more mysterious opposite. So, as I watched Domatilla push her hair away from her eyes with a rapid, unconscious flickering of her long pale fingers, and saw Titus reflected in that gesture, I sensed that he had been the forerunner, and told myself that Domatilla was the love of my life, that perfect other half, union with whom would bring me that harmonious joining of souls which Plato affirms is the supreme experience and the goal of love.

Such at least were my dreams, in that last early summer before Rome tore itself apart and I was forced into a premature and morally corrupting knowledge of the vileness of men, and found my character so deformed by what I learned that I emerged incapable of generosity of spirit, incapable of love but only of lust. That year – I tell myself now – killed most that was good in me, as in many others. As for Domatilla . . . what can I say? Even now the thought of her is too painful. It quickens my senses, and then I remember how, at last, she turned away from me, because (she said) I demanded everything, entire possession, and she was not to be possessed by anyone. Her husband, she said, was a man who asked little of her, only the appearance of virtue. 'When we were young,' she said, 'I loved you. Now . . .' she stroked my cheek with soft fluttering fingers, 'no, not now . . .'

Can I understand this? Can I make sense of the barriers that were erected between us? Not at all.

So I question the possibility of understanding another person. Yet Tacitus is certain he understands Nero – even Nero. Well, I had a closer acquaintance – too close on that occasion I have alluded to – with the tyrant than Tacitus, who indeed had no personal knowledge of him, and was only fourteen or fifteen when Nero fell, but I do not claim to know how or why the young man whom my mother remembered (before the murder of Britannicus) as 'charming, ingenuous, a little naive, shy, and lacking in self-confidence', should have been transformed into a perverted and vicious monster.

Tacitus believes that character is fixed, so that what emerges at one stage in life was merely hidden before. He may therefore conclude that the young Nero was merely a hypocrite concealing his true nature. I have indeed heard him make this argument. He takes the same view of the Emperor Tiberius.

Then, tracing Nero's degeneration, he will undoubtedly blame Greek influences. I remember how often in our late-night conversations over another flask of wine – and Tacitus in his early thirties was as hard a drinker as myself, or indeed as Tiberius is reputed to have been – he would curse the foreign tastes which were, he said, 'reducing our youth to a bunch of gymnasts, loafers, and perverts. The Emperor and Senate,' he would mutter, 'are to blame. They not only allow these vices and practise them themselves, but they even force Roman nobles to debase themselves by appearing on the stage to sing, declaim and dance. They indulge in Greek athletics, stripping naked, putting on boxing-gloves and sparring, rather than toughening themselves by serving in the army.'

The truth is that Tacitus, priding himself on his old-fashioned ways and, taking Cato as his hero, has always had a vulgar taste for blood and slaughter. He relishes cruelty, even though it may also repel him. Complicated fellow. I was too well-mannered to say so, and used to content myself with teasing him.

'I don't suppose,' I would say, 'that you have often been invited to strip and display your charms.'

'There would be trouble for anyone who made such a suggestion to me.'

Oh dear, I never could resist teasing him. I can't even now. It really surprises me that my old friend has become so great a man, if, that is, a mere historian can be thought great. He talks of greatness, writes longingly of greatness. But what has he ever done that was great?

Nothing disgusted him more than the story of Nero and his catamite, Sporus; and yet he could never leave it alone, but reverted to it frequently in conversation.

Sporus, a Greek boy, had been a slave in the household of my mother's sister when Nero first saw him. The boy was only twelve, but, according to my mother, already very pretty, with soft dark curls, silky skin, high cheek-bones, strangely narrow eyes. The young Emperor at once lusted after him and commanded him as a gift. What could my aunt do but part with the child? Nero had him castrated, on account, he said, of the purity of the boy's voice which he pretended was what had first enchanted him. A couple of years later he went through a form of marriage with him, the boy being dressed as a bride, and wearing a garland of red roses. After the ceremony, a parody of the real thing, he retired with him to a bridal chamber, and poor Sporus had to scream as if he was a virgin being ravished. I believe Nero even wounded him so that the sheets would be bloody. All this was perfectly disgusting, but it was rather harsh and quite unreasonable of Tacitus to speak with such contempt of the boy. What choice had he? My mother, having a better understanding than the future historian, always spoke sympathetically, even tenderly, of poor Sporus. I mention these circumstances now because of the part the boy subsequently found himself playing.

Nero's excesses are not my subject. Tacitus will revel in describing them. Let him do so. My memories of the last year of Nero's life are very different, and delightful. What did I care if he, in his mad extravagance, was taking advantage of the destruction wrought by the

Great Fire four years previously to create his new palace and rural landscape, with its groves, pastures, herds of cattle, wild animals and grottoes where the mean houses of citizens had once crowded about each other? What did I care if men said in bitterness that all Rome was being transformed into Nero's villa, and if satirists advised the citizens to flee to Veii, assuming, that was, the villa did not get there first? What did I care, even, if every week brought news of some plot against the tyrant, followed by the melancholy report of yet another suicide of some exposed and terrified conspirator?

For me that year was dominated by love. For me now, in cold and wretched exile, it is a time of sunlit afternoon. Summer afternoon, but summer afternoon with the freshness of spring.

Domatilla . . . I have only to form her name to find myself near to weeping.

There was the moment that summer when she was transformed from a girl I had always known and liked and been happy to amuse, to . . . how shall I put it? Not a goddess; I leave that nonsense to poets. No, but just as the Emperor's Golden House spread itself in unimaginable delights over the dull city, so my life too was made golden by this hitherto scarcely imagined girl. Perhaps intense love is never anything but a projection of the imagination on the other.

It was one afternoon at the seaside, and if I was to narrate what happened that afternoon, it would appear perfectly commonplace. Domatilla had some friends with her. We played some ball-game. Domitian lost his temper and shouted at his sister, accusing her of having infringed some rule of the game. She lowered her eyes and spoke gently, seeking to pacify him. But he, giving way to a mood which I knew only too well, refused to be mollified, turned away, and strode off towards the woods. She called after him, appealingly and then, when he paid no heed, her upper lip, which was long and a little too thick for perfect beauty, trembled. But she shrugged, scuffed her feet uncertainly in the sand, and suggested we resume the game, for which, however, no one now had any heart. 'Bother him,' she said, recognising and resenting her brother's ability to impose his sullen will on the company – even by withdrawing his presence.

Nothing, you see, nothing. Yet it was in that moment when she looked after him and scuffed her feet in the sand that she became no longer the girl I had known all my life, but someone quite new to me, whom I experienced the absolute need to know perfectly and thoroughly.

I followed her to the house, where I found her drinking a glass of lemon squash.

'He's so silly,' she said, and a tear escaped her eye, trickling down her cheek which was flushed, either from the game or as a result of her emotion. I wanted to take her in my arms, and lick the tears which she now began to shed in profusion as she gave way to great sobs. I was at a loss to understand why she was so moved, and I did nothing. I could speak no words to comfort her. But I felt much.

VII

You chide me, Tacitus, for being dilatory, as you call it. May I remind you that you are the historian, not me, and that I am doing you a favour, or endeavouring to do you a favour, in excavating painful memories?

But I am glad that you now at last ask me specific questions. In particular, you seek to know what it was like in Rome when Galba, who had been proclaimed Emperor by the legions in Spain, entered the city. You weren't there yourself, you say. Indeed you weren't, and I was. If this part of your History is to be authentic, you must rely on me. Don't forget that. No doubt you have other informants, and will study documents. But if you seek an eye-witness account from one who understands, or once understood, politics, then you must put your trust in me. For which reason you should remember your manners.

I don't pretend to know everything, but I can promise you that I won't pretend either to more knowledge than I truly possess. What you get from me is authentic, from the horse's mouth, as we say in these barbarian parts, where the horse is highly revered. And you must allow me to approach it in my own way. The years, and my bitter experiences, have deprived me of the literary skills I once was so proud of.

What, I wonder, do you really know of Nero's death? There are more than a dozen stories that have gone the rounds, not least, of course, those which assert that he didn't die then but escaped. You will remember that in the subsequent few years at least half a dozen false Neros presented themselves. And what will you make of that, if you happen to mention it? Perhaps you won't mention it, because it points to something which you will not readily wish to admit. These false Neros all gathered support from the common people wherever they presented themselves. Why? Because, outside the senatorial class to which we both belong (you uncertainly, if you don't mind me saying so) Nero was popular. And not only with the riff-raff. Respectable provincials had a high regard for him; he had done them no harm, they had prospered during his reign, and the Greeks especially admired and even loved an Emperor who so highly valued Greek culture.

Nero was at a villa on the Bay of Naples when he learned of the revolt in Gaul. Characteristically, he did nothing. Soldiers bored him, and he assumed that this was a mutiny which could be settled by the promise of a lavish donation, which he empowered the Governor of Gallia Ludgenensis, G. Julius Vindex, to offer them. That shows his indifference to what was happening. If he had listened to the report he would have known that Vindex himself was leading the rebellion. But he was busy chatting to his architect when the messenger brought him the news, and listened with only half an ear, if that.

It was several days before he learned that rebellion was not confined to Gaul, where however the issue was in the balance, for Lucius Verginius Rufus, the Governor of Upper Germany, opposed Vindex. That news was of little comfort to Nero, since it was not clear whether Rufus was still loyal or acted on his own account.

Rebellion is like an epidemic. Once launched, it breaks out everywhere, and spreads rapidly. The Spanish legions were not to be outdone by their colleagues in Gaul and Germany. They, too, were ready to reject Nero.

The Governor of Spain was Servius Sulpicius Galba, a veteran general, now over seventy, reputed to be a man of ability; and indeed at different points in his long career he had justified his reputation. Now he was compelled either to listen to his troops or suppress their mutiny. He chose the former course, and proclaimed himself 'Legate of the Senate and the Roman People', though neither Senate nor Roman People had appointed him their legate.

Meanwhile, in Gaul, Vindex and Rufus had come to an agreement. It wouldn't last long. The two armies fell out, and Vindex killed himself. But while the outcome there was uncertain Galba seized the opportunity now open to him.

So Spain was lost to Nero. At first he was little perturbed. 'Spain is a long way off,' he said, 'and the Praetorian Guard, for whom I have cared so tenderly, will not desert me.'

They might not have done so if he had immediately returned to Rome and gone to their camp and appealed to their loyalty – and naturally to their greed. Vespasian's brother, Flavius Sabinus, the City Prefect, was afraid that this was just what he would do. He had already determined that Nero must be disposed of. So he sent the Emperor a message saying that Rome was quiet, there was no cause for anxiety, and the word was that the rebellions in Gaul and Spain were already petering out. What's more, he got the Praetorian Prefect, Nymphidius Sabinus, to send a similar message; they were cousins and Nymphidius, I believe, hoped to gain the Empire for himself, though Flavius was determined he shouldn't.

This was just what Nero wanted to hear. So he abandoned any plan to come to Rome and gave himself up to revelry. But, in a gesture intended to impress people with a sense of his energy, he named himself sole Consul.

All this gave time for the Senate to act. Once they had received confirmation that Galba was in control of his army and was making for Rome, and been assured by Flavius and Nymphidius that the Praetorians were ready to desert Nero – for a suitable reward – they convened and, greatly daring, declared Nero 'a public enemy', to be punished 'in ancient style'.

'What does that mean, "in ancient style"?' Domatilla asked.

'I don't know exactly,' I said, 'but something disagreeable I should imagine. Our forefathers could be rather rough, you know.'

'I can tell you,' Domitian said. 'I can tell you exactly.' He smiled – you remember that smile of course, like a snake's? 'The executioners strip the condemned man naked, thrust his head into a wooden fork and flog him to death. We can be pretty sure Nero won't like it. I should think they'd hear his screams at Ostia.'

'Horrible. Poor Nero,' Domatilla said, 'poor anyone to suffer like that. What brutes our ancestors were. They won't really treat him like that, will they?'

'No,' I said. 'He is the Emperor, after all. The common people would lose all respect for us if an Emperor was put to death in so barbarous a manner. I imagine they hope the threat of such a death will be sufficient to persuade him to kill himself. Anyone must prefer an honourable death at his own hand to such ignominy.'

(How young I was, how naive. I know now that there are those who will endure anything, any humiliation, any pain, rather than surrender life. Sometimes I even admire such fortitude.)

'They say he fainted when he heard of Galba's revolt,' Domitian said.

'They say all sorts of things,' I replied. 'This afternoon at the baths, I was told first that Nero intended to invite all the members of the Senate to a banquet, and then poison them; second, that he was going to set the city on fire again, but only after letting wild beasts – lions, tigers, and so forth – loose in the streets to hinder the fire-fighters; and third, that he was going to buy off the Gallic legions by giving them permission to sack any city they chose. It's all rot, even though Nero is such a liar and fantasist. He won't do anything like that. People also say he's paralysed with terror.'

'I heard something else,' Domitian said, 'that he was intending to go to Gaul and confront the rebel legions. Only, instead of haranguing them in a manner worthy of his ancestors, he would fall on his knees before them and weep and weep. This, he says, would soften their hearts. They would be so moved to find their Emperor throwing himself on their mercy, that they would take him to their hearts. How contemptible can you get? Actually, I don't suppose they'd react like that at all. I imagine some centurion would step up and cut his throat, stick him in the gizzard.'

'I don't know,' I said. 'Soldiers can be very sentimental, I'm told. That might be the only thing that could save him, and he's such an actor he might even pull it off. But I can't suppose he would have any chance of getting to Gaul.'

'Poor Nero,' Domatilla said again. 'I do feel sorry for him. I know he's done terrible things, but all the same . . . I hate to see people humiliated.'

I think it was that night that, walking through the city, I came on one of Nero's statues, with a note attached to it, written in Greek: 'This time it's a real contest, Nero, and one you can't fix but are going to lose.'

Nobody knew what was happening. Some Senators began to regret their rashness when it was reported that Nero was calling on the common people to rise and arm themselves in his defence. Then, at the baths, one of my admirers – but I forget which – assured me that this was nonsense or, if it wasn't nonsense, the next best thing, since no recruits had presented themselves. 'Die for Nero? Not bloody likely. That's the popular opinion,' he said. 'Actually, I do know that Nero was preparing yesterday to go to Gaul, but his first concern was to find wagons to carry his stage-equipment, and then to arrange for his concubines to have their hair cut in a boyish style and be issued with shields and weapons such as the Amazons used. The man has taken leave of what senses he still retained. He's living in a dream world.' No doubt, I thought, but it may still turn to nightmare for the rest of us; and I hurried home to make sure that all was well there and my mother safe. I had already begged her not to leave the house till things were more settled. Though I couldn't imagine that anyone would harm her of choice, accidents will happen, especially when someone like Nero is at his wits' end, and the mob is excited beyond measure – as it might be at any moment.

Was it that evening or one a few days later that, shortly after I had retired to bed, where I lay sleepless, listening to the ever-changing sounds of the night city that refused to surrender to silence, I heard a scratching at the outer door of our apartment? It was a gentle noise, calculated, as I supposed, to alarm nobody. Yet its persistence suggested anxiety, even fear. I rose, put on a dressing-gown and, picking up the cudgel which we kept in a stand by the door, listened to the renewed scratching.

'Please help,' came a thin high voice. 'Please let me in.'

I did not recognise the young man who stumbled through the door, falling against me. I pushed him off, and he swayed, and would have fainted (as I supposed) had I not taken him by the shoulder and guided him to a stool by the table. He sat for a moment with his back to the wall, his legs quivering. His face was streaked with dirt and tears and what might have been blood, and his tunic was torn. Then he uttered a deep sob and buried his face in his hands so that I could not see his features but only the tangle of black curls now presented to me.

My mother, aroused by the sounds, joined us from her chamber. She took one look at the young man, who had, with a start of terror, lifted his head.

'Sporus?' she said. 'So the Emperor is dead?'

'At my hand,' he said. 'Perhaps. In part. I don't know. I hope not. It was terrible.'

My mother told me to fetch wine, while she busied herself heating up what remained of the broth we had had for our supper. Sporus gulped down the first cup of Marino wine as a parched traveller drinks water from a well, and held out his cup for more. I sipped mine and watched him. His hand still shook, and every now and then, though he must have known he was for the time being safe, he darted anxious looks at the door.

'Were you followed here?' I asked.

He shook his head, but there was no certainty, only hope, in the gesture.

'Let the boy be,' my mother said. 'Give him time. He's worn out, and no wonder. He'll tell what he has to tell when he has some food and drink in him.'

She placed bread on the table, and then soup. Sporus hesitated, as if the thought of sustenance disgusted him.

'Eat,' my mother said, 'then drink more wine.'

At last he was ready.

This is his account. I assure you it is authentic. I wrote down his story when he had finished speaking and fallen asleep. I have kept the document with me throughout the upheavals of life. You know yourself, Tacitus, that I have ever been an orderly man, and one who sets great store on documentary evidence.

He told the story haltingly, with false starts and changes of direction. I've tried to capture the way he gave it to us, but I admit I've tidied it up a bit. After all, it went on till dawn's pink fingers were touching the sky.

So he said: 'He was lost. I think he has been losing himself for a long time, and now he had lost the world. He knew that, but he wouldn't confront the reality. So his plans changed all the time, and he couldn't give his mind to them because his mind recoiled. Once he even interrupted a meeting of the loyal advisers who remained to him because one of Phaon's slave-girls, a virgin, ten or eleven, had caught his eye, and he had to have her without delay. It let him suppose things weren't as they were. Another time, when he was dictating a letter he was going to send to the Senate, a letter in very high and serious tones, he had me – I'm sorry, milady, but I have to try to tell it as it was, for my own sake, though I don't know why – he had me masturbate him as he dictated. When he got hard ... no, I'm sorry, I won't go on, I can see it disgusts you. But that's the life I've been compelled to live for years, you know, ever since ... let's just say, ever since he first caught sight of me. And yet, can you believe it, I was fond of him, he could be charming and ... no, let it pass ...

'This was when we were in Phaon's villa. That's four miles out of town, between the Nomentana and the Salaria. Phaon was one of his freedmen, you won't know him. We had come to Rome the day before, nobody knew that because we'd slipped in by night and nobody recognised him as we hurried to the palace. He'd a cloak over his face. I think that's when I knew it was all over, and the only questions remaining were how and when. I mean, that the Emperor didn't dare show his face in Rome, it was unthinkable. That night he had a new plan. He was going to appear on the rostra and beg the people's mercy – ask for pardon for all he'd done that had displeased them. It might have worked. That's what I thought then anyway. Whatever people say he was a good actor, nobody could play a part like him. I've never known anyone who could sound more sincere, when he chose, and you had to know him as well as I came to do to realise that when he was most humble and contrite he was laughing at the fools he deceived. I've heard that he could always convince even Seneca of his sincerity, and everyone says Seneca was one of the wisest of men. Till near the end he could convince Seneca, they say. Now he was so excited by the idea that he even dictated the speech he would make. He said, just before we went to sleep, "You never know, they might agree to make me Prefect of Egypt, even if they won't let me remain Emperor. We could have a marvellous time in Egypt, it's a remarkable country."

'I think that was the last real hope he had. He'd been drinking, of course. We all had. When annihilation stares you in the face, it's natural to turn to wine, isn't it?

'It was different in the morning. He woke before it was light, and discovered that his bodyguard had deserted him. They'd just slipped away. So had most of his friends. There were only half a dozen of us remaining. Imagine that, half a dozen in that vast palace, the corridors and all the dormitories empty. And still it wasn't light. That's when he first talked of killing himself. It's when I was first really frightened, too. He called for Spiculus to despatch him. That was one of his freedmen, a gladiator who had caught his fancy, a great brute of a German. But

Spiculus had run away. That was when Phaon suggested we returned to his villa. Nero agreed. "I need only some quiet place where I can collect my thoughts," he said. So we found horses and set off. Cocks were crowing in the suburbs and the mist lay heavy, promising a fine day. Odd that that was what I thought of. We passed quite close to the Guards' camp, which made the Emperor tremble. But when his horse shied at a dead body lying in the road, and the scarf he had tied over the lower part of his face to disguise him fell away, he was recognised by a veteran who, astonished, still saluted him. Nero didn't return the salute. I think he hoped the man would think he was mistaken. When we approached the villa, Phaon, whose teeth were chattering either with the cold of the morning or with terror, suggested we should hide in a gravel pit till someone went ahead to see if the villa was still safe. But Nero wouldn't have that. "I won't go underground till I die," he muttered. He went on repeating the line as if it was the chorus of a song.

'We got into the villa. But that, too, was deserted, except for Phaon's wife and daughters. Nero didn't even look at them. He sank down on a couch, saying, "This is the end, there's no way out for poor Nero now. Have they really declared me a public enemy? Poor Nero, poor Nero. And I had such wonderful plans." Phaon kept his head. He urged Nero to make for the coast, where (he said) they would be sure to find a boat. "Don't give up." We all told him not to give up. I don't know why.

'Then someone came in to say that he had seen a troop of cavalry approaching. Nero picked up two daggers and tested their points. "How ugly and vulgar my life has become," he said, but still couldn't bring himself to . . . "I'm such a coward. Set me an example, Phaon," he said. But Phaon shook his head. He didn't see any reason why he should kill himself to encourage Nero. By this time I was in tears, which pleased the Emperor. So was Acte, the slave-girl who, alone of his women, really loved him. "This is nice," he said, "someone at least is going to mourn for me. Someone at least is sorry to see me in this state. But it's no credit to me that I can't . . . Come on, Nero," he said, speaking as if we weren't there, "be a man, play the man." Then he held one of the daggers against his throat and began to sob, and his secretary Epaphroditus stepped forward and, taking his hand that held the dagger, thrust it into his neck. He gurgled, still tried to speak, lifted his head and managed to say, "What an artist . . . so great an artist to die like this."

Epaphroditus took the other dagger and stabbed him again, also in the throat.

'It was just then, while he was still alive, that the officer commanding the troop of cavalry found us. He looked at Nero, and said, "I'd orders to take him alive, but it's better like this." Acte threw herself at his feet, sobbing. She caught hold of his legs, and said that Nero had begged her not to let them cut his head off, but have him buried in one piece. I don't know when he made this request. I hadn't heard him say this. His eyes were bulging from their sockets. I wanted to close them, he seemed to be looking at me, and I couldn't. Acte then begged them to let her take charge of the body. The officer said it was nothing to do with him. He'd been told to take Nero alive, but since he was dead, it didn't matter to him. "I'd throw him in a ditch myself," he said. Then he hurried away. I suppose he wanted to be first with the news, and get some sort of reward. As for me, I couldn't stay, it was all too horrible. But I've been afraid all day that someone would recognise me as Nero's boy, and . . . So that's why I've come here, you were the only person, milady, I could turn to. You won't let them do anything to me, will you?'

'Of course I won't,' my mother said.

She was full of pity. She told me when she had put Sporus to bed, that he was a poor abused child, though of course he was older than I was myself.

She kept him in our apartment for a few days. Then one night when I returned home he had gone. For a long time she wouldn't tell me where. Eventually I learned that she had sent him to the house of one of her cousins in Calabria. Later I believe he kept a brothel in Corinth. I don't suppose there was much else he could have been expected to do. Though my mother was ignorant of the fact, I have reason to suppose that Sporus had hidden some of the jewels he had got from Nero and at some point retrieved them, thus financing his enterprise. In my opinion, he had earned the jewels.

VIII

I confess to having framed my last letter in such a way as to irritate Tacitus. The sympathy expressed for Sporus will infuriate him indeed. He hates everything that smacks of degeneracy, and talks sometimes as if poor things like Sporus are responsible for their unhappy condition. It's too ridiculous. Actually, for all his gifts, his History will suffer from his lack of imagination. He can never put himself in another's place.

Still, enough of Nero; a wretched tawdry fellow when all is said and done. One last comment is appropriate and I must remember to pass it on to Tacitus in my next letter: Nero was a liar to the last, claiming that he died an artist. The trouble was he was never an artist, he was merely artistic.

Now for Galba.

How much shall I tell him?

Quite a lot, because Galba has always been by way of being a hero of my friend Tacitus. In later years, when we were together in the Senate, I have heard him speak of Galba's nobility and of the great service he did the State before he won the imperial crown. He has even said that, given the chance, and better fortune, Galba would have made a great Emperor, being at heart a Republican and a respecter of the Senate. He was extremely displeased when I remarked that everyone would have thought Galba capable of Empire – if he had never been Emperor.

All the same, though he disliked what I said, he couldn't deny its truth. I even saw him make a note of my words. It will be amusing if he repeats them in his History.

Not, of course, that I care how much he steals from me. The more he steals the better his History, and I have no desire for literary renown. What would I do with it here?

Galba then: just the sort of jerk Tacitus would admire. Galba was immensely proud of his ancestry: so proud that he embellished it and, on a public inscription, traced it back to Jupiter on his father's side and to Pasiphae, wife of King Minos of Crete, on his mother's. I have never had patience with such nonsense. His great-grandfather was one of Caesar's murderers, joining the conspiracy because he had been passed over for the consulship . . . The future Emperor's grandfather wrote a huge unreadable work of history, but I can't recall the subject. And his father was a hunchback. The story went round that when he was first with his future wife – I think her name was Achaica and she was descended from that Lucius Memmius who disgracefully sacked Corinth, destroying much of historical and artistic interest – he stripped to the waist, revealing his hump and declaring that he would never hide anything from her. If he kept this vow he was unique among husbands . . .

The future Emperor was born some ten years before the death of Augustus. He had an elder brother who became a bankrupt and cut his throat because Tiberius denied him a provincial command which he didn't deserve, but had hoped to use to mend his fortunes by screwing the provincials in the fine old Republican fashion, as practised by that arch-hypocrite Marcus Brutus. Galba liked to put it about that when he was a small boy the Emperor Augustus had prophesied a great future for him, even that he would eventually be Emperor himself. This was fanciful; everyone knows that Augustus was determined to keep the succession in his own family and, in any case, always carefully described himself as Princeps, not Emperor, a title which (he said) had a purely military association.

There were signs that Galba was destined for great things, all the same. When his grandfather, the historian, was sacrificing one day, an eagle swooped down and snatched the entrails from his hands, carrying them off to an oak tree well laden with acorns. The hunchback said this portended great honour for the family. The historian was more sceptical: 'Yes,' he reputedly said, 'on the day a mule foals!' Later Galba let it be known that a mule had foaled the day he heard of the Gallic rebellion led by Vindex, and decided this gave him a chance to aim for Empire himself. This story was widely believed – such is credulity.

Somebody also once told Tiberius that Galba would eventually be Emperor, when an old man. 'That doesn't worry me a bit,' the real Emperor replied.

All this is by the way and I've no doubt Tacitus already knows these stories and will repeat them if it suits him.

One reason why my friend so admires Galba is that he saw him as an exemplar of old-fashioned Republican virtue. For instance, he was delighted to learn that Galba followed the old practice of summoning all his household slaves, morning and evening, to say good-day and good-night to him. A perfectly pointless exercise, if you ask me.

Galba toadied up to the Augusta, Livia, when he was a young man and I believe she left him something in her will. Some say it was to please her that, when he was aedile in charge of the Games, he introduced the novelty of elephants walking a tightrope. That's ridiculous; Livia Augusta was never amused by such nonsenses.

He had a long career of public service, and didn't do badly, but never so well as to arouse the jealousy of emperors. That he survived both Gaius Caligula and Nero is to my mind evidence of his essential mediocrity. But he liked to pose as a disciplinarian of the old school. For instance, when he was Governor in Spain he crucified a Roman citizen who was said to have poisoned his ward, even though the evidence was provided by people who had an interest in the man's conviction. He didn't respond to pleas that it was wrong to crucify a citizen, except by commanding the cross to be taller than other crosses and white-washed to make it still more conspicuous.

Galba married only once. He disliked his wife, who was also named Livia, as I recall, and ignored his sons, showing no emotion when they died young. But, hypocrite that he was, he gave the love he had borne his dead wife as the reason why he never married again. Actually, he had no taste for women, nor indeed for boys, but only for mature men. Since everyone despises the man who, though an adult, takes the part of the woman in bed, he concealed this taste as best he could till he became Emperor. Then he was so excited when news was brought him of Nero's death that he seized hold of his freedman Icelus, a handsome swarthy brute, slobbered kisses over him, and told him to undress at once and pleasure him. I wonder what Tacitus will make of that story. Nothing, I dare say.

IX

It was, all the same, my dear Tacitus, whatever you might like to think, with apprehension that we awaited Galba's arrival in the capital. Word came that his advance was slow and blood-stained. Those suspected of being less than enthusiastic for his elevation were, as the saying went, 'eliminated'. Varro, Consul elect, and Petronius Turpilianus, a man of consular rank, were both put to death, without trial. Or so we heard.

Then the Praetorians were agitated. They already regretted Nero who had treated them so indulgently. Their prefect Nymphidius saw in their mood his opportunity to strike for Empire. He made sure that they learned of Galba's response to their demand for the customary donative: 'I choose my soldiers; I do not buy them.' Domitian said to me: 'What a fool the old man must be; generals have had to buy their troops since Pompey's day. I know enough history to know that, even if I don't bury my nose in the stuff as you do. Tiberius alone could express such sentiments and survive them. But then Tiberius was a great general, which Galba isn't, and a man of matchless authority.' This wasn't the first time I had heard Domitian speak admiringly of that Emperor, on whom, as you know, he was to brood long and lovingly in years to come. Old-style Republicans (of your stamp, my dear) purred as they approvingly repeated what they termed 'Galba's most noble sentiments', which certainly inspired Nymphidius to promote a mutiny. For a couple of days he was master of the city; Flavius Sabinus told his nephew Domitian that for those hours he went in fear of death, even though Nymphidius was his cousin.

But then word came that Galba's troops were within a day's march of Rome. Those of the Praetorians who had lent an ear to their prefect's seduction now felt panic. For all their reputation, few of them had any recent experience of war, and all disliked its imminent reality. When Nymphidius entered the camp to harangue them, they shouted him down. He withdrew in alarm, followed by a hail of oaths and missiles. I saw him white-faced and trembling, jostled by crowds as he made his way through the Forum towards his own house where he hoped to find refuge. He did not attain it. A troop of cavalry, either Galba's advance-runners or specially commissioned by Republican senators – no one knew which, then or later – forced their way through the mob, which itself parted and then fled in terror, and cut him down. They dragged his body to the Tarpeian Rock and hurled it, already lifeless, over; a purely symbolic enaction of the age-old penalty suffered by traitors. It lay at the foot of the rock till nightfall, no one daring to remove it.

By afternoon the Forum was deserted. It was a grey winter day and fear hung heavy as frost. I was unable to return across the river; detachments of soldiers, under whose command, if any, no one could tell, were to be seen at street corners and also at the bridges. The poor wretches were doubtless as confused as the mass of citizens. But in their confusion they were dangerous. You could not guess what they might take exception to, whom they might turn on in their own fear. I withdrew, hoping merely that my mother had kept to our apartment. So, by narrow lanes and a careful circuitous route, I made my way to the house in the Street of the Pomegranates where Domitian and Domatilla lodged with their aunt. I was happy to find all safe, but, though Domatilla looked on me with eyes of tender love, we did not dare embrace in the presence of others. It was hard, in my agitated mood, to be with her, and forbidden to touch her flesh, hold her in my arms, feel her lips against mine, and be restored in the shelter of our love. Domitian sat by the window, at an angle to it, able to look out, and believing he could not himself be observed from the street. He drank wine and bit his fingernails. I told them what I had seen in the city, from which the winter light was now being quickly withdrawn. Domitian spoke out to prevent his aunt from lighting the lamps. It was, he said, safer to sit in the dark.

'But why should we be endangered?' the aunt asked.

There was no answer to that, for there was no reason why we in particular, people of no position then, three of us young and the fourth an old woman given to good works and the practice of religion, should know fear. Yet we did.

When it was quite dark, there were steps on the staircase and a knocking at the door, which Domitian had shut with triple bolts after my entrance. He made signs in the gloom that we should not respond, but then a voice spoke, announcing that it was their uncle Flavius Sabinus.

He had come alone, without slaves or any of the soldiers whom he had at his command. Though he would not say that he sought refuge, that, I even then had no doubt, was his purpose in coming to his sister's house. He might be in no danger. But, as a public man in a responsible position, he feared he was; and preferred to withdraw himself from sight till the situation, whatever it might be, had resolved itself.

It embarrassed him that he could not tell us what was happening. All he would say was, 'I warned Nymphidius that the Praetorians would desert him. To whom have they ever been faithful?' We sat wakeful through the night. My own feelings were confused, disturbed. One moment I knew the infection of Flavius' fears, the next, catching sight of the girl's profile or feeling the gentle pressure of her breasts as she leaned over me to look out of the window, I was seized with near intolerable lust. Is there, I ask you, in the autumn of life anything which sets the nerves throbbing more smartly than summoning up memories of youthful desire? Summoning up is not the right expression; they rise unbidden as urgent dreams. *Que de souvenirs, que de regrets*, as the Greeks say.

Galba entered the city the following day. Without hesitation he revenged himself on those troops which had not openly and immediately done obeisance to him. When some marines whom Nero had armed hesitated to obey an order to return to the galleys, Galba ordered his Spanish cavalry to charge into the protesting mob of men. They were then rounded up, lined against a wall, and every tenth man cut down. This was, as Galba's supporters announced, evidence of his antique virtue. 'Decimation is an old Republican measure,' they said, nodding their heads.

When the semblance at least of peace and order had been restored, and it was clear that Galba was in command of the city, Flavius Sabinus went to pay his respects and was, to his surprise, confirmed in his post.

'Nevertheless,' Domitian said, 'he is not at ease. He says Galba's grip is uncertain. He says, too, that the old man is completely controlled by three of his staff whom my uncle terms "the Emperor's nursemaids".'

'Dangerous,' I said, 'to speak of them in that way, whoever they are. Who indeed are they?'

'I don't know much about them. How should I? I've been kept in this vile obscurity. One of them's called Titus Vinius. I think he was also a general in Spain. Another is Cornelius Laco . . .'

'Oh,' I said, 'you must know who he is. He used to be a Treasury official, and you must have seen him at the baths, eyeing up the wrestlers. He's very tall, rather fat, bald, with a big nose, and walks like a woman. Well, his tastes are a woman's, too.'

'He should have plenty of opportunity to gratify them then,' Domitian said, 'for he has been appointed Praetorian Prefect in succession to Nymphidius. He can command any brawny soldier he pleases to share his bed. And from what men say of the Praetorians, he won't find any difficulty in securing compliance. It's quite disgusting,' he added, his nose twitching. 'And, of course, the third nursemaid is the freedman Icelus, whom everyone says is our new Emperor's bedfellow. He's been made an equestrian, by the way, and wears so many jewels and gold bracelets you'd think he was on the stage. It doesn't sound to me as though the new regime is any more virtuous than Nero's. I wonder how long it can last?'

Everyone was asking that question. There were already rumours going around the Forum and the baths that the German legions were refusing to acknowledge Galba, and were intent on selecting an Emperor of their own.

'That's bad news for us,' Domitian's uncle said.

I didn't immediately realise what he meant.

'Wouldn't that depend on whom they chose?' I asked.

He looked at me as if I was a fool.

This letter, too, must be sent in an edited form. There is too much in it that is personal, that cuts too close to the bone.

X

Tacitus also may think I was foolish. He has the advantage of hindsight. Historians, knowing what happened, can make harsh judgements easily. But even now I do not think I was obtuse in not realising in the first weeks of Galba's brief reign that my Flavian friends had already set their sights on Empire. Why should I have done so? I had never been given occasion to think of Vespasian as other than an ill-bred mediocrity. Though Titus had talked of his own ambitions, I had never supposed they reached to the supreme power; and though he had always spoken of 'the old man's talent for always getting that bit further than anyone expects him to, and doing a job better, too, than was looked for', yet I couldn't conceive that a man whom provincials had pelted with rotten vegetables could aspire to wear the purple.

As a matter of fact, from various conversations, hints and speculations, of which there was an abundance in that fevered time, I was persuaded that if the Eastern armies were to follow the fashion and elect an Emperor of their own, they would choose L. Mucianus, not Vespasian. As Governor of Syria, Mucianus was nominally Vespasian's superior. He excelled him also in birth and achievement. Yet when I suggested as much to Flavius Sabinus, saying that if Galba failed to establish himself, his successor might be Mucianus, rather than whoever the German legions chose, his reply was brusque.

'You know nothing about it, boy. For the moment anyway there will be no movement from the legions stationed in the East. They will wait to see how things develop in Rome and beyond the Alps. But Mucianus wouldn't do. We've had more than enough of that sort of

..ing. The soldiers want a real man as their Emperor, and preferably one with sons of his own.'

Then he smiled, and patted my shoulder.

'Sorry to bite your head off,' he said, 'but it would be better if you didn't go around talking up Mucianus. Safer for you also.'

That was Flavius Sabinus' way. He could be crushing but, because he was naturally kind, always sought to mollify his reproof. He had a natural courtesy and polish of manner that his brother Vespasian lacked. Yet he had passed as much of his life in the camp as Vespasian himself. He had served under Corbulo in Armenia, and, despite distinguishing himself in battle, survived Corbulo's disgrace and retained Nero's confidence. Even Nero recognised that this stocky man with his close-cropped hair and down-turned mouth, which expressed freedom from any illusions, was trustworthy and honourable. Nero never even made jokes at his expense. In the next months I came to understand the selfless determination with which Flavius Sabinus advanced his family's interest – I say selfless because he never sought the first place for himself. But, equally, I never doubted that he was also driven by his understanding of what was best for Rome and the Empire.

When he spoke of the need to wait and see how events unfolded in Rome, this was, as I came to realise, because he was maturing a plan by which he hoped that his family could secure the Empire without further civil war.

Domitian broke the news to me.

'It's not fair,' he said. 'Do you know what my uncle is trying to do? He is working to persuade Galba to adopt my brother as his heir. Why Titus? Why is it always Titus? Why am I forever cast aside, or ignored, as of no account?'

'You have,' I said, 'the misfortune to be a younger son. It's the fate of younger sons to take second place.'

'It's not fair,' he said again, and again.

How tired I was of hearing this refrain.

Domatilla said he was unhappy and couldn't help it. He was not to be blamed for his discontent.

I had a letter from Titus, written in the cipher we had agreed. I have it before me, but shan't send it to Tacitus, it's too personal. Reading it now embarrasses me. But there is one paragraph I might let him see.

'. . . I rely on you to keep me abreast of a s.
be changing with an almost inconceivable rapidity
keen intelligence that allows you to penetrate below the
understand the significance of what others see only sup
What, then, is afoot? I know that my uncle hopes to pe.
Galba to name me his heir, and this hope, I must tell you, is
shared by my esteemed father. But it won't do. I have discussed
the possibility with L. Mucianus, who has, you will be amused to
learn, developed a special *tendresse* for me, even though I am some
years older than the beardless ganymedes with whom he chooses
to surround himself and who delight his rather excessive hours of
leisure. (He has many merits, this Mucianus, but the ability to work
long and hard is not among them.) Be that as it may, I admire his
sagacity, the penetration of his intellect. He is clear that it would not
be to my interest to be named by Galba as his heir. "The Empire," he
says, "is not now in any single man's gift. It is carried on the point of
the soldiers' swords. To be nominated by Galba is to be condemned
to failure and an early death. Caesar and Augustus won their supreme
position by force of arms, and the exercise of their political skills. We
are again in the same position as they were: the Republic in ruins, and
all to play for. But believe me, dear boy, it is only when much blood
has been shed and battles fought that stability can be restored." It is
remarkable that one who loves to lie in perfumed softness should
speak with the accents of a cold clear morning. But I am not asking
you to dissuade my uncle from his endeavours, if only because you
must fail to do so, and he would think it strange, even suspicious, that
you should make the attempt. In any case, it won't do our cause any
harm, if people hear my name mentioned in that context. Meanwhile
the urgent matter here is to quell this ridiculous Jewish revolt, that we
may be free to march to Italy when the time is ripe.'

XI

Tacitus complains that my accounts are disjointed, that I veer off into personal reminiscences irrelevant to the great matter of his History. No doubt he is justified. Yet, as I sit here, there is more pleasure to be had, a quickening of the blood, in remembering how I occupied myself with Domatilla, and with fancies concerning her, than in recalling the dismal and brutal catalogue of crime and misery that goes by the name of history. Besides, it is only when I lose myself in memories of erotic moments, that the past seems real to me. But to work.

Tacitus: you do well to chide me. I shall strive to keep to the point.

I was in the Forum the day that the news of the revolt of the German legions was confirmed. It was bitterly cold, being the first week of January, and there was snow on the hills above Albano. The confirmation came from the Procurator of Belgica, in a dispatch to the Senate. I think his name was Pompeius Propinquus, but what his relation was to the great Pompey escapes me. He reported that the troops on the German frontier had refused to accept Galba as Emperor. He gave, prudently, no reason. Some said it was on account of Galba's age, some on account of his reputation for meanness. Most however thought it was simply because he was not their general; and that they had therefore little to hope from him. They had not yet elected an Emperor themselves, but instead required the Senate and the Roman People to name one agreeable to all.

'That's the official line,' Domitian said, tugging my sleeve, 'but I know better. I have it on good authority that while they have sworn an oath of loyalty to the Senate and the Roman People, they have other plans.'

'Well, they must have,' I said. 'Everyone knows that the way things are such an oath is perfectly meaningless. Do they intend that the Guards should choose the Emperor?'

'That is not my uncle's opinion. He says they do not know what they want, only that they don't want Galba.'

'Who is there else?'

Domitian laughed: 'I thought you would be sure to know. You always pride yourself on being a couple of steps ahead of the game. This time you are well behind me.'

And he went off preening himself.

The truth was, it seemed to me, young and confessedly ignorant, that my question was good. The new commander of the legions in Germany was Aulus Vitellius, and it was to me impossible that soldiers could suppose that he was capable of Empire. It was true that I had never encountered Vitellius, but I had often heard my revered mother speak of him, and always with contempt. He had been, she remarked, the favourite in succession of Gaius Caligula, Claudius and Nero, 'which proves him to be a man of mean and despicable character'. He had often acted as procurer of virgins for the first and third of these Emperors, and it was his addiction to every form of vice which had secured him the continued favour of Nero, who could forgive anything except virtue. It was said that he had run through three fortunes, the last brought him by his most recent wife, and that he had had to pawn her jewels in order to finance his journey to his German command.

Yet in the fevered atmosphere of the Forum nothing was impossible. In any case, men said, Vitellius will be a puppet, and his two legates, Fabius Valens and Alienus Caecina, are able men and popular with the troops.

So rumours ran this way and that and everyone was calculating which way to jump.

It was in these days of unreality and fear that Titus suddenly arrived in Rome, sent when his father yielded to his uncle's insistence that there was a real chance that Galba would take a fancy to the young man and name him as his heir. His arrival perplexed me, on account of his most recent letter.

He had been in Rome two days before he came to see me in my mother's house, where I was confined with a heavy cold. My mother, having made him welcome and supplied us with wine, left us alone.

For the first time distance stretched between us. In the thirty months since we had last met, Titus had grown fleshy, I had acquired a beard. It was impossible to feel what we had previously felt.

By unspoken consent we did not dwell on what had gone before, though Titus thanked me for my letters which had, he said, been of more use to him than any other reports he had received.

'My father thinks well of them, too,' he said.

'Surely you didn't . . .' I paused, recollecting some of the passages in my early letters, before Domatilla had supplanted her brother in my affections.

'Father cares nothing for any of that stuff,' he said and, stretching out, pinched the lobe of my ear between thumb and forefinger. 'I haven't been faithful to you,' he said carelessly. 'Greek boys, of whom there is an abundance in Antioch, are too fetching and willing also. Greek girls, too, if it comes to that. Lustrous curls and glistening skin. Delightful. You should come to the East with me. I'd take you back with me, if it wasn't for this mess here in Rome – and the value I set on your reports, and your judgement. I hope you can stop my little brother from making a fool of himself.'

'Would it still,' I asked, 'be against your interests to be named by Galba as his heir and partner in Empire . . . ?'

'"The partner of my labours". That,' he said, 'as you will doubtless remember, my dear, is what Tiberius called Sejanus – just before he did for him. No, I don't want that. Galba is an old cunt who can't deliver anything.'

'You're right,' I said, 'he's finished, almost before he's started.'

It amazes me that I could have been so certain. But then, you must admit, my dear Tacitus, that, till I miscalculated in a manner that I now find explicable, if not pardonable, I showed a rare ability to judge men. Galba himself had outlived his abilities. He showed no understanding of the world in which he found himself: that claim to command soldiers, not to buy their loyalty, was sufficient evidence. And the men with whom he surrounded himself were third-raters. There was indeed no future in Galba; he was an actor waiting to be howled off stage.

'The question is,' Titus continued to fondle my cheek, in an absent-minded manner, as if the touch of once-desired flesh stimulated his mental processes. 'The question is,' he repeated . . . and then laughed. 'For the moment, my dear, the question that really concerns me is whether we should have another bottle of wine.'

Later in the evening he spoke of the Jewish Revolt. It fascinated him, while the struggle for the succession here in Rome seemed only to fatigue him. 'Little men,' he said, 'with no conception of the meaning of Empire.'

'I don't understand that myself,' I said. 'I mean, it seems to me that we sort of stumbled into Empire, acquired it even in a fit of absence of mind, with no desire other than immediate gratification, and perhaps the chance to grab the spoils of Asia.'

'There is that,' he said, 'but there's more to it also; and that's why I view the likes of Galba and Vitellius with such contempt; and know that, if we bide our time and keep our nerve, they will trouble us for only a little.'

As I listened I felt what I had not known in Titus before: a strength of will was now added to his keen intelligence and charm. It even frightened me to think of what had passed between us, for I saw that, if the memory of this were ever to embarrass him, he would rid himself of me without compunction.

He said: 'We are in danger of slipping back into the old politics when men competed for glory as well as office. Augustus destroyed Republican virtue, as men chose to call this strife. Tiberius suppressed it. The feebleness of his successors has allowed it to flourish again, like a noxious weed. I should not complain, since I shall be the beneficiary of this new, or rather renewed, struggle to get to the summit of riches and power over things. I have no doubt of that. But when I myself reach the top, I shall act like Augustus. And I shall do so for no selfish reason, but because Rome requires it. I have seen our greatness in the East, and I know that when Virgil had the gods promise Aeneas 'limitless empire', they promised what was good for the world. But now, here, we slide back into the sterile contest between factions, indifferent to the civilising mission of Rome.'

Then he spoke of the Jewish Revolt, and of the Jews themselves. They were, he said, a remarkable people, remarkable for the intensity and narrowness of their views. They held, he told me, that they were the chosen people of the one true god. It was nonsense, of course. Everyone knew that the gods were many – or none; and that they aligned themselves with different races and individuals, quarrelling among themselves, if the poets were to be believed. He smiled to show that in his opinion such credulity was fit only for children. And yet he couldn't but admire these narrow bigots of Jews. 'There is,' he remarked, 'something splendid in their obstinate stupidity.' They made, too, for worthy adversaries. Naturally, Rome would crush them. 'I shall destroy their temple myself,' he said, 'but only because their monotheism and intolerance have no place in our Empire – as I understand it. All the same I can't but admire them, they die so well.'

So we talked, long into the night. The city fell to a murmur beyond us. Titus, drinking two cups of wine to every one I drank, exposed his deepest thoughts and ambitions to me. Yet, as the night wore on, and the first shafts of light awoke the morning sky, I felt him grow away from me. He had experienced what I had only imagined. He was hard and foreign to me. I was glad when, a day or two later, he left Rome and returned to his Jewish War. The last thing he said was: 'I've stopped my uncle's meddling in my career. That's what I came home to do. Remember, I rely on you to keep me posted – and try to keep my little brother out of mischief.'

XII

You will have, Tacitus, your own version of the events of that January, and I have no doubt it will be more favourable to Galba than my memories. All the more reason to offer you what will not please you. A historian should not be a partisan of one party in the State.

What will you say of Otho, I wonder?

I can't imagine you will find much to praise there.

Yet Otho was not wholly contemptible. I have that from my mother who had known him as a young man. She used to say that there was nothing malicious in his wildness; that his manners were naturally good; and that his wit was delightful.

The family was distinguished, boasting descent from the old Etruscan royal house. Of course, I know that the further back you go, the more distinguished ancestry usually becomes. But people seem to have accepted them for what they said they were, even though our Otho's father, Lucius, was reputed to be the bastard son of the Emperor Tiberius, whom he resembled in appearance. Our Otho – Marcus Salvius – was born while Tiberius was still alive, in the year that Camillus Arruntius and Domitius Ahenobarbus were Consuls. His father frequently rebuked him for wildness – he used to stalk the city at night with a gang of friends and toss any drunks or disabled men they encountered in a blanket, just for fun. When his father died, leaving him already in debt – for the father was as good at wasting money as the son, though he did so by silly investments rather than extravagance – the young man pretended to have a passion for one of the Empress' freedwomen who was ugly as sin and twenty years older than he was. Naturally this made him an object of mockery: he didn't care. It had secured him entry to the inner circle of the Empress Agrippina, and so he was able to become a bosom friend of her son Nero. It was difficult to say which of them showed a greater talent for debauchery. Yet my mother has always said that Otho was essentially good-hearted. And her judgement is to be respected.

The day Nero had fixed for the murder of Agrippina, Otho provided a distraction by hosting a lavish luncheon party. This doesn't mean that he necessarily knew of Nero's proposed crime. It could be coincidence. Certainly Agrippina had never ceased to show her liking for Otho.

Later Otho went through a form of marriage with Poppaea Sabina, who was already Nero's mistress. I put it like that because that was the way people used to describe it. But, in my opinion, Otho and Poppaea were really in love. Only they couldn't escape Nero. Certainly, I have heard that from the first night Otho bedded Poppaea he conceived a violent hatred and jealousy of the Emperor; Poppaea was beautiful as whatever you like, and not a woman any man of spirit would willingly share, especially with a creature like Nero.

He even tried to keep Nero from Poppaea, and so was charged with adultery – his partner being his own wife. Absurd, isn't it? Given your views, Tacitus, you should have some fun with this situation.

Whether because he still had some affection for him, or because he feared other consequences, Nero didn't have Otho murdered. Instead he despatched him to Lusitania as Governor – and forbade him to take his wife with him. There was nothing Otho could do but submit and, though he may have been distressed to abandon Poppaea, he was quite happy to leave his creditors behind. Lusitania wasn't a disagreeable posting, even for a dandy like Otho; and by all accounts he governed the province with restraint and good judgement.

He was one of the first to join Galba in revolt, probably because he had never forgiven Nero for kicking Poppaea to death. (She was pregnant at the time, but I am assured that the child couldn't have been Otho's. Or Nero's for that matter; he was sterile by then, a judgement of the gods whom he had outraged, some say.)

No doubt another reason for adhering to Galba was that an astrol- oger had assured Otho that he was destined to be Emperor and he thought also that Galba, being old, could be persuaded to adopt him as his successor. What he hadn't reckoned on was that, first, as soon as he returned to Rome, he would be beset by his creditors demanding payment of loans swollen huge by unpaid interest; and, second, that neither Icelus nor Laco supported his claim.

I don't know what their objections were, and can assume only that they thought Otho hostile to them, or too strong-minded to be controlled by them.

That then was the situation when word came during the first week of January that the German legions had rejected Galba, and had asked the Guards to choose an Emperor.

The word straightaway went round that Galba intended to strengthen his position by associating a younger colleague with him in the Empire. After all, he was held to believe, it was only his age that caused men to hesitate to commit themselves to his cause. Once the succession was assured they would naturally do so. He was encouraged in this belief by Laco and Icelus, whose own continued power depended entirely on his, and also by the Consul T. Vinius, a man of inordinate ambition, with a reputation for double-dealing. The question was: whom would the old man select?

Everyone discussed the probabilities. Domitian was so carried away by the excitement that, absurdly, he even put himself in the aged Emperor's way, addressing him in a flattering poem (written unfortunately in limping hexameters, for, unlike me, he had never benefitted from our rhetoric master, and could not turn an elegant verse). When I told him, roundly, with that candour which has always been my wont, that his hopes were ridiculous, since, in the first place, Galba had no reason to choose him and, in the second, even if by some miracle he did so, then his father Vespasian would not permit him to assume so dangerous a role, he bit his lip till the blood started from it, and his tongue flicked out to lick the blood away.

I mention this incident, trivial as it was, merely to remind you, Tacitus, that those January days were ones when even the most absurd and outrageous of possibilities seemed, to many, not improbable.

Had Galba had his wits about him, or even had he been left by his courtiers in possession of such wits as remained to him, he would have selected Otho, without whose support and help he would never have been able to seize the purple. But, as I say, Laco and Icelus disliked Otho. Some claim that they resented the fact that one so effeminate in manner and certain habits as Otho (he was, you will recall, accustomed to shave all his body-hair, and scented himself like a Corinthian brothel-boy), should have been indifferent to their charms. But I think this nonsense. The real reason was that they were determined to choose a successor whom they could control as they controlled Galba; and they knew that Otho would not permit this. The Consul T. Vinius did favour Otho, but, finding opinion against him, kept his views to himself, an act of prudence which would cost him dear; nevertheless he opened secret negotiations with Otho.

My source for this information is, or rather was, Flavius Sabinus. Later Titus confirmed what his uncle had said.

Otho fully expected that Galba would select him; and he had reason for his confidence. This led him to give assurances to his creditors that he would soon be in a position to satisfy them. Which promise added to his subsequent desperation.

Now Laco and Icelus produced their candidate: Gnaeus Licianus Piso. You know all about his ancestry, which was distinguished, so there is no need for me to dwell on it. No doubt he would have made a fair enough choice, being, as I remember you saying once, 'a young man, but in appearance and manner one of the old school' – if, that is, anyone still cared for the old school, or if anyone had heard of this Piso. Few had, though he was the nephew of the Piso who had been the figurehead of the conspiracy against Nero.

I was indeed an exception, for Piso, before he went into exile for fear of Nero, had been a friend of Lucan, with whom I used to see him at the baths. He had many admirers there, for he was tall, well-built, with close-cut black curly hair, high cheek-bones, a flat stomach, and long shapely thighs. Only the small, pursed-up mouth spoiled what would otherwise have been perfect beauty. Lucan used to say that the mouth was the true indication of his character, for Piso (he said) was of a chilly and secret nature. 'As far as I know he's never been in love with anyone, except himself,' he once said.

'But he's a friend of yours nevertheless?'

'There are friends and friends,' Lucan said with a smile. 'I've known him all my life and I can't dislike him, but . . . Besides our mothers are great friends, so we've lots in common.'

This then was the young man – still young, for he was only thirty or thirty-one – whom the aged Galba had selected as his companion in Empire. There were those who, noting the resemblance in physical type between Icelus and Piso, supposed Galba would take him into his bed also. But that was nonsense. Piso had far too much pride and self-esteem to be willing to satisfy Galba's senile lust. As it was, the whole thing was done with the utmost formality, as was Galba's style, and he decided to adopt the young man.

So, he took him by the hand, and said, 'If I were a private citizen and were now adopting you according to the Act of the Curia before the Pontiffs, then it would be a high honour to me to introduce into into my family a descendant of the great Pompey and of the no less to be honoured Marcus Crassus . . .'

(This, by the way, was the first time I had ever heard anyone suggest that Marcus Crassus, who carved up the State at Luca with Caesar and Pompey and whom my great-great-uncle by marriage Mark Antony always used to call 'that fat booby', was worthy of any special honour; but let that pass.)

'Likewise,' Galba continued, 'it would be a signal honour for you to add to the nobility of your family the honours of the Sulpician and Lutatian houses.'

Yawn, yawn was the general reaction to this speech. I know, my dear Tacitus, that you have a tenderness – a tenderness which I find touching – for the old nobility; but, speaking as one of far nobler birth than yours, it didn't take the indifference displayed by those who heard Galba's words to persuade me that the day of that sort of aristocracy was dead. Frankly, in the New Rome, nobody at heart cares a damn who your ancestors were. We may be better or worse for this, I can't tell. But that's how it is. If you pretend otherwise in your History, you will be lying to your readers.

Then Galba went on to explain that, in adopting Piso, he was following the precedent set by the Divine Augustus, who had 'placed on an eminence next his own first his nephew Marcellus, then his son-in-law Agrippa, afterwards his grandsons Gaius and Lucius, and finally his stepson Tiberius Nero'. If I had been Piso I wouldn't have found this catalogue of heirs, all but one of whom never succeeded, of any comfort; but Piso looked so much as if he took his elevation, which he had done nothing to earn, as his due, that the thought probably never occurred to him.

Then Galba proceeded to give his new son advice about the trials of his new position.

'Hitherto you have been tested by adversity; now you must confront the keener temptations which prosperity brings you. You will be assailed by adulation, by that worst poison of the heart which goes by the name of flattery, and by the selfish interests of individuals.'

All this was no doubt very true – or might have been. Piso inclined his head. No smile flickered across his face. He was perfectly respect-ful.

Galba raised both arms aloft and cried out in a louder voice so that the crowd which had gathered round could hear his words:

'Could the vast and mighty frame of this Empire have stood and preserved its balance without the direction of a single controlling spirit, then I, on account of my lineage and my deeds, might have been thought not unworthy of restoring the Republic in its pristine splendour. But, alas, this cannot be. Therefore we have been long reduced to a position in which my age can confer no greater good on the Roman people than a worthy successor, your youth in its turn no greater than a good Emperor. Under Tiberius, Gaius and Claudius, we were the inheritance of a single family. Now we have made a new start, a renewal of Rome, and the choice which begins today with us will be a substitute for Republican freedom.'

Then he went on to explain how it was not the legions that had revolted against Nero, but Nero himself who, by reason of his profligacy, cruelty, self-indulgence and neglect of duty had proved himself unworthy to rule.

Nero, in short, had betrayed himself, and those who had rebelled against him were innocent of any disloyalty. This was quite a clever suggestion for it was intended to render any refusal to acknowledge the legitimacy of Galba's position out of order, Galba being, unlike Nero, virtuous. It was, I'm sure, prompted by T. Vinius.

Finally, to allay any doubts, he said grandly that Piso must not be alarmed if, after a movement which had shaken the whole world, a couple of distant legions had not yet resumed their duty and acknowledged his authority.

Piso certainly showed no sign of alarm, nor of elation either. Did it, I wonder now, cross his dull conventional mind that in accepting the gift of Empire from the aged Galba, he was entering a dark wood from which he might not emerge?

These formalities being completed, Galba resolved that he should lead his new son to the camp of the Praetorians that they might learn, even before the Senate, of how their Emperor had arranged the succession. No doubt that decision was wise, being an admission that the Praetorians, and not the Conscript Fathers, had the power to make and unmake Emperors. Nevertheless it cast a dark ironic

shadow on Galba's pompous and all but Republican pronounce-
ments.

Domitian and I resolved to follow in their train.

It was only an hour after noon, but darkness was already imminent.
Black clouds hung over the city, shifted only by a sullen gusty wind,
which then however blew up still more dark and heavy successors.
Even while Galba spoke to Piso the palace had been illuminated by
shafts of lightning; thunder rolled like the noise of battle round the
hills. Heavy rain prevented departure for the camp for at least half an
hour. Some said that the thunder and lightning were evil omens, and
that Galba should put off the address to the soldiers till the morning.
Others recalled how, as legend has it, the night before great Julius'
murder had been as wild as, but no wilder than, this afternoon; and
what did that portend?

At last the rain stopped. Galba was helped to a litter, for, as a result of
an attack of gout, he could not walk any considerable distance without
emitting shrill cries of pain, which detracted from his dignity. Piso
walked beside the litter, tall, impassive, bound up in his thoughts;
and an excited crowd, Domitian and myself among them, followed
the litter.

The soldiers were assembled. Not then having experience of the
military life, I was unable to judge their mood with any certainty. The
silence with which they greeted Galba's announcement that he had
adopted Piso, following the precedent of the Divine Augustus, and
also the custom by which a soldier chooses a comrade, might only
have been evidence of their stern discipline. But I could not think so. I
caught the eye of one centurion, a grizzled veteran with a scar running
from his right eye across his cheek and even as far as the throat; and,
though there was no expression, the eye being dull as a beast's, I read
there either scepticism or indifference.

Galba then said: 'Soldiers, you know me for what I am, a straight
man. So I shall not conceal from you the news that two legions, the 4th
and the 18th, led astray by a handful of factious officers, are refusing
to acknowledge my authority. Mutiny is too strong a word to use. At
any rate, it is premature. But they are guilty of insubordination. I have
no doubt however that when they learn of my arrangement for the
succession and of how these have been approved by you, the best
of soldiers, they will soon come to heel and return to their duty. For
duty, soldiers, is the watchword of Rome.'

Domitian was disposed to admire these sentiments. You may not believe that, Tacitus, for you judge him by the Emperor he was, and you have often said to me that men are forever the same, their character fixed, and only its appearance and revelation changing. But I disagree. Why should I not? I am conscious that I am not now what I once was. So, you must believe me that Domitian was generously moved by Galba's sentiments.

However Domitian was also acute – at least when his own interests did not distort his judgement. So, observing the soldiers as they talked among themselves after the parade was dismissed, and as they formed into little huddled groups and hung around discussing what had been said that afternoon, instead of hurrying off to the barracks and thence to the wine-shops, Domitian said, 'All the same, they're not content. He should have given them money, or at least promised a substantial sum.'

'I think you're right. They're remembering that boast, "I choose my soldiers, I do not buy them."'

'Yes,' Domitian said, 'it's not something I'll forget when my time comes.'

I thought him, again, a foolish fellow. Why should he suppose he had a time that would come?

XIII

A bitter and scornful letter from Tacitus: if only there was as much sense as style in what he writes!

He upbraids me for my characterisation of Galba. Galba, he tells me, was a man who belonged to a more virtuous age. In our degenerate time it was his virtues rather than his vices which destroyed him: his old-fashioned inflexibility and his excessive sternness. And so on. The truth is that Tacitus himself has a view of Rome which was out of date centuries ago. He would play Cato charging the great Scipio with treason because he introduced Greek culture to Rome.

In any case, I have my own opinion concerning antique virtue, which is that it was deficient in generosity and humanity, rooted in fear of the gods who, in truth, no more concern themselves with the fate of men than with the leaves that are torn from the trees by autumn gales; it was narrow and harsh in temper, even to the point of brutality.

Moreover, even Galba understood that the great frame of Empire had rendered Republican institutions inadequate for its government.

Yet this letter disturbed me, more than for some days I dared to admit to myself.

Is it because I am no longer a Roman?

I snarled at my woman, betook myself to a wine-shop, and soaked my questioning spirit in liquor. There was a German boy serving whom I had not seen before. Was it because he appeared modest and shy that I commanded a chamber and had the woman of the inn send him to me? Or was it his so red lips and dark troubled eyes that aroused my brief demanding lust? I stripped him of his tunic, ran

69

my hands over his thin body, felt his revulsion, and compelled him to submit. He cried a little when I gave him gold.

'You would not understand,' I said. 'I am searching for something which I lost many years ago.'

His name is Balthus. His arms were so thin I could have cracked them. There was a delicacy to his behaviour that intensified my lust and brought me shame.

Tacitus denies that Galba took Icelus as his lover. He was not that sort of man, he says. Does he not realise that everyone is more complicated in his nature than he would have the world know? Does he not realise that if we knew the thoughts and desires of our companions, we would shun all society?

Balthus is in no way like Titus. But, without Titus, would I have arranged to have him again next week? He was born a slave, I a free man and a Roman noble. But what is freedom, what slavery, when the passions are aroused? Yet I was almost perfunctory when it came to the moment. Afterwards I felt a rare tenderness because I had wronged him.

And actually it was like what I came to feel for Domatilla when I knew we had, without willing it, so deeply wronged each other.

I didn't tell Tacitus all I might have said of Piso. I might for instance have mentioned that there were those who said then that the young Piso, only exiled on account of his complicity in his uncle's plot against Nero, was thought by some to have been among those who laid information against the conspirators.

I have no proof that he did so. What I do know is that Lucan distrusted him and expressed jealousy of him. He told me that this was because they had quarrelled over a woman. It may be so. Piso however was never otherwise known to have taken any interest in women. Nor in boys either; I can be sure of that because the first or second occasion I met him at the baths, I embarked on a little flirtation with him – entirely on account of his beauty and before I had taken note of his mean mouth – and he rebuffed me coldly. When I told Titus of this, for in those days I told him everything, or near everything, he was greatly amused and assured me it was common knowledge that Piso was addicted to masturbation because he could never love or trust anyone except himself. Lucan's story he refused to believe.

I shrink from giving my account of the 15th January. Wine is a comforter, wine and my Greek-Scythian woman, Araminta. I rely on her, she satisfies me, she arouses no feeling in me; and that is a species of, at least, contentment.

XIV

Flavius Sabinus sent to us before dawn, advising us to keep the house that day. Domatilla and the aunt added their pleas to this counsel, which was undoubtedly good. But Domitian and I were young and bold. At any rate each was eager to impress his courage upon the other; and we would not obey.

What is strange is that we never questioned why Flavius Sabinus should have so advised us. It was not till later that I realised he must have been privy to the conspiracy.

Not, of course, that we knew there was any such thing brewing, or not precisely, or what form it might take. It was rather that the hum of rumour in the city was irresistibly disturbing. Every day for the last week more reports of the mutiny of the German legions had excited the Forum. Though it was impossible that they could have advanced even to the northern Alps, men talked as if they might be in the city any day. The price of bread and wine and oil soared as traders took advantage of the public alarm.

Then a second message came from Flavius: there had, he said, been talk the previous evening of seizing Otho, and putting him to death. Otho, he added, was desperate. He had been heard to say that he might as well be killed by an enemy in battle as by his creditors in the Forum. The streets, Flavius wrote, were no place today for us.

So naturally, dismissing such fears, we sallied forth. I have to say that Domitian showed no sign of cowardice that day.

We learned in the Forum that the Emperor was sacrificing in the Temple of Apollo. The word was that the omens were bad. The priest told him the entrails had a sinister colour, that an enemy threatened and that he should stay at home that day. Everyone in the Forum seemed to know of this.

'Have they arrested Otho, then?' a fat equestrian called out.

'Not yet, but the Senate are about to meet in order to declare him a public enemy.'

'But that's wrong,' another cried. 'What harm has Otho ever done? He's a true friend of the Roman People, that's for sure.'

'Galba, Otho, Piso – what difference will it make to the likes of us?' the keeper of the tavern into which we had retired demanded. 'The question is only, who will keep the German legions from marching on the city?'

'They say Piso has already set off to negotiate with them – with full power to conclude a bargain.'

'Piso? He's a long streak of piss, if you ask me,' said another. 'Conclude a bargain? Him? Pardon me if I fart.'

In fact, as we now know, Otho himself had been at the Temple of Apollo, and had seen and heard what the priest said. There he had been approached by friends who told him that his architect and the contractors were waiting for him. So he excused himself, saying that he was thinking of buying a property, but, being unsure of its condition, had ordered a survey. I suppose this was a joke as well as a deception. He was certainly thinking of taking over a property.

Why Otho had attended the ceremony in the Temple of Apollo I do not pretend to guess. By doing so he had put himself in great danger. But it may be that, uncertain whether the troops would indeed rise in his support, he thought it safer to disguise his disaffection by attending. For, if he had not done so, and if the troops had refused to move in accordance with the prompting of his agents, then his absence, being remarked on, would have been taken as evidence of disloyalty. But it may simply be that the gamble of attendance appealed to his peculiar sense of humour; he was ever a gambler.

Now, leaving the temple, leaning on a freedman's arm to suggest that he felt no urgency, despite the speed of his departure, he passed through the Palace of Tiberius to the Velabrum, and from there to the golden milestone which stands near the Temple of Saturn. All this we learned later.

Had it been immediately known that scarce two dozen of the Guard were there to salute him as Emperor and raise him aloft on a gilded chair, then Galba could have snuffed the conspiracy before it was properly underway. But Otho's agents were active, and it was at once the talk of the Forum that the whole of the Praetorians had revolted, and were marching on the palace to make an end of their aged and despised Emperor.

Word came confusingly to Galba, so that he did not know which report he should believe. It was resolved that the loyalty of the cohort stationed in the palace should at once be put to the test. If it was involved in the revolt, then all was lost. So they were paraded before the palace to be harangued by Piso.

I have no doubt, Tacitus, that, favouring Piso and wishing to honour his memory, you will compose a noble speech supposed to have been given by him. But I was there and the truth is that he spoke haltingly and in a confused manner, as one who has been overtaken by events which he does not understand. His only sensible act was to promise the soldiers a donative for their loyalty – better late than never – but he spoiled this by adding that it would be at least as great as any payment they might receive for treason. This was feeble. It put the idea of desertion in the minds of any who were not already entertaining it.

Messengers were then sent to the troops belonging to the army of Illyricum who were stationed by the Portico of Vipsanius Agrippa in the Campus Martius, and to those legions recruited to serve on the German frontier which were then encamped by the Hall of Liberty on the Aventine. But they hesitated to send to the legion levied from the fleet, for it was known that these troops hated Galba on account of the murder of their comrades who had remained loyal to Nero. Yet, so feckless had been Galba's short rule, these soldiers had not been disarmed. Within the hour it was known that they had declared for Otho. Finally, tribunes were despatched to try to recall the Praetorians to their duty: a hopeless, if necessary, endeavour.

How argument raged among those around Galba I do not know. But it is probable that some were for barricading themselves in the palace, and defying the conspirators to storm it. This plan had something to commend it, since, in order to approach the palace, Otho would have had to force his way through the swirling mob of citizens, drawn to the events of the day as to the theatre. Domitian and I were among them and, at this moment, their sentiments were still inclined to Galba. A butcher near me was shouting again and again for Otho's head, and each time his words were greeted with cheers. But even then I was aware of the fickleness of a mob.

Others in the palace were for action. Galba must gather such troops as he had and march out against Otho.

Whether either party gained the mind of the aged Emperor, no one knows. Some say Galba was rendered speechless by the shock of the revolt, others that he conducted himself boldly. From my knowledge of him, and from what I learned later, I suggest that he swayed from one view to another.

Be that as it may, Piso was seen to lead a detachment of soldiers from the palace. The crowd parted to let them through, still encouraging them with protestations of loyalty. 'That's our boy,' the butcher yelled, 'you go and sort these fuckers out.' The mob will ever applaud what appears to be decisive action. But Piso's face was a frozen mask.

Piso had hardly gone – to the camp of the Praetorians? or wherever? – when someone cried out that Otho was slain. He had seen him fall with his own eyes. A great cheer was raised. Many were relieved to think that there would be no great shedding of blood.

Domitian said: 'We must get into the palace and display our loyalty.'

Others had anticipated him. Several Senators and equestrians, who had been hovering uncertainly on the fringes of the crowd, now had their slaves clear them a way forward. They burst open the doors of the palace (Domitian and myself in their wake) and thronged round Galba, protesting their loyalty and crying out that they had been denied the opportunity to display it, denied also their revenge on the traitor Otho. It was a contemptible exhibition.

To his credit Galba seemed unimpressed by their performance. That was how it first seemed to me. Then, observing the blankness of his eye, and his wrinkled face quite without any expression, I wondered if the old man had any firm understanding of what was happening. Not that that was clear.

Someone, not the Emperor himself, gave an order, and a slave began to fasten him into his cuirass. This was not easy. He could scarcely stand. Then, when he was armed, it was evident that he was in danger of being knocked over by the turbulence of the crowd, more and more of whom were still invading the palace to assure him of their undying devotion. So, at the order of Icelus, he was placed in a chair, and raised on the shoulders of four Nubian slaves above the level of the people. He was in this elevated position when a member of the bodyguard shoved his way forward, his sword extended and dripping blood. The sight silenced the babblers.

'Whose blood is that?' Icelus asked.

'It is the blood of Otho, who I have slain,' the soldier said.

If he expected a reward (as he must have), he was disappointed.

'Who gave that order?' Galba said.

'What a stupid old man,' I whispered to Domitian. 'Come on. This is not where we should be.'

He followed me out, reluctant and puzzled.

'I don't understand,' he said, when we were beyond the palace. (I'd had to take him by the arm and half-drag him with me.) 'Why shouldn't we have stayed? It could have done me only good if I had had a chance to impress Galba with my loyalty. Now you've deprived me of the chance.'

'You'll be grateful one day,' I said, and hurried him down the flight of steps that serve as a short-cut to the Forum. It wasn't till I had got him into a wine-shop, and sat us down before a flask of Marino that I was ready to explain.

'There's something wrong. I don't know just what, but there is. For one thing, that soldier was lying. Oh, he may have thought it was Otho he killed, I can't say, but I don't believe it was.'

'You're crazy,' Domitian said, 'and I'm to lose my chance of impressing myself on the Emperor because you take a foolish notion in your head . . .'

'Remember what your uncle advised,' I said, 'that we should keep the house. Today's not over yet. Now let's drink this wine and wait on events.'

For the moment there was a lull. The crowd still jostling to and fro in the Forum was tossed on waves of anxiety. It was certain Otho was dead; it was not certain. On the contrary, the Guards were even now advancing from their camp and preparing slaughter for the city. Not so; they were indeed coming but to express their loyalty to Galba and do obeisance to him. Piso had collected a troop of cavalry and was hunting down the last of the rebels; Piso had been seen fleeing the city disguised as a woman. In short everything was said, and for a moment everything was believed, till it was contradicted by what was said next. So, knowing nothing, the crowd was held in a state of constant apprehension.

There was a cheer when a litter bearing Galba was seen to emerge from the palace, and begin the descent to the Forum, guarded by the cohort that had been stationed on palace duty that week.

'Galba has come to give thanks to the gods for his deliverance,' some cried. 'Long live the Emperor.'

Though many had come to see him destroyed, all now felt it prudent to applaud his deliverance; and those who hated him most cheered loudest. Domitian, too, would have cheered, but I laid my hand across his mouth.

'It's the cavalry.' That was the new cry, and the crowd was seized with terror. I drew Domitian into the portico of a temple, I forget which now. As I did so I saw the standard-bearer of the cohort that guarded the Emperor seize Galba's effigy, hold it aloft, and then hurl it to the ground. It was a moment of horror, affecting all. The populace fled the Forum seized with panic sudden as a thunder-storm. And indeed it began to rain, heavily, the rain flung by a gust of wind in the faces of the slaves who carried the litter. The bodyguard hesitated, then with one accord, cried out, 'Otho for Emperor.' The terrified bearers ran now this way, now that. Near the little lake which goes by the name of Curtius, Galba was thrown out of the litter. He lay on the ground, then I could see him no longer as he was surrounded by the soldiers who had sworn to guard him, and they hacked at his head and body with their swords.

I had heard accounts of murder, seen gladiators killed, often. I had never seen anyone who mattered butchered. One soldier cut through the throat, trampling his sword down on it. They vied with each other to acquire merit.

Others died also. Vinius cried out that Otho had not commanded his death. He attempted flight. A circular swing of a legionary sword caught him behind the knee. He fell to the ground and another legionary pinned his body to the earth. This happened just outside the Temple of the Divine Julius. Laco was, I believe, murdered soon after his master. Icelus, being a freedman, was reserved for public execution.

The whole thing was over in less time than it takes to tell it. We had a new Emperor, Otho, who later in the day, when it was already dark, attended the Senate where he was greeted with cheers and acclamation. They hurried to confer the tribunician power on him, rendering his person inviolate.

'Like Galba's,' Domitian muttered.

Piso survived till near night. He had crept into the temple of the
Vestal Virgins and remained hidden for some hours. But information
was laid and a soldier belonging to the British auxiliary infantry (and
therefore indifferent to the crime of sacrilege) forced his way in,
disregarding the protest of the priestesses, dragged that morning's
deputy-emperor into the street, and cut his throat. Otho is said to
have received Piso's head with unmingled joy.

By this time Domitian and I had returned to his aunt's house. It was
from Flavius Sabinus that I later received the full and exact account of
these murders or executions – call them what you will. During the day
we had been buoyed up by excitement and the quivering uncertainty
of the changing moment. We had not even felt the cold tremble of
fear. Now, safe before the stove, nursing goblets of mulled wine and
listening to the scolding of the aunt – she had a voice like a seagull
when alarmed – I found I could not stop shaking. Domitian sat still as
a monument but for a nerve that twitched in his right cheek. Twice he
lifted his hand and placed it on the side of his face, as if to arrest that
movement. But, when he lowered it again, the twitch still zig-zagged.
    A rap at the door brought us to our feet. My hand stretched out in
search of a weapon. But it was Flavius Sabinus who entered. And he
was smiling.

XV

I cursed Tacitus for making me relive that day. He will judge (when he has doctored my account) that its horrors were the consequence of the degeneracy into which the loss of Republican virtue and liberty had thrust us. 'Never surely,' he wrote in a recent letter in which he urged me to delve more deeply into the putrid sink of memory, 'was there more conclusive evidence that the gods take no thought for our happiness, but only for our punishment.' I would not dispute that, merely observe that licence was as unbounded in the days of the Republic from which only the wise government of Augustus and Tiberius rescued us. The horror of the years that succeeded Nero was not the result of one particular form of government, as my old friend, so full of imaginative sympathy with the distant past, supposes; it was the ineluctable consequence of the failure of government.

Philosophers have argued much concerning the nature of men, whether we are actuated by virtue or by fear. For my part, I know from bitter experience, from reflection and self-study, from the observation of others and from my reading of history, that men are born wicked; that virtue is something only laboriously achieved, in spite of nature; and that the driving force in any man who has achieved any degree of power – even power over his own household, family and slaves – is fierce, dictatorial, destructive, even if also self-destructive. Pride, jealousy, anger, the desire for revenge on account of slights real or imagined, are forces few can, or wish to, resist.

Consider Galba. At the age of seventy-three he had enjoyed prosperity all his days. He was rich, had won the esteem, or at least the respect, of his peers. Why should he put all that at risk merely to wear the purple and be saluted as Emperor?

And Otho? A man you would have said formed for pleasure. Was that not enough to content him? There are pleasant orange groves, soft breezes and lovely docile girls in Lusitania. Yet he, too, would be called Emperor, by men no one of intelligence or taste could respect.

'Isn't it the case,' I remember saying to Domitian – perhaps not that evening, but one soon after – 'that the condition of man is a war of everyone against everyone?'

I did not believe this. That is, I did not believe it should be so. Or did I? Should be? What is there to form 'should be'?

Domitian said: 'If you are right, and life is warfare, then it behoves one to make sure of winning.'

Flavius Sabinus laughed. 'You speak like a child,' he said. 'It is not in mortals to command success. Therefore . . .'

'Therefore, what?' I said. 'Trust to the gods? They are deaf. Seek to deserve it? I have not noticed that merit is rewarded.'

Flavius picked up the dice-box and threw.

'A pair of sixes,' he said.

'There's no merit in that, sir,' I replied.

'Who said there was?'

Domitian said, 'It is wrong to speak against the gods. I myself have a particular devotion to Minerva, Goddess of Wisdom, and I believe she rewards her devotees by guiding them on the true path.'

'The bird of Minerva flies only by night,' I said.

'What is that supposed to mean?'

'I don't know, I'm sure,' I said. 'It's something I heard a philosopher, a Greek sophist, say once. It may not mean anything, like most that philosophers say, but it's stuck in my mind and I daresay it makes as much sense as your belief that Minerva has a care for you. If she does, why' – and I threw, I recall, a cushion at him – 'are you such an ass?'

Flavius Sabinus again rattled the bones and once again threw a pair of sixes.

'Do it a third time, and I'll be Emperor,' Domitian cried out.

'Silly,' Domatilla said. Turning to me she added, 'What will you be if uncle throws again and Dom wears the purple?'

'His fool, I suppose,' I said and, turning, smiled to her, as the dice-box rattled, and a pair of sixes were disclosed on the table.

The German boy Balthus tells me he belongs to the tribe of the Chatti, and that his father was taken captive in Domitian's campaign against them. I remember that campaign and the sweet valley of the Neckar and a German woman I took as my concubine. Remembering made me sentimental. I drank wine with the boy and did no more than stroke his cheek and kiss him a couple of times. He protested, but gently. Then he looked at me in fear, aware of his slave-status.

XVI

A letter from Titus, undated but received (I surmise) early in February:

Dear Boy: your account is riveting. What a catalogue of folly! I am grateful to you for restraining my little brother, but I do wish you had sent me a copy of his poem in praise of Galba. I have become a connoisseur of bad verses.

And of other things too, for I have a new diversion of which you are not to be jealous, for, be assured, you retain a special place in my heart. This diversion is a lady, a queen indeed, Berenice by name. She is the daughter of Herod Agrippa who was reared in the court of Tiberius and befriended by the Emperor Gaius. So Berenice knows our ways, for she was not herself brought up to respect all the narrow superstitions of the Jews. She is, I confess, somewhat older than I am, and has been married two or three times – sometimes she talks as if she has had so many husbands she has lost count. Moreover, when I first heard of her, I was told she had lain incestuously with her brother the king, Herod Agrippa II. Add to this that she is as beautiful as the loveliest depiction of Venus you have ever seen, and is possessed of more arts of love than Ovid told of in that poem which you will remember reading with me, delightedly, on the shores of the Bay of Naples, and indeed of more than I have ever found in any Greek courtesan, even from Corinth, and you will understand that she is, to one of my temperament, utterly irresistible. In short, if that great-great – is there one more great? – uncle of yours, by marriage as I don't forget, Mark Antony, of whom you have so often spoken to me with a very natural and unstinted pride, thought the world well lost for love of his Eastern beauty Cleopatra, why then, I too – the Antony of our days – am utterly consumed with passion for Berenice, and would let war, Empire, glory, reputation go hang themselves, if they were to be found in competition with my love.

Fortunately, it is not so, for Berenice is herself a politician!

So congratulate me and when at last I am able to bring you to this East – a garden where all we have ever dreamed of is given to us – see if I don't supply you with a girl who will offer you whatever you desire; my Berenice has two daughters ripe for gentle plucking.

Is love not better than Empire? Is it not the true empire of the heart? Ah, my dear, in the words of a Persian poet which my Berenice has taught me, 'God planted a rose and a woman bloomed.'

'But,' you may say, 'this outpouring of delight is poor return for the grim and grisly chronicle I sent Titus. Does he not reckon what is happening in Rome equal at least in the balance to his bed-tumblings?' So you will chide me, Best (in his own way) Beloved.

Therefore I shall desist from one seriousness – for love is . . . oh, hang it, I am out of such language. Let me just say, love is one thing, war and politics another, and for the moment you, dear boy, are caught up in the latter.

So, first, what of the war here? We make progress. We have reduced most of the cities and strongholds of Judaea: wearisome work of sieges, and much digging for the troops. But we get on top of the revolt. The better class of Jews have returned to their duty, chief among them their most able general, one Josephus. You would be impressed by him, as I am, for he has none of the bitter temper characteristic of the Jews, but is possessed of a breadth of knowledge and a rare capacity to weigh what is essential against what is inessential, and to judge the advantages and disadvantages of a case. So he has concluded that, since our Empire cannot be overthrown, it must be the will of the Jewish god that we prevail, and therefore it behoves him to collaborate with us; and this conclusion is very helpful to our cause.

Furthermore, Josephus understands what he has learned by experience: that the revolt (in which he formerly took part) is aimed not only at our rule, but at the overthrow of all that is worthy of respect in Jewry itself. 'For,' he says, '"the Zealots",' which is the name given to the most extreme and violent enemies of Rome, 'seek not only to throw off your yoke, but to effect a social revolution also. They would destroy the authority of the High Priests, and raise up the poor and malignant to a position of power. Therefore if we are to defend what has long been established among our People, and the natural order of society, we must ally ourselves with the Romans against these maniacs, who can build nothing but seek only to destroy what has been the work of centuries approved by Almighty God.'

You won't, of course, make any sense of his conception of this 'Almighty God', for whom by the way the Jews have no name (or, if they have, it is one which they dare not utter). You must understand however that this strange people see the purpose of their god in every unfolding of history. This is odd, but makes some sense to them as I cannot doubt, having spoken at length with this Josephus whom I have come to respect.

Moreover, at certain moments anyway, Josephus understands that the day of small nations, or small nation-states, is over. He sees, too, that if the narrow exclusivity of the Jews has maintained their sense of themselves and of their religion (which, as I say, is unlike any other, for they have no image of their god and call the reverence we pay to images, idolatry), it has also denied them opportunities of acquiring a greater culture, and also prosperity. We have had long talks, and I have opened out to him my theory of the new Imperialism which, though it derives from Rome, is more than Roman, and would be diminished if it was only Roman. Consider, my dear: that a huge Empire has grown up around us, full of problems on which our previous experience sheds little light. Our motives in winning this Empire were not admirable. I can't pretend they were. We were driven on by greed and lust for power. Nor was our government good in the days of the Republican empire. Then the only thought of our Proconsuls was to exploit their provinces and enrich themselves. They were extortioners. The noble Marcus Junius Brutus, making loans to the provincials under his care in Cyprus, levied interest at the rate of eighty per cent; deplorable and, by any standard you choose to apply, unethical. It was, as I have learned from my studies, that much maligned Emperor Tiberius who succeeded where even Augustus had struggled in bringing an end to such practices. He said the provincials were his sheep, and must be only sheared, not skinned.

Now things must change, Tiberius' way. No state owes its greatness in any true sense to its material strength, but to the ideas it embodies. And at the heart of our Roman world is the belief in Law, not the Law that is imposed by tyrants, but the true Law that regulates relations between free citizens; and the basis of that Law is contract.

Josephus accepts this, but then he asks, provocatively, why it was necessary for us Romans to range the world and add states and kingdoms, once free and independent, to our Empire. I could enquire of him what their freedom meant – without an understanding of the law of contract; but I choose not to, and I admit that, as I have said, we acquired Empire for no noble motive. And yet, to you, I may say that the extension of our Empire was also necessary to cure the disease of the Roman State. We were like a man fainting from foul air and revived under the winds of heaven. Indeed, I shall put this argument, which I have just thought of, to my friend Josephus and invite him to apply it to his own nation – pestilential narrow-minded monotheists, who in their own eyes are ever right and all the world wrong. Will they not, I shall ask him, expand and fructify if liberated from their narrow estate and set to roam in the lanes and highways of the world? That indeed is why this Jewish War, which I detest, must be carried to a successful conclusion: that the Jews may also become part of the great imperial scheme.

The Empire is Roman, but it is not merely Rome; and if it was it would be a mean thing. I am not, as an Imperialist, inclined to any cheap complacency. On the contrary, I burn with ardour when I consider the magnitude of our task. For, ultimately, the Empire is peace – peace, justice and that prosperity in which alone true liberty, the liberty of the untrammelled philosophic mind, can flourish.

You can tell, can you not, that it is late at night, when I write like this. Indeed it is so late that the hills of Galilee are touched with dawn's rose-pink fingers.

Yet, excited by my rhetoric, and reassured that you, my audience of one, will understand my sentiments and feel them with me, I can scarce bring myself to stop.

The aim of Imperialism then is not conquest, though conquest was needed to make its realisation possible. But conquest was the preliminary to the great task of consolidation and development, and the still greater task of bringing all the subjects of the Empire into citizenship, that they may share in the traditions, faith and liberties of Rome.

Read Virgil, and you will find the meaning of Empire stated more clearly than I can define it.

I believe that I am destined to make the dream of Imperialism a reality for all within the borders of the Roman world. There is great work to be done, by me or my successors. For example, one evil that I see is that too many men are rich beyond their needs and too many miserably poor. There is a great work to be done in reorganising what I call the world economy. Prosperity should benefit all, not merely fat, greasy bankers and speculators, and those granted the farming of the taxes.

Oh, I have so many ideas . . .

But – you will say – Titus is mad, he is running ahead of reality. He is not Emperor, he is not even a provincial Governor, only the son of Vespasian who was pelted with turnips by citizens, and meanwhile Rome itself is like a beautiful woman threatened with rape by conflicting suitors. Indeed the poor lady is being raped daily; the city brought into being by the kindness of a she-wolf is now laid waste by wolves that know not, or have forgotten, the very word kindness; forgotten humanity, forgotten duty, and think licence liberty.

Your account of the fall and death of Galba was pitiful, because it was evident that Galba had no understanding of his position, that, lacking such understanding, he had recourse to ancient manners and modes of thought meaningless today. He was a man born to play a subsidiary role, as a mere functionary, thrust by his own foolish ambition into a part that had not been written for him – you were right there, in questioning why he did not turn aside the offer of the purple, which he was incompetent to wear.

And to have chosen that Piso as his son, heir, and companion in Empire, bespeaks a mind that was dull and conventional.

And how, I ask myself, could Piso have supposed himself capable of Empire – Piso who had never commanded an army in his life, not even a legion, who had no imagination and never once entertained a generous thought.

Now there is Otho . . . well, he will be popular for a few months – and then? Then he will be revealed for what he is, a clever fellow, witty, charming, everybody's friend – and respected by nobody. It is impossible to govern if you are not respected.

Meanwhile the German legions are on the march, as if we were back in the days of the Republic and the Civil Wars. Which indeed is where we seem to be.

But don't be deceived. Either a strong Emperor must emerge, which won't be either Otho or – save the mark! – Vitellius, or the Empire will crumble and disintegrate – which is impossible, since our Destiny, promised to the pious Aeneas, has not yet been fulfilled.

Hence my confidence and my serenity.

There are three words I would have you lodge in your mind, for they express my purpose, which is Rome's: Humanity, Liberty, Felicity. If we are guided by the principles incorporated in these words, then Rome will indeed be the Eternal City.

But, though I am sure in my destiny, I am not so great a fool as to suppose that it is wise, or even possible, to succeed if one neglects tactics and even base information.

So, though you are not base, it is what you may learn of the mean ambitions and base practices of those who compete for power in this wounded Italy of ours that I require of you – if you love me, as I am happy to believe you do.

Continue then, my dear, to send me all you can glean of what passes in Rome – and when happier days return, why, I shall introduce you to Berenice's daughters, and give you the pick of them.

I send you all my love or all the love it is proper that I send, and then more. You are part of me for ever and I of you. Titus.

So in all my wanderings I have kept this letter, which I shall not send to Tacitus.

XVII

You don't, you say, Tacitus, want my opinions, but only my memories. Dear man, do you suppose the one can be distinguished from the other?

The strange thing was that Otho's reign seemed for a few weeks to be an exercise in virtue. He set aside the pleasures in which he had extravagantly delighted. He behaved with more dignity than any Emperor since Tiberius. That was my mother's opinion, which you will therefore respect as you always respected her. The competition since Tiberius was not, admittedly, stiff. Nevertheless, I suppose you will say that Otho was a hypocrite and that in time his vices would have re-emerged, all the more powerfully and disgracefully on account of their period of suppression.

But virtue was expressed in acts. His treatment of Marius Celsus was only one example. He had been a faithful friend of Galba who had arranged his nomination as Consul elect. The mob demanded that he should follow Galba to the grave. Otho hesitated to save him, and ordered him to be loaded with chains and carried to the Mamertine prison, that execution chamber from which, throughout Rome's history, few have emerged alive. But Otho made Marius Celsus an exception. As soon as the fickle fury of the mob had spent itself, Otho released him, and even appointed him to a military command. That was honourable.

Nero's favourite, the freedman Tigellinus, whom he had made commander of the Praetorians – a man who had prompted Nero to every cruelty, wickedness and act of folly – had escaped punishment from Galba, being protected by Vinius. The reason given was that at some unspecified date Tigellinus had himself placed the shield of his protection over Vinius' daughter, saving her, though whether from disgrace or death I cannot recall. No doubt this was policy, for Tigellinus, fearing a reversal of fortune, was careful to cultivate some private friendships which he trusted might preserve him from the justice to which he would then be exposed. Now, his protector gone, Tigellinus found he must answer for his crimes. Otho sent to tell him he had cumbered the earth too long, and to advise him that the mob was ready to tear him limb from limb. Tigellinus received this unwelcome news with unexpected courage. He bedded the current favourite among his mistresses – all well-born girls whom he had seduced when they were under age – and then, dismissing her, cut his throat.

This news added to Otho's popularity, and many said he would prove a good Emperor. Even his decision to spare the life of Gallia Crispinilla, one of Nero's mistresses who had fomented rebellion in Africa and – it was believed – attempted to prevent the corn ships from sailing to Rome, was soon forgiven. As my mother said, 'The woman is a trollop and utterly unprincipled, Otho's enemy too, but to consent to her execution would have been barbaric.'

In many ways indeed he suggested that he might make at least a tolerable Emperor – if he did not tire of the part, as my mother, though indulgent to him, advised me he would. He did not interfere with the public appointments and pleased the Senate by granting positions to elderly Senators of eminence. Young nobles who had returned from the exile to which they had been condemned by Nero or which they had fearfully chosen were greeted warmly and invested with priestly honours held by their fathers and grandfathers. If Caesar's watchword after his invasion of Italy had been clemency, Otho's appeared to be conciliation. For instance, he sent ambassadors to Vitellius who, with the German legions, had marched deep into Trans-alpine Gaul, with instructions to discover their grievances, and propose remedies. They were also to assure Vitellius that, if he collaborated in the restoration of peace, he should have an honourable position as second man in the Empire.

Had Vitellius been left to his own devices, he might well have accepted this proposal, even with joy. This is speculation, I admit, but Vitellius – flabby, self-indulgent, weak-willed and cowardly – must have known in his heart that no man was less fitted than he to engage in a bruising and desperate struggle for Empire; even if he emerged victorious, he would then be compelled to assume a burden he was incapable of bearing. Vitellius was not a bad man, merely a soft one. Or so I think now.

But Vitellius enjoyed no independence, though the legions had invested him with the purple. On the contrary, he was the puppet creature of the legates Fabius Valens and Alienus Caecina. Neither had acquired the reputation sufficient to compensate for undistinguished birth, that would make him a credible candidate for Empire. Both were young, able and ambitious. Caecina especially was a favourite of the troops on account of his handsome stature, courage, audacity and eloquence. Both had been originally protegés of Galba, but had turned against him: Valens I know not why; Caecina, on account of Galba's order that he be prosecuted for the embezzlement of public money while he was quaestor in Baetica. Both saw that Vitellius, on account of his rank and open-handed manner which made him popular with the soldiers, could afford them the means of rising to power which they could not attain in any other way. At the same time his malleability, sloth and self-indulgence which, even on the march through Gaul, generally saw him half-cut by midday, ensured that they must dominate him. Yet, in some curious manner, he retained the esteem of his troops who even hailed him as *Germanicus*, a title associated with that beloved of the legions, the father of the Emperor Gaius. It was absurd; nevertheless it was so.

It could not be expected therefore that Valens and Caecina, the animators of this charade, would welcome the approach of Otho's ambassadors, who promised honour and position to their nominal chief, and nothing of substance to them. So, either by threats or inducements, they suborned the ambassadors, impressed by the might and resolution of the German legions and by the danger of their own position.

In Rome meanwhile, before we heard of these tidings, Flavius Sabinus, though he had been again confirmed in his office, grew anxious. Good government and pacification were no doubt admirable, to be desired, but good government and pacification of the Empire by Otho ran counter to his plans and ambitions for his family. He assured us it would not last. I thought he was right, though my reasons were not his. Domitian was less convinced. 'Am I to be sacrificed,' he muttered, 'for the ambitions of my father, and still more my brother and uncle, ambitions which the present trend of events suggest are vain?' He thought it in his interest to make overtures to Otho and his friends, though he was, of course, so insignificant, so young, and his record so barren of achievement (no fault of his, I admit) that his approaches either went unnoticed or aroused no interest.

The calm of the first fortnight in February was illusory. The riot that broke out in the middle of the month did much to restore Flavius Sabinus' spirits.

In its origins it was a trivial affair.

Otho had given orders that the 17th cohort be brought to Rome from Ostia and gave the charge of arming it to a tribune of the Praetorians, named Crispinus (or perhaps Craspitus; I do not remember). For some reason of his own, this officer chose to order that the move be carried out by night, when the camp was quiet. But the hour provoked suspicion that something more sinister was afoot. There was a disturbance, and the sight of arms inflamed a drunken crowd. They cried out – someone cried out – that the arms were being taken to the houses of those Senators who were opposed to Otho, and that a coup d'état was underway. The soldiers, some of whom were drunk, joined in the accusation. Fighting broke out, among those who were trying to enforce or obey the harmless order of the Emperor and those who were seized with the idea that the arms were to be used against him. The tribune, Crispinus – Craspitus? – attempting to do as he was ordered, was cut down and trampled in the gutter, and several centurions who stood by him were also slain. Then the soldiers, convinced that they had foiled an attempt on their Emperor's life, mounted their horses, bared their swords, and galloped to the city and the palace.

There Otho was holding a reception for some of the most distinguished men and women of the city. I was among them, on account of my birth; and Domitian had been seized with jealousy, not having had an invitation himself. The confused and frightening noise of the soldiers' tumult in the courtyard created consternation. Nobody knew what was happening. Some feared it was an attempt on the life of the Emperor; others that Otho himself had planned a massacre of his guests, or at least their arrest. Few behaved well; most like poltroons. Some fled, losing themselves in the corridors of the palace or finding the doors barred and guarded – for Otho's bodyguard was likewise in ignorance of the cause of the tumult. Some did escape by side-doors or windows and, hastening from the Palatine by whatever route they thought most obscure, regained the city, where however (as I was later told) many did not dare to go to their own houses, but either wandered the streets lamenting the evil days or took refuge in the lodgings of their humblest clients.

I confess I was alarmed myself, though logic, rarely any help when the apprehensive emotions are awakened, told me I had nothing to fear. Yet panic is infectious, and I do not know what I would have done if my attention had not been caught, and held fast, by the spectacle of the Emperor himself.

Otho was hurrying about the room, seizing remaining guests by the sleeve, and talking urgently to them. A few minutes earlier he had been rosy and convivial, though not without dignity, happy in his role of host. Now he was white as a virgin's sheets, and sweat stood out on his forehead. His eyes darted round and I read in them a fearful perplexity. Or so I think now; so I remember.

Then an aide approached him, conferred with him, and they withdrew from the banqueting chamber to an inner room, Otho glancing two or three times over his shoulder as he left us.

There came a crash, loud yells, screams of renewed and more urgent terror, and the chamber was full, as it seemed, of soldiers, brandishing swords, some of which dripped with blood. The tribune, Junius Martialis, boldly demanded what they wanted, and was thrust aside, but not before he had been slashed in the groin, so that he fell, moaning and bleeding on the marble, and was trampled under advancing feet.

Those of the guests who remained huddled in corners, each man and each woman trying to find another to use as a shield. Nobody knew the purpose of the incursion, and everybody feared it. The soldiers cried for Otho to present himself to them and, again, we could not tell whether they were about to kill him or merely sought reassurance as to his safety. What discussions went on in the little room where he had taken refuge, I have never learned. But I believe that it was Otho himself who determined that he must show himself to the soldiers, and accept whatever fate had in store for him.

So he emerged stiff-legged, and pale of face, yet with an odd boyish resolution. I felt a surge of admiration; I remembered poor Sporus' account of Nero's abject terror. I have seen the look on Otho's face on the countenance of defeated gladiators stretched out on the sand consenting to death.

No one moved. Otho looked on the spectacle, looked on Junius

Martialis, the wounded tribune crawling towards him, bent down and put his arm round him, with pain and labour eased him on to a couch, and then, mounting the same couch beside him, let his eyes walk with unconscionable slowness round the chamber where candles still burned on those tables that had not been overturned, and where wines and plates of delicacies were still displayed . . .

'Comrades,' he said, very gently, 'what is this? What is this you have done? What strange ideas have enflamed you? If you have come to kill me, here I am. No other blood need be shed. If you are labouring under the delusion that my life is in danger, and have nobly come to protect me, I respect and cherish your devotion – even while I deplore your eagerness to act without true knowledge, and your insubordination . . .'

Then the soldiers threw down their swords, or lowered them, or returned them to their scabbards, and crowded round their Emperor, kissing his hands, pressing against him (so that the poor wounded tribune was now in danger of being smothered) and protesting their devotion.

The next day the city was quiet as a house in mourning. Shutters remained up, shops were closed, few moved in the streets; you might have thought plague had struck or that Rome – even Rome – was an occupied city in the hands of a terrible enemy.

XVIII

The next evening, when I had returned from news-gathering at the baths to my mother's house, to see that all was well with her, and to reassure her as to my own safety, we were disturbed by one of her slaves who came running to warn us that a detachment of soldiers had entered the courtyard and were demanding where my lodging might be found. Had I been alone, I believe I would have attempted flight. But it was inconceivable either that I should leave my mother to answer for me, or show myself afraid in her presence. So, speaking as calmly as I could, I commanded the slave to go fetch the soldiers, and thus ensure that none of our neighbours was exposed to any danger that might threaten me; for my mother was so respected, even in her poverty and distressed condition, that it was probable that some at least of the people in the building might think to deceive the soldiers, in the hope that they would spare her their attentions. They would be the more likely to do this, since I had entered the house cautiously, and few could have known that I was there.

The look of pride that shone from my mothers's eyes was reward for the danger I supposed I had invited.

But the centurion who entered our apartment, at the head of a detachment of only four of the Guard, was immediately civil. He apologised to my mother for this incursion on her privacy, remarking that, in less evil times, he would not have contemplated breaking in on so great a lady. My mother received this as her due and gently enquired what they sought of me.

'Orders from the Emperor himself, ma'am,' the centurion said. 'He commands the presence of this young gentleman, and desires it so urgently that he sent me with these men to ensure that he arrives unmolested at the palace, for the streets are unruly and those who guard the palace are so on edge, if I may put it this way, you might say they are having kittens, that we are thought necessary to act as the young man's safe-conduct. And the Emperor bade me – expressly bade me – to assure you that he means the young man no harm, but rather the contrary. And he also required me to convey to you – these are his own words, precisely – his most profound respects, and – I forget exactly – hopes you are well, anyway.'

Then he wiped his brow with a red bandana, as if he had rehearsed this speech and was glad to have got it out.

My mother insisted only that I must first wash, shave (though my beard was still light and I scarce needed to do so more than twice a week), and put on a clean toga before she could think me fit to enter the presence of the Emperor. In her mind, despite all she knew to Otho's discredit, the office demanded respect, and respect required clean garments. The centurion assented and, while I retired to obey her instructions, she served them with wine, not apologising for its quality being inferior to that which she would have been accustomed to provide before misfortune laid its icy hand on her; for to do so would, in her view, have been to demean herself.

Then we embraced, she bestowed a blessing on me, and reminded me to acquit myself in a manner worthy of my ancestors (by whom she meant her noble family, and not my real father Narcissus). And so we set off for the palace.

I thought it beneath me to enquire of the centurion whether he had any idea why I was sent for; but, as we moved through the snarling streets, I felt my blood run with excitement, as if I had at last fully entered on adult life.

Nevertheless, despite the honour apparently paid me, I was thoroughly searched at the palace door, for fear I was carrying a weapon which I might employ against the Emperor.

'Sorry about that, sir,' the centurion said, when I was passed clean. 'It's the way as is now, even Senators get frisked.'

I was led through a labyrinth of passages and an armed sentry stood at each corner-turning. I remember thinking that, lacking Ariadne's ball of wool, I would be unable to find my way out of this maze, should things go against me and I sought escape.

At last I was shown into a small chamber beyond the third court of the palace, as I judged. The light was dim. There was indeed only one lamp, and at first it seemed the room was empty. Is this to be my prison? I thought. Then there was movement from a couch beyond the lamp, and therefore in more obscure darkness, and a voice which I recognised as Otho's thanked the centurion for his services, told him to wait outside, and greeted me by name.

The Emperor did not rise. Nor did he speak again till the centurion had given a smart salute with a great stamping of feet, and retired. As my eyes grew accustomed to the dim light, I saw that the Emperor was lying on a couch, soft with many cushions and that his body was covered by a richly-embroidered blanket.

'There should,' he said, 'be wine on that little table. Give yourself a cup, and fetch me one.'

His voice was weary, and a little thick, as if he had already drunk.

'You will be wondering why I have sent for you.'

'Since I could not guess, I thought it vain to speculate, my lord.'

'Spoken like a true Claudian – save that "my lord". I had a great respect for your mother when she lived at court. She was kind to me as a boy. I observed you last night. You behaved well in that – what shall I say? – ridiculous and frightening business. In a manner, again, worthy of a Claudian. Are you a good Claudian or a bad Claudian?'

Of course I understood the question, as you will, Tacitus, but you may have to remind your readers (if you make use of this dialogue), that there were reputedly two sorts of Claudians: those who served the Republic dutifully, and did the State great service, and those who . . . well, didn't; but were self-willed, domineering, reckless, dangerous to others and to themselves.

'I am not yet nineteen,' I said. 'It is too early to know.'

He laughed.

'I think,' he said, 'that is the most honest thing said to me since I began to play this part; and the wittiest. Usually it is only licensed fools who jest with Emperors. That at least is a tradition not yet abandoned. So your answer pleases me. You're a handsome fellow, too. Come, sit beside me.'

I obeyed, with misgivings. Not this, I thought.

He laughed again, reading my mind.

'You've nothing to fear,' he said. 'I have no intention of practising a perverted species of the *lex primae noctis*, a custom which, even in its normal form, disgusts me. Women should be won, not taken; that is my opinion as an ageing debauchee, now satiated in the lists of Venus. But I think we could do business.'

I remained silent. He questioned this.

'My mother taught me,' I said, 'that if you have nothing to say, then say nothing.'

'Good advice. Follow it and you will be a politician. Or a general. Silence is a good weapon. There is nothing so disconcerting as silence. Unfortunately, I have always been talkative. It's done me harm . . .'

Candour is charming, and to be distrusted.

'I never had any great taste for boys anyway,' he said. 'When you have learned to enjoy a woman, no boy can ever fully satisfy. Have you discovered that yet? Come, don't blush. The light is dim but I can still feel your blush, there's a glow in your face. You were, I'm told, the lover of Titus, son of Vespasian. Are you that still?'

I hesitated, like a man on the threshold of a dark house, through which the wind is blowing. Danger can have no smell, not being corporeal; yet often I have scented it. Fear, of course, has a smell – the smell of cold sweat; and danger and fear are close blood-brothers.

'We were boys,' I said, 'now we are men.'

'And Titus fucks an Eastern Queen, Berenice, they say. Are you jealous?'

'Titus is my friend. What makes him happy pleases me.'

'You choose your words with care. I like that. My life would have been more fortunate had I possessed that ability.'

'You are Emperor, sir. What more can fortune grant you?'

'It could start with sleep. Yes, I am Emperor. But for how long? Galba was Emperor. So was Nero, once my friend. So was Claudius, murdered by his wife. At least I have no wife now. I had one once, you know, and loved her, though she was a whore, dissolute as myself in those days. Nero killed her, as an angry child might kill a puppy. Now, I have no wife, nor son either.'

Jupiter, I thought – this is genuine, Tacitus, I swear it – he's not about to adopt me, is he, make me his Piso. No thanks. But how could I evade him if he made the offer?

'But your friend Titus still keeps a troupe of dancing-boys, Syrians, they say, and what he does with them requires no guessing. You're not jealous of that either?'

'If you were not Emperor, sir,' – I couldn't bring myself to say 'my emperor' – and left the answer hanging in the incense-scented air of the little room which now seemed to enfold the pair of us with a nauseating closeness.

'If I was not Emperor, you would tell me to go hang myself – eh? Is that it? Good. I like your spirit and your unspoken response.'

He lifted his cup, emptied it in one gulp, as drunkards drink, or men in the grip of sorrow or despair, and passed it to me to fill again.

'It's a lonely business being Emperor. I've discovered that already, in a matter of weeks. Nero enjoyed it, of course. But then Nero was a fool, a clever and often amusing fool, but still a fool. Tiberius, who was a wise man, loathed it. So my father used to say, and he knew the old man well, and revered him. He used to hint that he might be the Emperor's bastard. I don't know. His father, my grandfather, was a client of the great Livia Augusta. He owed his place in the Senate to her. There are not many men left in Rome who know more about emperors than I do, or what it means to wear the purple.' He paused and drank again. 'I know what you're thinking: that I sought the crown. So I did. Who wouldn't when the chance presents itself? Even that dull fellow Piso yielded to the temptation. Even Vitellius, and of all those I have known, none has been less fitted. But that does not restrain him, and now, thanks to the energy of his legates, Valens and Caecina, he is a danger to me. What do you say?'

'What can I say? We are reared to thirst for glory, and to compete for posts of honour. Mark Antony was my great-great-uncle, if only by marriage. Is that answer enough?'

'It will serve. There were two Triumvirates, formed to dominate the State. Each left only one survivor, after terrible wars: first, Caesar, then, Augustus. I should like to avoid war. Romans killing Romans is a beastly business. Civil war sets brother against brother, destroys friendship, which we are also taught to prize. But . . . I have sent ambassadors to Vitellius. They have not returned. Perhaps they have chosen to remain in his camp, perhaps they are held there. Who can tell? But the conclusion is clear: Vitellius – or the men who control him – are determined on war, with all its terrible and unknowable consequences. We are perhaps evenly balanced, Vitellius and myself, our forces being equal in strength and valour. But there is a third force in the East, another great army, whose influence may be decisive. Mucianus, Vespasian, your bosom friend Titus – what do they want?'

'I am not in their confidence, sir. I am not privy to their ambitions.'

'Don't try to deceive me, boy, don't play the fool with me . . .' A note, as of metal ringing on stone, entered his voice. He pulled himself up to lean on his elbow and regarded me searchingly.

I felt his power, like the cold wind of winter dawn.

'Come,' he said, more gently, 'let us understand each other. I've no wish to have secrets between us. We live in evil times, when liberty is perforce constrained. You carry on a regular correspondence with Titus. Sometimes he employs the imperial post, and then his letters are routinely intercepted, deciphered – the code you use is simple and presents no problems to the imperial agents – and copied before being sent on to you. If you examined the seals more closely you would have been suspicious. Sometimes he sends you more private missives by the hand of one of his freedmen. Last week one such was arrested at Brindisi. The threat of torture persuaded him to surrender the letter he was carrying to you. I have read it. While it is not positively seditious, a man more given than I am to seeing conspiracies around him would find there sufficient grounds to order the arrest and even execution of Titus. Here is the letter. You see, he makes no bones about his determination to wear the purple, nor of his expectation that he will do so. 'Otho cannot last,' he says, 'Vitellius is a clown. The way will soon open before us.' Well, I do not dispute his judgement of my rival, Vitellius. How it disgusts me,' he drank more wine, 'to call that thing my rival. But what do you say? Your friend is rash indeed, his rashness matching even his ambition. And some might call that inordinate. How old is he? Not yet thirty? Twenty-six? Twenty-seven? Too young to be Emperor, too old to be so foolish. What do you say?'

'It was a private letter. To a friend. People talk loosely to friends. Not all they say is to be taken seriously.'

'A gallant answer, but you know it won't do.' He took my hand, squeezed it twice, and let it fall. 'I've no wish to quarrel,' he said, 'and I haven't brought you here to punish you, not even to upbraid you for carrying on a correspondence which verges on the treasonable. The times are disturbed. It's no wonder if many men entertain ambitions which at other seasons might be taken as seditious if they found expression. Indeed, I almost admire Titus for his audacity. But it won't do either.'

He bit his nails, and was silent a long time.

'Three forces,' he said. 'In any battle of three, it's two against one, unless . . . unless one of the three stands aside and waits to feast on the carrion. That wouldn't be your Titus' way, I can tell that. But his father, Vespasian? Nobody ever took much account of Vespasian. Nero thought him a joke, he used to mock his accent, his habit of saying *o* for *au*, provincial and lower-class. He was in the mule trade once, you know, and his mistress, Caenis, is even commoner than the man himself. Then he offended Nero by falling asleep during his recitals, and even snoring, an act which showed a judgement that was aesthetic rather than prudent. But he's survived. He's a mangy old cur, but a wise dog. Which way will he jump? Will he stay in his kennel? Vespasian puzzles me, and troubles me. I don't reckon on Mucianus, he lives for pleasure, as I once did, and his pleasures are perverted and degenerate as mine weren't. But Vespasian? I'm thinking aloud, boy . . .'

The thinking aloud was an act, or in part an act. I felt that even then, for I guessed he had already made a decision which he was approaching by this circuitous route. Even so, I was excited by his apparent candour, and felt that I was on the verge of some great enterprise.

'I need Vespasian,' he said. 'I need Titus. Rome needs them. What Rome does not need is a protracted war, and what Rome may not need is the government of a single person. That's why I've brought you here. I am sending you as my emissary to Vespasian and your friend. I'll furnish you with the quickest and easiest passage. You will have letters to carry, but this is what I want you to say, with all the persuasive eloquence you can muster: that Otho offers an alliance, that he will share the government of the Empire with Vespasian – and also, if they choose, with Titus, or even Mucianus, if Vespasian thinks that necessary, if they will join with me to defeat Vitellius and the German legions. You will say that, though my forces and Vitellius' are evenly matched, I am confident of victory, because I shall be fighting on the defensive, but that Rome requires that this victory is complete, and so I need Vespasian's troops. The Third Triumvirate, tell them that . . .'

He paused. Had he forgotten – did he expect me to have forgotten – what he had said of the first two such compacts?

'I am sending you,' he said, 'precisely because you are not my boy, but theirs, or Titus' anyway. You understand how I am reposing trust in you? That I have shown you my weakness? Or what men might think my weakness? But remember this: I do it for Rome which cannot afford protracted and terrible wars, but needs stability.'

'Does Flavius Sabinus know of your intentions, sir?'

'Sabinus is a man I do not understand, and therefore cannot trust. You will therefore say nothing to him. At an opportune moment, when

I learn of Vespasian's first response, then I may consult Sabinus. For the moment all must be confidential. My position here in Rome requires that. It is another reason why I have selected you for this mission. If you will forgive me for saying so, you are, on account of your youth, a person of no consequence. Nobody will therefore suspect that your departure is of any significance.'

I smiled: 'Nobody but my family and friends will notice I am not here.'

'Oh,' he said, 'I am sure you have admirers who will miss you. And a girl perhaps?'

'Perhaps.'

He resumed the nibbling of his nails.

'Vespasian has a younger son here in Rome, hasn't he? Domitian? Is that right? I must bring him to the palace and employ him in some way. In some way or other.'

There was no necessity for him to say that Domitian would be a hostage for the success of my mission. Nor did he need to tell me that I must inform Vespasian that Otho now held Domitian – as a sort of inducement. So I felt no need in my turn to say that, in my opinion, Vespasian had never cared a docken for Domitian: that all his love was given to Titus and all his ambition bound up in him.

'My secretary will give you a note of your travel arrangements and a letter of transit. You will then be escorted back to your mother's house and leave Rome in the morning. Say nothing to anyone but your mother, and to her say no more than the least that a loving mother need know. My respects to her. Good night, and may the gods grant you safe passage, and us a happy outcome.'

XIX

Shall I send that last letter to Tacitus, or not? It would correct his view of Otho which, since this would disturb him, would please me. But I have never, over years of conversations with him, found him willing to credit that I was employed on such a mission. He might not credit it how, assume I have gone soft in the head. That is so often the response of people to what they either don't wish to hear or find impossible to believe.

It reminds me of a story Vespasian used to take pleasure in telling. His father, after sacrificing one day, was impressed by his inspection of the entrails which, the priest assured him, betokened greatness for his family. Indeed, the priest said, he would have a son who would one day be Emperor. When Sabinus (Vespasian's father, not his brother) passed this good news on to his own mother, the old woman laughed, and said, 'A grandson of mine Emperor? Fancy you going soft in the head before your old ma!'

Vespasian himself can hardly have believed in the omen, when he was a young and undistinguished soldier, who so mismanaged his affairs that he had to mortgage the estates he inherited from his father. But eventually there were lots of such stories. There was one about a stray dog which picked up a human hand at the crossroads, and carried it into the room where Vespasian was breakfasting and laid it down at his feet. This was significant because a hand is a symbol of power. At the time however he probably cursed the dog for a dirty brute.

We are all superstitious, even the philosophers among us; and I have been driven to philosophy by misfortune. Titus sometimes said that Fortuna was the only god we need have a care for, and that even that care was vain, since Fortuna took no heed of the actions of mortals, but played dice with our lives.

I have grown weary of visits to the wine-shop to see the boy Balthus. So I purchased him from the woman, at an exorbitant price which she was able to demand because she saw I was prepared to pay it. I have brought him home and installed him in the chamber next mine. Araminta is indifferent; it is enough for her that she is mistress of the household, and that our sons and daughters grow sturdy.

It is not lust I feel now for Balthus. That was the brief flurry of old age, like a thunder-storm in fine weather. And the boy himself made clear his repugnance. So I do no more than fondle him. His presence calms me; there is an inner serenity to him. It is better this way. Had I followed the demands of lust, then soon enough habit would have dulled appetite, and I should have been led to that uninteresting port where life lands its exhausted cargo. What I feel for him is different from what I have known before – except perhaps with Domatilla.

One day I asked him to account for his serenity. How could he, a slave, torn from his own people, look so acceptingly on the world? When I put the question, he was stretched out on a couch, for I find myself allowing him liberties I have never granted another slave; he looked like Hermes, or the young Eros drawing his bowstring, the arrow directed at my heart. But though I might invest him with such fantasies, he was also the thin boy who had recoiled from my touch, and then, knowing his station, submitted, tearfully, to my first advances.

Now he exclaimed, haltingly, but as one who fears he may not be believed rather than one ashamed of his words, that he trusted in the love of the one true god to deliver him from evil.

'The one true god?' I asked. 'Who is this strange being? You Germans worship many gods, I know that, spirits of the forest and warriors hurling thunderbolts.'

'I know better than my people did. I worship God the Father, maker of heaven and earth, and Jesus Christ, his only begotten son, and the Holy Spirit that inhabits any heart that opens itself to the Word.'

'You must excuse me,' I said, 'but that sounds like three gods, not one . . . Jesus Christ . . . are you then one of that criminal sect of Jews known as Christians?'

His dark eyes searched out mine. His tongue flickered over these so red lips that had first aroused me – lips of that strange dark-red, promising the softness of roses – and that promise, as I had learned, was kept. He hesitated, then confessed, 'I am. But,' he said, 'in Christ there is neither Jew nor Gentile, only those who believe and are saved.'

I did not understand that 'saved'. I set it aside; that is, I had heard Christians use the word before, and had taken it for esoteric jargon of the sect. But Balthus, in his simplicity, seemed to have an understanding of its import which gave the word a certain concrete reality.

Then I recalled how, when Nero was alarmed by the Great Fire of Rome, and by the people's anger directed at him, he had seized on these Christians – adherents of a slave religion which our Jewish friend Josephus would, years later, impatiently dismiss as 'a perversion of Judaism, practised by men as mad as those Zealots we destroyed at Masada' – and pronounced them guilty of incendiarism. I was young then, and my mother forbade my attendance at the Games where the Christians were slaughtered, singing hymns (I was told) to their god. 'Crazy folk,' the door-keeper of our *insula* told me. But not all the care of my mother could shield me from the sight of these depraved wretches (as we took them to be) who were made by Nero into burning candles to light his gardens; the stench of burnt flesh hung in the air for days after; and I often heard Flavius Sabinus say it so disgusted him that, though a soldier, those nights illuminated by flames of flesh cured him of any disposition towards cruelty.

'What is the basis of this Christianity?' I asked Balthus.

'In one word,' he said, 'it is Love.'

'That's not so strange then, nor so new. Men have sought and worshipped Love since poets first sang, and before them, I'll be bound.'

'We do not worship Love, though our God is a God of Love, nor do we seek it. Rather we are filled with love, and expressing it, extend it to each and everyone, and to all mankind as God's creation.'

XX

Love. On his voyage back to Syria Titus had called at Cyprus, in order to visit and inspect the great Temple of the Paphian Venus, known to the Greeks as Aphrodite, the Goddess of Love. She is of especial significance to us Romans also as the mother of Aeneas, father of our race, and this temple in Paphos is said to be her oldest place of worship, since, after she rose in birth from the sea, she was wafted thither and, though often found elsewhere, has yet never departed. The temple was consecrated by one Cinyras, many years before the Trojan War, and the sacrifices and divination are still conducted by the descendants of Cinyras. 'Or so they maintain,' Titus told me.

Whatever the truth of this, the place of worship is of unfathomable antiquity, as may be demonstrated by the fact that the image of the goddess is of no human shape; I surmise that the art of sculpture had not yet been learned. Instead, it is a rounded mass rising in the manner of a cone from a broad base to a narrow circumference. No one knows the significance of this now; which again is proof of antiquity. Also it is forbidden to pour, or spill, blood on the altar, the place of sacrifice being fed only with prayers and pure flame. Though it stands exposed to all weathers, yet the altar is never wet with rain.

I mention all this now, in the perplexity occasioned by that conversation with Balthus I have related; and none of this, of course, is for Tacitus who would jeer, having no spirit of the philosopher, at the metaphysical speculations which the contrast between Balthus' words and my memory of Titus' account of his visit to Paphos provokes in me.

When questioned concerning my religious beliefs, I was accustomed for long to brush the interrogation aside with some such remark as, 'My religion is the religion of all sensible men' and, if pressed to elucidate, would add merely, 'Sensible men never tell.' Such a response is satisfying, but unsatisfactory. There are days when I believe in nothing, others when I say that the only real questions are ethical – how we should behave – and since we can know nothing certainly beyond that, all speculation is vain. Yet we are by nature given to both speculation and worship. Titus, who had talked of Fortuna as the only god, nevertheless went out of his way, and at a moment of extreme political urgency, in order to satisfy his curiosity at the oldest of Temples to Venus; and I do not think that his motive was connected with his affair with Queen Berenice, which required no divine sanction and no encouragement, divine or human.

I pressed him on this point. His answers were vague. He talked of 'the numinous', a word that to me then was only a word, such as poets use, with no precise meaning, if they are bad poets anyway. That is to say, it is a word which, even if the poet is good, affords one an agreeable shiver of the spine, and no more than that. Yet Titus was no poet. The word meant something to him. I could see that, for it embarrassed him to employ it. And indeed he was embarrassed when I pressed him close on his experience at Paphos.

He said: 'I do not know. But I felt something. Was it what Virgil calls *lacrimae rerum* – the sense of tears in mortal things? Perhaps. I felt greater than myself, and also less. I was inhabited by I know not what. I was assured of a glorious destiny and yet felt that I was drained of all the satisfaction I should have expected to derive from that assurance. In short, dear boy' – he spoke this flippantly as if to divert me from any sense that he was truly serious, but his eyes were clouded as when a man looks inward and is surprised and puzzled by what he sees – 'in short, dear boy, I felt myself to be more than I have ever been, and yet less also.'

What he said made no sense to me, and Titus, embarrassed as if he had been caught in some shameful act, turned away, provoked some diversion, called for wine or suggested play – I forget which. But now, I recalled his words, and the expression on his face, half-proud, half-bemused, and I put what he had said to Balthus, even while I was both irritated and perplexed to think that I sought wisdom from this boy, all the more so since his face, body and manner had first attracted me precisely because they promised an encounter that would for the brief moments of sensual delight annihilate thought and so free me from the disturbances that made demons in my mind.

'Is that what your god – your religion – means to you?'

'I'm not intelligent,' he said. 'I'm not educated. I can't use big words. Not Latin ones anyway. Like that – what was it? – "numinous"? It doesn't mean anything to me. But when I'm with Christ, or when I know Christ is within me, then I know peace. The only thing to be sacrificed is my will, but we say "surrendered", not "sacrificed". That is what I know. Maybe that's why you Romans think ours a slave religion, though there are Romans who follow it. It would give me great joy, master, if you would open your soul to my master, who is Lord of all.'

XXI

There was a reserve in Titus' manner. Though he had embraced me warmly on my arrival, the frank affection characteristic of his letters was missing from his conversation. When I explained how I had come to be there, I felt, sensed, his distrust.

He reclined on a couch and dipped his hand in a bowl of water scented with rose petals.

'My father wants to see you,' he said. 'You haven't met him since you were a small boy, have you?'

During supper he ignored me and carried on a conversation with the Jew Josephus, a lean dark man with a pointed beard. They spoke in Greek, and Josephus' accent being unfamiliar to me, and obscurely provincial, I found it difficult at first to follow his side of the conversation. But it seemed that Titus was more interested in the religious practices of the different Jewish sects than in the disposition of the rebel armies. I wondered if the matter of the talk had been chosen simply to exclude me.

Josephus gave no sign that my presence either interested or disturbed him. As far as he was concerned, I was merely a young Roman noble of neither achievement nor significance. I began to fear his view was justified. My interview with Otho, and the commission he had given me, seemed ridiculous and remote.

Titus said: 'Your explanations, my dear Josephus, are admirably clear, and it's evident that you yourself are pious in your faith. But hasn't it occurred to you how strange it is that, alone among nations, you refuse to recognise that other gods and other faiths may have their merits – their apprehension of ultimate realities – or that, again alone among nations, you refuse to make an image of your god which may appeal to the senses, and thus stimulate the piety of worshippers?'

I thought: this is deliberately unkind; what have I done to chill the love you have so often protested that you feel for me? It seemed that I had never been to Titus anything more than a sort of toy, a trivial amusement. I bit my lip to prevent it from quivering and tried to conjure up an image of Domatilla. I told myself it was absurd to feel aggrieved, since I had long decided that I wished no further sexual relations with Titus. And yet I wanted him still to admire me, and put me in the centre of his world.

Josephus said: 'You are accustomed to tease me with this question, my lord, which must bore your young friend here excessively.'

'That is immaterial,' said Titus. 'In any case it will be good for him to learn that adult men can concern themselves with intellectual matters.'

'I do not understand this "intellectual matters",' Josephus said, 'though of course commentaries on the sacred books require the exercise of the intellectual faculties, faith itself is not a matter of intellect, but of history. The Lord God made a covenant with Israel, and named us his Chosen People.'

'If I may intervene,' I said, aware (with permissible pride) of the purity of my Greek, 'from what I have heard of the present war, it would seem that your god has broken any covenant he may have made with you. For certainly the actions of the rebels seem to be driven by folly, and to be without the sort of wisdom which you might expect from people guided by a god.'

'The Lord chastises those whom he loves,' Josephus said.

Titus smirked. That is the only way to describe his smile.

When we were alone, he said, 'I was nasty to you. You didn't like that. It serves you right. You deserve punishment, for you have disobeyed my instructions.'

'What sort of language is this?' I said. 'Disobey . . . instructions . . . am I your servant, your slave? We may no longer be lovers but I thought our friendship secure.'

'I needed you in Rome,' he said, breaking off the leg of a roast pheasant and gnawing it.

'How could I remain in Rome when the Emperor commanded me to come here?'

'Emperor? Otho?'

'Emperor for the time being at least . . . besides, I bring you news of Rome such as it might be dangerous to write . . .'

'So you say. But why should I believe you?'

I wept that night. I am not ashamed to remember, and say so. It seemed that friendship was a mere bubble, and I had trusted in friendship. But the next morning Titus was in a different mood. We rode into the desert. Josephus accompanied us. But this time he was the third member of the party, the superfluous one. Titus talked to me alone, and with a gaiety and affection that caused my last night's fears and misgivings to fall away. I thought: he is a creature of mood, and last night I was merely so unfortunate as to find him in a mood where I had no place.

He pointed to distant hills, rising purple-black against an azure sky.

'That's where the rebels lurk,' he said, 'the so-called Zealots. There are innumerable bands of them couched in those hills like wild beasts. They are fanatics and death means nothing to them. Civilised men respect Death and give him a wide berth, unless Necessity demands otherwise. But these young men – they are mostly very young who form these bands – are infatuated with Death. It makes them difficult to deal with. They don't understand the rational arguments of civilised men. They don't understand that when two opposed interests clash, it is wise and expedient to seek a middle way.'

'Yes,' I said, 'I think that's what Otho is seeking. I found him likeable, you know.'

'Oh,' Titus said, 'almost everybody has always liked Otho. He's never found any difficulty in being liked. It's a matter of whether he deserves respect or trust, and that's rather different.'

A hawk hovered overhead. We drew rein and watched it. Then it dropped true as a stone.

You were always curious, I remember, Tacitus, about this journey of mine to the East. When I told you, once, that I had undertaken it at Otho's command, you were incredulous, and ascribed my statement either to my vanity or my lamentable habit of making jokes. As it happened I was more amused than irritated by your inability to accept the truth. Now I wonder if this lack of simplicity in your nature will impair your History. Do not think me impertinent if I tell you that you are too inclined to look for hidden meanings lurking behind straightforward words and actions. Such are not always there. Lucan once said to me that 'only shallow people do not judge by appearances', and I thought that a characteristically clever-silly remark. But there is something in it. I would never call you shallow, but you suffer from a psychological deformity which apparently makes it impossible for you to accept the simple and obvious explanation.

However I shall give you more details now, instead of teasing you with silences and hints of I-could-if-I-would with which I sought to tantalise you in the past.

The suspicion with which Titus received me was not shared by his father. And yet it is possible that beneath, or rather behind, his bluff, even coarse, exterior Vespasian was a more subtle man than his elder son.

Titus accompanied me to the Governor's palace which Vespasian had made his headquarters. Mucianus was there, too. The generals made a compelling contrast. Vespasian was on his feet when we entered or, rather, bounded to his feet when we were announced; you will not have forgotten how difficult he always found it to keep still, and how he would disrupt the reception of, say, ambassadors by scratching himself, bobbing up and down, pulling his ear, twisting in his seat, and then getting to his feet and circling the chamber. Now he clapped me on the back, ruffled my hair, told me I had grown, looked quite soldierly now (which I didn't, but the compliment pleased me) and then started scratching under his armpits.

Mucianus reclined on a couch, resting against cushions. His long pale fingers, with their painted nails, toyed with the stem of a wine-cup. He fluttered his other hand feebly in my direction.

'Knew yer father, boy,' he said, 'you don't resemble him, fortunate for you. Bit of a shit, yer father, if y' don't mind me sayin' so.'

As if exhausted by the effort of speech, he sipped wine and then fanned his face with a kid-skin fan decorated with cupids.

Everything about him spoke of lethargy. Five or six little dogs shared the couch with him, now and then crawling over his body to be fondled, licking his hands, face, and even lips. He made no move to restrain them, and neither Vespasian nor Titus appeared to find anything remarkable in the spectacle their colleague offered. So I concluded it was customary.

Vespasian was never one for long speeches, or for approaching a subject delicately.

'My brother tells me you've a brain in your head, and that your mother's brought you up to be honourable. That so?'

'I'm grateful he should think so.'

'Don't fence, boy. Are you honourable?'

'I hope so. I believe I am.'

'Poor dear,' Mucianus said, 'and you such a beauty. Honour belonged to the days of the Republic, my dear. The Divine Augustus stifled the idea of honour as he stifled liberty and all virtues. So nowadays we all look after number one, don'y' know that?'

Vespasian flapped his hand at his colleague, and scratched himself again, this time in the belly.

'That's as may be,' he said. 'Not going to argue with you. Waste of time. Point is, this young man comes here with a message. From Otho, he says. Question is, do we believe him?'

'No reason not to, darling,' Mucianus said. His voice was a languid drawl; he drew out the syllables of some words as if loth to let them slip, and abbreviated others as though the effort of speech was too wearisome. 'Boy's not a fool, you say. So there's no reason to question his coming. Point is, do we believe Otho? Just what did the man say?'

I gave them, in as brief and military fashion as I could muster, Otho's proposals.

To my surprise they were ready to discuss them in my presence. Now, I wonder to what extent their arguments had already been rehearsed, since Titus had certainly informed his father and Mucianus of the gist of Otho's offer; and therefore whether the intention was that I should repeat to Otho the doubts and hesitations they now expressed. Yet certainly they could not have wished me to report everything, for all three spoke of Otho with unmingled contempt. To my further surprise, this irritated me. Though I was accustomed to think of myself as bound to Titus, and therefore to his party, I had been touched by something in Otho's manner and speech, which aroused in me the desire to protect, or at least stand up for him. But now I kept silence when I heard him derided.

'In my opinion,' Titus said, 'we should hasten slowly. That was a favourite saying of the Divine Augustus, I've been told, and it remains a good one. It certainly proved a good principle in his case.'

Vespasian said, 'What do we have to lose if we assent to Otho's proposals?'

Mucianus said, 'There's Vitellius, of course. A buffoon, admittedly, but not backed by buffoons. He's their puppet, y' know. Suppose he wins.'

Titus said, 'Suppose Otho wins, even with our help? Will he pay his debt? How long can a Triumvirate last? The history of the two earlier ones . . .'

Mucianus said, 'I know Otho. He's weak. He would like to be loved. Ol' Tiberius never cared a pigeon's fart for that. He knew the nature of men: that they hesitate less to offend a man who has made himself loved than one whom they fear. For love binds only by a chain of obligation, which is easily broken, but fear by dread of punishment, which never fails. What a long speech! I'm quite fatigued. But the words came to me and I couldn't hold them back . . .'

'So Otho's weak,' Vespasian said. 'Better he win then, with our help.'

Mucianus fondled his dogs, Titus smiled, we drank wine.

I shan't send this passage to Tacitus. It's too shameful to confess myself a gull. The truth is, men are blind throughout their entire lives. The Jew Josephus said that to me once when I had the audacity to ask him how it felt to be a traitor. He added, 'Look in your own heart; recall what and whom you have betrayed in life. No one is innocent of some act of treachery.'

I spent two days with Titus before a ship could be found to carry me back to Italy. Titus was in sunny mood, regretting only the absence of Berenice, which denied me the promised chance of meeting her daughters.

'Believe me,' he said, 'the secret of reaping the richest harvest from life, and the most intense enjoyment, is simple: it is to live dangerously.'

'If you and your father had decided otherwise,' I said, 'your brother Domitian would be in mortal danger.'

'Domitian has too little imagination to live dangerously,' Titus said. 'He's not like you and me. Trust in me, my dear, and I shall lead you to wonderful times. You must return now, to give our message to Otho, and then perhaps you will come back here to help me suppress these wretched Jews, who fight with a fanatical determination and then, who knows? The world is ours, our plaything, our oyster. On such a day as this I feel unrivalled strength. Open yourself to chance and the future . . .'

It was then that he told me of his visit to the Temple of the Paphian Venus.

XXII

I assume, Tacitus, you are relying principally on my memories to enable you to catch something of the mood in the city during the weeks of Otho's ascendancy when, at his command, I was lodged in the palace. You were, of course, still a boy yourself – fourteen or fifteen if I calculate rightly; and, as I recall you once telling me, your mother had prudently removed herself and all the household, including you and your sisters – what by the way became of the most beautiful of them, Cornelia, with whom I once engaged in a charming flirtation in your father-in-law Agricola's Sabine villa? Now I have lost myself in this sentence. Where was I? (You see how rusty my command of the written language is; it runs with my thoughts in no ordered rhetoric. I apologise; no doubt you will, sternly, despise my incapacity and apology alike.) Ah yes, your mother had removed you to the safety of her father's estates in Campania. I believe you have always resented this – as, if I may say so, so much else. Indeed your resentment was formerly so great that I have heard you speak as if you had indeed been in the city that spring and summer, and a witness of all the horrors then enacted. But I knew otherwise, though I kept silent then.

So I shall now give you what will be of certain use in your great work, and something which you could not have without my assistance. For you can learn of actions from records, and you can dissect character from what you read, from letters and speeches which were recorded, as well as from public documents. But for that shifting and evanescent thing we call mood or atmosphere, you require the testimony of one who lived at the time and saw and

119

felt all. Furthermore, I can supply you also with the gossip and wild stories that did the rounds; and these will lend animation to your History. Some of them were, as you may imagine, choicely absurd.

For instance, prodigies were daily reported. It was said that in the porch of the Capitol, the reins of the chariot on which the Goddess of Victory rides eternally to battle, dropped from her hands, a gloomy omen; that the statue of the Divine Julius, on the Tiber island, turned from the west to face to the east, and this – it was added with many shakes of the head – on a day when there was no breath of wind, as though it would have required a gale to shift the statue east-facing. Someone else had seen a form bigger than any man burst forth from the Temple of Juno bearing a mighty sword. Others reported that an ox in Etruria had spoken, in hexameters moreover, and that a goat had given birth to a calf (predominantly white, with black patches). In short rumour ran on winged feet, and no story was too absurd to find creditors. Domitian, who had been given a post of some sort in the palace, was torn, when we conversed, between credulity and disdain. His intellect told him such tales were nonsense; his fears denied the reasoning of his mind.

A sudden thaw melted snow in the mountains and, being succeeded by three days of incessant rain which led fools to assert that the heavens wept for Rome, caused the Tiber to break its banks and flood. Not only the low-lying and flat districts of the city were under the turbulent waters, even parts long thought safe from flooding found the water lapping at their doors. I required a boat to visit my mother and bring her supplies, which however were scarce. Scores of people were drowned, many more were marooned in shops, their workplaces or their homes. The foundations of countless slum dwellings were sapped by the force of the waters and gave way when the river returned to its usual channel. It was impossible for the troops to parade in the Campus Martius; they would have had to swim.

The capital was astir, and the ravages of the flood only mirrored the disorder in men's minds. It was said that Vitellius had infiltrated soldiers into the city, in civilian disguise, who were ready, at a given signal, to assassinate the partisans of Otho. So suspicion lurked behind every sentence spoken, and men dared not look each other in the eye. The state of public affairs was even worse. Nobody knew what the future held and opinions shifted with every rumour relayed. When the Senate was in session, many Senators absented themselves on grounds of ill-health. Those who did attend flattered the Emperor who, accustomed from his days as Nero's favourite to such language, treated it with the contempt it merited. But the next minute the flatterers, realising that their words might be held against them, should Otho lose the war that could be only a few weeks distant, tried to give them a double meaning; and so, in most cases, rendered them senseless. When they were called upon to brand Vitellius a traitor and public enemy, the more cautious did so in such general and indeed hackneyed language that none could think them sincere, for their words appeared as a parody of the genuine accusations of treason of which our history already afforded so many shameful examples. Others employed a more cunning ruse. They arranged that, when they rose to speak, their friends and cousins should raise such a hubbub of noise as to make them quite inaudible. So they could subsequently claim that they had done their duty, whoever enquired of them; and they could not be gainsaid.

Otho still hesitated. He received the report of my embassy to Vespasian and Mucianus with equanimity rather then pleasure. He commended my speed and my honesty, then, as if thinking aloud, said, 'All war is ruinous; civil war most ruinous of all.' He recollected my presence, smiled, and said, 'You may find these strange thoughts of an Emperor committed to the defence of his cause, who has just received, thanks to you, the welcome news of the goodwill that the commanders of the Eastern armies feel for me. Yet I would still wish to avoid war, and I wonder whether this assurance can be employed to that purpose. For surely, if Vitellius learns that I have joined Vespasian and Mucianus with me in defence of the Republic – as for convenience we may still call it – then perhaps he will desist and be ready to negotiate terms. Vitellius is no man of war. He's a lazy fellow, timid too, and I can't believe he has stomach for the fight.'

'That's as may be, sir,' I replied, 'but you yourself, when you gave me my commission, said that there were those behind Vitellius – Valens and Caecina you named – who were determined on war. You suggested Vitellius was their puppet, and I have never heard that the feelings or fears of a puppet count for anything.'

'Alas,' he said, 'you do well to remind me of my own words. Yet your readiness to do so makes me sad – so young and already so hard. I hope to avoid war because any war will be my responsibility, a weight on my soul and a blot on my reputation. Consider . . .' he paused and, without summoning a slave, poured wine for us both. 'I should never,' he said, 'have consented to assume this burden of Empire. And yet what else could I have done? You may say that I might have remained Governor of Lusitania, loyal to Galba. Would you say that?'

'It is none of my business, sir.'

'There were powerful reasons against such a course. My debts for a start. You're a young man, you can't know the demoralising weight of debt. When I was your age, I borrowed without thought of the morrow, or repayment. I had almost as many bankers as mistresses, and they were equally lavish with their favours, I assure you. They seemed to think it an honour to lend me money – as Nero's friend, you know. Then, when Nero turned against me, or I against him – it's a long and complicated story, for we wronged each other, I see that now – and I fell from favour but was bought off as it were with Lusitania, I felt the first chills of bankers' suspicions. So to repay the respectable bankers – just enough to keep them quiet – I resorted to the less reputable moneylenders, whose rates of interest were extortionate. They expected me to repay them by fleecing the poor provincials, my already sufficiently wretched Lusitanians. But I couldn't do so. Couldn't. Do you understand that? Shall I tell you something strange that I have learned? The men who behave well at certain points in their life anyway are not always those who have had a high opinion of themselves and their own virtue.'

He stopped his pacing, lay down on a couch, gazing up at the ceiling where a disagreeably muscle-bound Apollo tangled with an auburn-haired Daphne even as she was being transformed into a bay tree. The vulgar exuberance of the painting suggests to me now, in memory, that it was a Corinthian work. The artists of that city have always had a weakness for the florid and an impure taste. I confess I've always rather liked such work.

'So,' the Emperor continued, talking to keep me with him and save himself from solitude, 'my debts grew, vaster than empires and a good deal quicker, like monstrous vegetables, marrows or pumpkins. When I followed Galba to Rome – at his request, after I had declared my support for him – I was positively besieged by clouds of mosquitos whom I identified without difficulty as creditors. What was I to do? They threatened to strip me of all I possessed, make me bankrupt, disgraced and debarred from public life. Which I was weary of, I assure you. I could have borne exclusion and disgrace, but for one thing: my pride would not let me display to the world the miserable condition to which my extravagance had reduced me . . .

'Are you still listening? It's good of you to listen. What am I saying? I've forgotten for a happy moment that I am the Emperor. You can't walk out on me, or go to sleep, as you would if I was a private citizen. Still, you're a good boy to listen. Come and sit beside me.'

He ruffled my hair, stroked my cheek, and sighed.

'Poppaea was the only person I ever truly loved, except that, when I was with her, I could also love myself. No more; Otho's despicable, a sad piece of work. Relax, boy, I have no designs on you. I had designs on Galba. He half-promised to make me his heir and his partner in the Empire. That was one night on the journey to Rome. He was in his cups, but not heavily drunk, though many nights the old general was carried sodden to bed. For my part, I have never found pleasure in heavy drinking. It destroys all other pleasures and abilities. Galba – that model of old-fashioned Republican virtue – propositioned me. Well, Julius Caesar may have consented to be bedded by the King of Bithynia, but Galba . . . He had a taste, you know, for mature men, like that brute Icelus, who shared his bed and did who knows what to the old man. That sort of thing has never attracted me. I can see the point of a boy and can understand men who run after boys, though it's never been my taste since I was a boy myself. But to take your sexual pleasure from some hairy brute – no – it disgusts me. Galba even in his cups understood the repulsion that I felt. He called for Icelus and dismissed me, and with my refusal my chances of being adopted as his heir went out of the window – where, as you might say, my creditors were lurking and clamouring. So there it was. I had a choice: dishonour and poverty, death at my own hand, or a bid for Empire. When some officers of the Guard approached me and told me how the Guard detested Galba on account of his stinginess, what could I say? It's one thing to turn down an Emperor, quite another to turn down the Empire itself. And so I said yes. Should I have done so? What else could I have done?'

Had I known then as much of men and affairs as I do now, I would have realised that Otho's future as Emperor was likely to be brief. His self-pity corrupted any determination and ability he might possess. Even his winning of Empire had had no more moral significance than a gambler's lucky throw. Yet because I was young and inexperienced and of a generous nature, I warmed towards him. I was flattered, too, that he had unburdened himself to me, and I did not consider that a man who would so abandon the reticence that dignity demands – and before one who was little more than a boy, a mere youth, however admirable my breeding, bearing and intelligence might be – was unlikely to be more restrained in other company. In short, I should have realised that Otho, expressing his regrets and misgivings, even to casual acquaintances (for I was in reality no more than that) was certainly dismaying his supporters and proving himself incapable of giving that impression of serenity and steadfastness which is necessary if soldiers are to be ready to die for a cause.

In passing, Tacitus, let me urge you to consider the significance of the numerous desertions that occurred in this turbulent year. Was it not the case that the legions had only one interest in these wars: to finish on the winning side? Few held their generals in affection or respect; few were wedded to them as Caesar's, or Mark Antony's troops to them. So, for instance, Otho would embark on his campaign at the head of an army some of whose legions had only a few weeks earlier hailed Galba as Emperor, and had indeed marched from Spain to install him on the throne. Now they were to fight for Otho, who was responsible for the murder of Galba. How hard would they fight? What loyalty was to be expected from men in their position?

XXIII

Domitian was furious. As usual – this will not surprise you, Tacitus – his anger was inspired by resentment and self-pity. He had had a letter from his father informing him that he had written to Otho requesting that Domitian should not be included among the members of his staff, but be permitted to remain in Rome 'to continue his studies'. Otho had 'graciously' consented. He had in any case developed a dislike for Domitian, whose restless look and quickness to take offence were, as he told me, 'intolerable'.

'It's not fair,' was Domitian's refrain. 'I have no studies worth the name and, even if I had, my father has never given a hang for them. You're going to the war, with a position on Otho's staff. It's not fair.'

'Well,' I said, in what I hoped was a conciliatory manner, for in truth I had some sympathy with Domitian's resentment. 'You forget that I have no father to make such a request. It's true that I have a guardian, my mother's brother, who may still claim some notional authority over me, but then he has never cared a tinker's cuss whether I live or die. So there's no reason for him to start doing so now. But I'm sure you wrong your father. It's natural he should be concerned for your safety. Indeed, he said as much when I was with him recently. He spoke very warmly of you,' I lied.

'It's not fair,' Domitian said again, 'and I know who to blame. It's Titus who has persuaded my father to take this attitude. He's jealous in case I win a renown in battle that would put him in the shade.'

'That's ridiculous,' Domatilla said. 'As if you could! Everyone knows what a hero he is. His soldiers adore him. Don't they?' she turned to me and flushing, sought confirmation of what she could not have known, but nevertheless believed, for she herself 'adored' her glamorous elder brother, and could never suppose that Domitian might be in any way his equal.

'He is certainly very popular,' I said. 'As I daresay, Domitian, you yourself will be too, when the time comes. In any case, surely you see that it is in your father's interest – whatever reason he may have given Otho – that you remain in the city as his representative.'

'Oh, fine words,' Domitian said, 'awfully fine words. Do you think I'm stupid? Do you think I don't know that my uncle Flavius Sabinus is also to remain in Rome, and that he will be the man to receive confidences and instructions from my father?'

He continued in this vein interminably, till at last Domatilla told him to 'grow up' – a piece of admirable, if impracticable, advice which sent him into a deeper sulk.

At the time I shared her irritation. Subsequently I have wondered whether Vespasian's treatment of Domitian wasn't in truth prompted by Titus' determination that his little brother should be denied any chance to distinguish himself. If this was indeed the case, then Domitian's resentment was justified. It is regrettable that Rome, and my own career, should have suffered on account of resentment becoming his dominant characteristic.

XXIV

Near the beginning of March word came that the first army of the German legions had crossed the Alpine passes, under the command of Caecina. Orders given to the Danube legion based at Poetevio in Styria to intercept them had either gone astray or been ignored. So Otho found himself in a position similar to Pompey's at the opening of the campaign which led to Caesar's dictatorship. There were those who advised him to act like Pompey, abandon Italy to the invader, and carry his legions to the East, where they could join with those commanded by Vespasian and Mucianus, and so return, strengthened, in triumph.

Otho considered this advice and sought other opinions, hoping (I believe) to find that a majority of his advisers favoured this course. It was not that he was a coward, however effeminate and unsoldierly he might be in manner. But he doubted his abilities as a general; he detested the prospect of civil war; his sleep was made wretched by nightmares in which the ghost of Galba appeared to him; and he was temperamentally inclined to favour any course which would postpone the day of decision. In private conversation with me, he repeatedly bewailed his misfortune in being saddled with the load of Empire, and reverted to his favourite theme: that it had been forced on him by circumstance rather than by his own will. Everything in his speech was such as my Stoic upbringing had led me to condemn. And yet I could not do so. It was not merely that I was flattered (as any young man might be) by being singled out, as I supposed, to be the recipient of the Emperor's confidences. It was also that I responded to Otho's charm and vulnerability. Moreover, as I have said, my mother had always had a tenderness for Otho and this naturally inclined me in his favour.

Yet I did not abdicate my judgement to his fears or futile hopes. When he pleaded with me – with looks as well as words – to advise him that this course of withdrawal from Italy was wise and right, I could not, or would not, do so. On the contrary I pointed out that it had been fatal for Pompey, that it would be wrong – I may even have said 'unmanly' – to abandon Rome to the doubtful mercies of the Vitellian troops, all the more so because the Guard, whose duty it was to defend the city as well as the person of the Emperor, had committed themselves to his cause, and were reputedly loathed by the German legions. Then I added:

'Believe me, sir, I know Vespasian and Titus – the latter well, as you yourself know – and I have met Mucianus. If you abandon Italy and seek to unite your army with theirs, you will find that you have in reality surrendered the Empire to them. At best you will be the third or fourth man in the Empire. The only way in which you can maintain your position and make use of the friendship which Vespasian at least feels for you, and the good will which all three have expressed, is by meeting them in the character of a victorious general who has driven the German legions back beyond the Alps.'

'So young and yet so stern,' he replied. 'I'd like to get drunk, but I can't, however much wine I take. If I could get drunk, then I might sleep. And if I could sleep, my resolution might return.'

Otho's weakness and indecision were pitiful. It is therefore, surely, the more to his credit that he was able to overcome his fears, or at least to give his troops the impression that he felt none. Summoning up whatever resolution he could command, he gave the order to advance and seek out the enemy. As he buckled his armour on, he sighed. Then he wept a little, when he had dismissed the slave who had helped dress him as a man of war, and told me that he wished to keep me by his side throughout the forthcoming campaign.

'You may bring me good fortune,' he said. 'I have a notion that you may.'

'I have read,' I said, 'that Caesar himself used to say that Fortune was the only goddess a commander should concern himself with.'

Having come to a decision Otho embarked on the campaign with the utmost urgency, lest, perhaps, he should have second thoughts, or his nerve should fail him again. The speed with which he now determined to move disturbed many. For one thing the shields had not yet been returned to the Temple of Mars after the annual procession; which, a centurion assured me, was 'traditionally a bad sign, sir, if that is you take any heed of such traditions. I don't meself of course. To my mind it's a lot of balls, but I'm bound to say many of the men don't like it, sir.' It didn't please them either that the order to move was given on the day when the worshippers of Cybele, the Great Mother, commenced their annual wailings and lamentations, as they mourned the death of her lover Attis, nor that the priest who took the auspices after a sacrifice to the God of the Underworld, found the victim's intestines were in prime healthy condition – just what they shouldn't be on such an occasion – in the opinion of the superstitious anyway. More to the point, as I saw it, was that the march north was delayed by floods in the vicinity of the twentieth milestone from the city, and that we then found the road blocked by the rubble from buildings which had collapsed as a result of the flooding. All this disturbed the nervous.

For my part, however, I was in a state of high but controlled excitement. All my life I had longed for the chance to emulate the achievements in war of my Claudian ancestors, and now this was being given me at an enviably early age. I sang as we marched, and the soldiers cheered to see an officer (even an honorary one) in such high spirits. But they could not fail to observe that the Emperor's face twitched and that he rode silent and seemingly indifferent to what happened around him. Since soldiers are as affected by the mood of their commanders as schoolboys are by their master's temper, this was an omen far more serious than any of those which had excited the fears of the superstitious.

Yet the news of the first actions was good. A detachment sent north to try to intercept the army which Valens was leading down the valley of the Rhone gained a victory near the colony of the Forum Julii. Then there were rumours of a mutiny in the camp of the enemy; these were premature, though in truth such a mutiny did break out in a few days, for reasons which I have never discovered. The word came to us that the advance of Caecina and his legions through north Italy was resented by the citizens of the towns where he quartered his troops, and that they were particularly angered by the conduct of his wife Salonina, who rode through their towns garbed in the imperial purple. Of course, the dissatisfaction of these citizens could be of little immediate benefit to our cause. Yet the unpopularity of an invading enemy is always to be welcomed. For one thing, it may demoralise the troops who, in a civil war, always hope to be received as liberators.

Then came the news that Caecina's assault on Placentia, which the Vitellianists considered of the first importance, had been repulsed after a desperate struggle, in the course of which the beautiful amphitheatre beyond the city walls was set on fire and utterly destroyed. The ardour of our troops within the city was however such that Caecina despaired of taking it and so raised the siege. And then, as we moved to concentrate our forces near Cremona, we learned that one of Otho's most able lieutenants Martius Macer had won a victory to the north of the city.

It seemed therefore as if success attended our arms everywhere, and I began to be anxious lest the Vitellianists should soon see the hopelessness of their position, and either surrender or withdraw beyond the Alps, and that I might therefore be denied the chance to add lustre to my family name in battle.

Yet, it was at this moment that Fortune first frowned on our cause. Having scattered the enemy, Martius Macer prudently checked the pursuit, for fear that the enemy might be strengthened by reinforcements, which spies had warned him they were bringing up. I say 'prudently', for by every law of war, his action was indeed prudent. And yet its consequence was evil. For there were those in our army who immediately described this act of prudence as a display of cowardice, while others said that it showed Martius Macer to be less than wholly committed to the cause, and even a traitor who had deliberately refrained from destroying the main army of the enemy. This was ridiculous, but good sense is an early casualty of any war.

The soldiers were disturbed. They did not know whom they could trust. They were uncertain whether the generals who gambled with their lives were determined on victory, or whether some at least were already preparing to defect to the enemy. Such was the evil consequence of the rumours circulated by his personal rivals concerning Martius Macer's conduct. So harsh things were said of the other generals, Annius Gallus, Suetonius Paullinus and Marius Celsus. The officers of the Guard who were guilty – or most guilty – of the murder of Galba, however that might have been prompted by the old man's arrogance and folly, were chief amongst those who now employed the wildest of language. They alone, in their own minds, were fully committed to Otho's victory, and, in their disordered state, were ready to accuse others of treason. In so doing they undermined the cause, the success of which offered them their only hope of security and future prosperity.

Otho could not fail to be affected by the mood of suspicion that surrounded him. Without good reason, he fell into distrust of some of his most able commanders. I cannot blame him altogether for this; the rumours of treason had thrown him into a state of perpetual alarm. He sat for hours in his tent, sipping the wine that failed to intoxicate him, but which nevertheless numbed his critical faculties. Time and again, I heard him bewail his unhappy lot. 'If you ever dream of wearing the purple, dear boy,' he said to me, with many heavy sighs, and on the verge of tears, 'wake from that dream. It is a crown of thorns, not of laurel, that presses on my brow.' Yet in public he strove, not always in vain, to appear cheerful.

There was a consequence of the dissension and the rumours still more damaging to his cause than their effect on his state of mind. That is not the best way of putting it, for the consequence was provoked by the distrust and dismay that clouded his judgement. Believing that if so many men spoke ill of his generals he could not know whom to trust, he resolved to hand over the management of affairs, and indeed the whole conduct of the campaign, to his brother Titianus, a man with neither experience of victory nor the capacity to inspire the soldiers with confidence. Of all Otho's mistakes, this was the most serious. Soldiers who trust their commanders will fight bravely, to the death, even when the cause is failing. Those who neither trust nor respect them will lose the battle in their hearts, even when the disposition of the forces may yet be in their favour. For the truth, Tacitus, is that morale is the determining factor in war; perhaps you have heard your father-in-law Agricola say so.

Yet on the ground things still appeared to go well. Caecina, perhaps because he was unnerved by the failure to take Placentia and his discomfiture in other lesser actions, perhaps because Valens was now bringing his untested army up and Caecina feared that he would gain the glory of the campaign, now made a rash attempt to regain the credit he had lost with his troops and with his imperial candidate, Vitellius.

He posted some of his veterans – auxiliaries as we later learned – concealed in the woods that overhang the road twelve miles from Cremona, at a place called Castors. Then he sent forward a cloud of cavalry, with orders to provoke a battle and then withdraw to lure our men into the trap he had laid for them. It was a pretty scheme, but dangerous in the circumstances of a civil war in which spies and deserters abound. No doubt, had he been engaged against a foreign enemy, his plan would have met with success. But in a civil war there are always many men whose commitment is wavering; they have friends and relations in the opposing army, and so there is habitually a communication between the armies of a sort which is not found in foreign wars. So his scheme was betrayed, or revealed to us.

Titianus was, fortunately, some miles in the rear, and neither Paullinus nor Celsus felt the need, or desire, to consult him. As it happened I was then in the front line, having been sent forward with a message from the Emperor. I was therefore in a position to observe the disposition of our troops and to admire the assurance with which this was made.

Paullinus commanded the infantry, Celsus the cavalry. The veterans of the 13th legion, men who had fought with Corbulo in Armenia before that greatest of generals was discharged, disgraced and destroyed by Nero on account of his jealousy of any other man's virtue and success, were drawn up to the left of the road. The raised causeway through the marshes was held by three cohorts of Praetorians, in deep columns, while the right was occupied by the 1st legion and a few hundred cavalry. Several troops of cavalry were sent forward, and more cavalry held in the rear. I myself, with the general's permission, sent my horse to the camp-lines and stood by Paullinus.

Paullinus was a general of the old stamp. His first care was to throw up defence works, so that he could secure himself against defeat before venturing in search of victory. So the first part of the battle was fought some distance ahead of us, and I know of its course only from hearsay.

The Vitellianist cavalry having provoked battle then withdrew. But Celsus, aware of the ambush, checked the advance. This caused some alarm, especially when a handful of Illyrian cavalry galloped back to our lines, calling out that all was lost. They would have inspired a panic, had Paullinus not quickly intervened, and ordered his men to stand their ground. Baffled, the Illyrians wheeled about, and for some time galloped to and fro in front of our line, neither seeing a way to safety nor daring to try to force the barrier we presented to them, forbidding their flight.

Meanwhile, the Vitellianists, believing that the battle was in their favour, surged from their concealed position to give battle to Celsus. He gradually withdrew, making an orderly retreat, the most difficult manoeuvre in war, especially for cavalry. But he moved too slowly, and so found himself surrounded. It was at this moment that Paullinus gave us the order to advance. I did so myself at the head of a cohort of the Praetorians, whose officer had been wounded by a stray javelin.

I have been in so many battles since this first one that I have learned to distrust all accounts of conflict. There is no narrative of a battle, rather a phantasmagoria of discordant impressions: the look of surprise on a dead man's face, the glint of a horse's hoof raised above you, the grunts of men thrusting with swords, sounds strangely like those emitted in love-making, the sudden face-twisting fear as a man struggles to free his weapon from the body of a fallen man which, holding it fast, renders the killer for the moment defenceless.

Most of all, though, it is the smells which linger vilely in your nostrils for days after a battle: the stink of fear, of sweat, blood and ordure, for terror can cause a man to defecate, and shit to rush down the wavering legs of even the victors. The idea of war has its beauty, but there is nothing pretty about battle.

As the infantry came together we thrust and slashed and pushed. Close combat gives you strength, adds also to fear, since there is no escape unless the hindmost ranks give way to panic and turn to flee. Then you find your back naked.

That morning the close fight lasted only a short time which, nevertheless, was endless. I had no notion we were winning, for at first we seemed to be pushed backwards, and I stumbled twice, thrice, over fallen comrades. Then I felt a weight behind us, a great press of men and, without warning, the soldier with whom I had crossed swords, each hacking at the other's shield, glanced over his shoulder. His mouth opened in a wordless cry and he took two steps backward, then, before I could launch myself at him, turned tail and ran. And I saw that the whole line of the enemy was in flight.

We pursued them with cries for some half a mile, and then the trumpet sounded and a grey-haired veteran seized my shoulder, checked my attempt to free myself, and said, 'That's enough, young sir. That's the recall. Run on and you'll find yourself alone. And that'll be the death of you.'

Later, there was fierce criticism of Paullinus for halting the pursuit so abruptly. Men said that if he had not done so, we would have achieved a complete victory, that Caecina and his whole army might have been destroyed. The critics may have been right. There is no doubt that a general panic had spread through their ranks. I myself had heard many cries such as 'It's every man for himself.' But Paullinus justified his caution. He said that he did not believe that the whole army of the enemy had been engaged, and that their commanders might throw reinforcements forward, who, attacking our men after they had lost order in the pursuit, might reverse the decision of the day. In short, he asserted that it was enough to have inflicted so much damage on the enemy and that it would have been folly to risk throwing away the advantage we had won. No doubt there was much wisdom in what he said, and events might indeed have turned out as he feared. Yet his policy dismayed the army. They thought they had had a chance to settle the campaign in one afternoon, that the opportunity had been lost, that the enemy had been only bruised and would soon recover. So, instead of celebrating a noble victory, men talked more readily of what had been thrown away. Their mood was such that you might even have supposed we had lost the battle.

Nor was that all. Paullinus, though he had master-minded the victory, and shown such skill in the disposition of his troops, and such control over their movements, yet lost credit on account of his decision to halt the pursuit. Those who had already been putting it about that he was less than completely committed to Otho were confirmed in their suspicion. Some even went so far as to say that his halting of the pursuit was an act of treachery.

For a few days the war was suspended. This allowed the enemy time to repair the damage done. More significantly, it permitted the union of Caecina's army with that of Valens. Though our intelligence assured us that the two generals were now bitter rivals, each fearing that the other would become the chief man in the army, and indeed the State, when Vitellius was victorious (for nobody regarded the so-called Emperor himself or thought him anything more than a figurehead), yet the coming together of the enemy made it necessary for Otho to call a council to discuss strategy.

'The question,' he said, fingering a piece of material merely to keep his hands occupied, and perhaps to prevent anyone from observing their tremor, which was occasioned not by fear, but by some nervous complaint that I had observed to afflict him in moments of excitement, 'the question is whether we should seek battle or wage a defensive campaign and so draw out the war longer, in the hope of exhausting the enemy.'

He invited Paullinus, as the senior commander – in years, that is – and as the victor of the most recent battle to give his opinion first.

Paullinus spoke with an old-fashioned formality. His conduct in the recent battle had won my respect, however I might think the prudence which had caused him to halt the pursuit to be ill-timed; and I was therefore displeased to observe that his manner of speaking gave rise to some amusement. In particular, the two ephebes who were customarily in attendance on Titianus, and who were assumed to be his catamites, though they were at the council in the capacity of secretaries, giggled and nudged each other, and smirked and pulled faces in imitation, as they thought, of Paullinus' grave manner. During the course of his speech I sidled round the room, and, coming up behind the two little beauties, jabbed each hard in the ribs with my knuckled fist; they yelped, and fell silent, rubbing themselves where I had struck.

'Vitellius,' Paullinus said, 'has now assembled his entire army. He can hope for no further reinforcements. Nor has he any strength in his rear, for Gaul is restive (as I hear) and he can strip no more troops from the Rhine frontier lest the Germans break through. He can get no reinforcements from Britain either, unless prepared to abandon that rich province to the barbarism of its northern wilderness. There are few troops left in Spain. Narbonnese Gaul has been reduced by the action of our fleet. Italy, north of Padua, is confined by the Alps. It cannot be supplied from the sea where we still have mastery; and, lastly, his army has already stripped the towns, villages and farms of the last grain. He can get no more corn, and without supplies an army cannot be kept together. Then the German auxiliaries, who are among his finest fighting men, will suffer, should we drag the war out till the summer, from the heat of our climate to which they are unaccustomed.'

He paused, and cleared his throat. (It was at this moment that I silenced Titianus' catamites.)

'Many a campaign, beginning well in the fruits of its first impetuosity, has crumbled, become nothing, when subjected to delay. Was that not how the great Fabius Maximus wore down Hannibal, the most formidable enemy Rome ever faced? But our position is very different. We have Pannonia, Moesia, Dalmatia and the East, with armies that are fresh and ready for action. We hold Italy and Rome, the seat of Empire and of government. We have at our disposal all the wealth of the State and of countless private men. We control the corn route from Egypt and we have a vast supply of money at our disposal. Money may be a sharper and mightier weapon in a civil war than the sword. Did not Antony and the young Octavian, later the Divine Augustus, prove that when they moved against the Liberators, Brutus and Cassius?

'Our soldiers are accustomed to the climate of Italy and the summer heat. We have the River Po on our front, and strongly garrisoned and fortified cities, any of which will withstand a siege, as the defence of Placentia has demonstrated. Therefore, for us, the wisest course is delay. Let us protract the war or, at least, if there is to be a battle, let us compel the enemy to come at us. Then we shall fight in a prepared position, while they endure the hazard of open ground. In a few days, or weeks at most, the 14th legion, laden with battle honours, will arrive from Moesia. We shall then be even stronger than we are now and if, sir,' – he turned to Otho, who started, as if till that moment he had abstracted himself from the company and permitted his mind to wander through a world of dreams – 'if you are eager for battle,' Paullinus said, 'we shall fight with increased strength and a greater assurance of victory. For this is my final word: the wise general delays battle till the odds are overwhelmingly on his side. And with every day that passes the balance of advantage tilts towards Otho.'

Otho thanked Paullinus for his advice, and for speaking so frankly. Then he bit his nails while he waited to see who was eager to follow the first speaker. Marius Celsus got to his feet.

'I've had my quarrels with Paullinus in the past,' he said, 'and I still hold that he was wrong to halt the pursuit in the last battle. But what's done is done. You can never alter yesterday's course. Now Paullinus talks sense. Everything comes to he who waits, as the proverb says. All we have to do is sit tight, hold our position, and Vitellius will be like a rotten fruit that falls from the tree. Why risk defeat in battle when victory is ours if we do not do anything rash?'

A young blond legate, who had nodded to me approvingly when he saw me silence the catamites, and whom I now recognised as one whom I had been accustomed to see, years previously, in Lucan's company at the baths, now stood up. He wore the short military tunic and rubbed his hands down his thighs as if they were sweating. His thighs, I recall noticing, were shapely and free of hair. Not many men have the cool self-esteem to shave their legs on campaign. He addressed Otho in a dandified voice, with a note of haughty reserve.

'Permit me,' he said, 'to introduce myself, for few of you will know me, while those who do may be surprised to see me at this council. My name is Caesius Bassus, and I am attached to the staff of Annius Gallus. As you know, my general had a heavy fall from his horse a few days ago, and is presently laid up. Therefore he sent me here, that I might read to you a paper which he has written giving his views of what should best be done. I see no reason not to say straightaway that he is in substantial agreement with Paullinus. Nevertheless, since his reasons for advocating this course are not identical, which you may consider adds weight to the argument, I request your permission, sir, to proceed.'

As he read his general's document, a line of verse floated for a moment just out of reach. Domatilla had quoted it, I knew that, and named the author as Caesius Bassus, which meant nothing to me then. Now the three things came all at once together, Domatilla's lips framing the line as we gathered our things and looked round the garden before returning to the villa, the line itself – 'Stark autumn closed on us, to a crackling wind from the west' – and the image of the poet stretched out on a bench at the baths, caressing himself, as Lucan urged in a voice that grew sharper the more his friend ignored it, some wild course, but what I know not. How strange, I thought, to find him here, so untouched by war, untouched even by time, for he, who was several years older than myself, now appeared to me to be my equal in age.

He finished speaking, made a curt bow towards the Emperor, and turned away, as if indifferent to the effect of his words which, I suspected, might have been written by him, for Annius Gallus was not reputed to have any skill in rhetoric or letters.

It seemed to me that the argument for delay was cogent, and I also believed it would accord with Otho's own predilection for postponing. But I had reckoned without the influence of his brother Titianus, who spoke up for immediate war. He was supported by the Prefect of the Praetorians, one Proculus, an ignorant and short-tempered man. Their chief argument was that delay in a civil war encourages desertions and that the troops should not be given time to consider whether they might find better fortune in Vitellius' army. This argument, though expressed inelegantly and without any attempt to appeal to reason, nevertheless prevailed. It did so because it played on men's fears, and fear is a more potent advocate than good sense. Even as Proculus spoke, I could see Otho begin to twitch; he had told me only that morning that he had dreamed of waking, naked but for a single sheet, in a vast desert; a cold wind was blowing and vultures hovered in the air. Poor man, he had no confidence in the loyalty of either his soldiers or their officers. Having won the Empire by an act condemned as treasonable by so many, he saw traitors lurking at every corner of the road he was compelled to travel.

Then Titianus, either because he sought to reserve glory for himself, or perhaps because he had a certain affection for his brother Otho, which I find hard to credit, proposed that the Emperor should not command the army in person – or rather should not remain with the army command of which he had surrendered to his brother – but should withdraw to Bedriacum some dozen miles to the rear. There, he said, the Emperor would be secure from danger and able to occupy himself with the administration of Empire.

Otho received this speech with a blank expression on his face. I don't think he knew what his brother had been going to propose; and the words pained him. They suggested that he was useless, an embarrassment to the troops, some of whom would have to die to maintain him as Emperor. He looked around as if seeking someone to oppose his brother's motion. His gaze fell on Caesius Bassus, who held it a moment and then lowered his eyes. Otho's mouth trembled. When he saw that no one was going to demand that he remained with his army, he gave a little shrug of his shoulders, clapped his hands, and called for wine for the council. Unusually, there had been none provided beforehand, perhaps because Marius Celsus was known to be intemperate.

The gathering broke up into little groups. I felt a hand laid on my shoulder. I turned to see Caesius Bassus.

He said, 'So we've made two bad decisions.' He smiled, as if making bad decisions was matter for indifference. 'You're attached to the Emperor's personal staff, I think,' he continued. 'So I'm afraid you will see no immediate action. But I hear you have already distinguished yourself. I congratulate you. To display virtue in war is all that is left to us, now that civic virtue has been outlawed. You must not be surprised that I know of your doings. It is not just that they have been much spoken of. I had my eye on you in any case. You were a friend of my friend Lucan, I think.'

'That does me too much honour,' I said. 'I was a mere boy. We were not equals. Therefore we could not be friends.'

'No?' he said, and smiled. 'At any rate, he admired you greatly.'

'I admired his verses,' I said.

'Yes, of course.'

'One of your lines ran in my head as you were reading your general's dispatch.'

I quoted it to him.

'Do you know,' he said, 'I can't for the life of me remember the next line. A poet who forgets his own verses – not, I assure you, a being you are often likely to encounter.'

'I'm afraid it's the only line of that poem I know. It was a girl who quoted it to me. The girl I'm in love with actually.'

'Ah, yes, my verses appeal to lovely girls. And to some boys also, I'm glad to say, even some lovely boys.'

He laid his hand on my shoulder again, and squeezed it gently.

'I often think I should have died with Lucan. I'm rather ashamed I didn't. Well, I don't suppose it will be long now. Not after the decisions taken here tonight. Take care of yourself, and remember me. Get your girl to recite the rest of the poem. It was rather good, I think. Sad that I've forgotten it myself.'

That night Otho dictated to me for a long time, letters to the commander of the 14th legion, to Vespasian and to Mucianus. He spoke confidently of his expectation of victory and of how he looked forward to their meeting to discuss the government of the Empire.

But, every few minutes, between phrases, his eyes shifted and he looked into the night.

XXV

I do not know why I sent these last pages, with the record of that conversation with Caesius Bassus, to Tacitus. I regret it. I feel as if I had given something of myself away. But how can that matter? Do I care whether Tacitus thinks well or ill of me? I have no reason to. I am cast up here. He writes again that there is no reason why I should not return to Rome, now that law has been restored, and no one is condemned merely by the caprice of the Emperor. No doubt he speaks truth. He still does not understand that exile has become my choice – or my destiny.

Besides, what would I do in Rome? Who would I know? Who would remember me? Who would greet me kindly?

Even my friendship, such as it is, with Tacitus is one that can be maintained only at a distance, by post. With several hundred miles separating us, I can be amused by his narrow puritan censoriousness. It would bore and irritate me if we met and spent time together. That used not to be so; I was then delighted by his wit and intelligence. But now I could not abide his certainty of being always right, of being justified; I scorn his consciousness of his own virtue. Actually, I find I dislike him. But he amuses me – at a distance.

In his last letter he said, 'You forget that the murder of Galba made Otho odious and terrible.' Strange adjectives to use of that unfortunate man.

Balthus is lying stretched out before the fire, asleep. One of my hounds has placed his leg over the boy's thigh, pushing the skirt of his tunic up to reveal a long line of naked flesh. The skin is pale, though the flames dance red-gold over it. It is deep night. I kept the boy with me rather than being compelled to solitude. Minerva's bird utters its warning cry. Bitterns boom in the reeds by the inland sea. From the bedroom beyond comes the, as it were, answering snores of my woman. She has never had a disturbed night in her life, and she tells me she never dreams. Indeed I once, years ago, had to explain to her what a dream was.

There are pictures in the fire. Some nights they frighten me. Balthus utters a little moan. It sounds contented. But it may have been the hound that uttered.

Two nights after that staff council, I was released by Otho when he declared himself at last ready to retire. He had talked of doing so several times, and I was beginning to think we would see the dawn, as we had done on other occasions. But this night he said, 'I really think I may sleep', and let me go. We were lodged in a villa, from which the owner had fled, or which he had perhaps been persuaded to surrender to the Emperor, and I had secured for myself a little room by the gatehouse.

When I entered, I found Caesius Bassus reclining on my couch with a wine-flask by his side.

'I had your servant stoke the stove,' he said. 'You don't mind that I've come here? Look, I've brought wine.'

He poured me a cup.

'I'm very tired,' I said, ungraciously.

'Who knows? I may be dead tomorrow. I've remembered how that poem goes.'

He recited it to me.

'It's good,' he said, 'isn't it? One of my best. I can't think how I came to forget it.'

'It's sad, certainly,' I said, 'and beautiful, like the last colours of the evening sky. But you didn't ride here to recite a poem to me.'

'Why not? I am a poet, after all, with all the poetic vanity. And being a poet, writing poems, that's the best of me, the only good in me, I have often thought. And I was touched that you remembered that line your girl quoted to you, even if you would not perhaps have done so but for the girl. But I admit, the poem was an excuse. I wanted to see you again. To talk. To unburden myself. To speak to someone who knew Lucan and was loved by Lucan, and to kill the night with talk of Lucan, and life, and love and this awful war, this so uncivil civil war.'

'Lucan talked, to seduce me,' I said. 'That was all. He didn't succeed.'

'You can't reproach him for that ambition,' he said. 'You were very desirable. You still are, if you don't mind my saying so. To me, you are in that most delicious of stages, no longer a boy, not yet a man. But that's not why I've come here. Oh, if you were to invite me to tumble you on your bed, I should accept, of course. But I don't expect you to do so and, even if you did, and we took pleasure in each other, what would that amount to? The brief opening of a window in the blank wall of weariness, no more than that. For me now, even satisfied lust tastes sour, like new wine poured yesterday, drunk today.'

He fell silent. I could not read his expression, for his face was in half-shadow. A moth fluttered against the lamp, burned its wings and fell to the table.

'"The shadow of a great name",' he said, quoting Lucan. 'I think he meant Caesar, but the great name in whose shadow we all live is Rome itself, and Rome is now, like Troy, in flames. Nothing that was Rome remains – except the name. We were Republicans, you know. We dreamed that it might be possible, Nero dead, to restore the Republic. It was only a dream, foolish and insubstantial. We proved that, betraying ourselves and each other in our fear. No one in our generation has the fortitude of our forefathers. They tortured me, you know, but only a little. That was all that was necessary to make me betray Lucan. And Lucan himself tried – oh, so meanly – to cast the blame for his conduct on his mother. Perhaps he had Rome in mind. I should like to think so. For we had – it was a bond between us – a certain idea of Rome, which however in no way corresponded to the reality. I crawled to Nero: to save my life which, ever since, has seemed to me worthless. And so now, we are caught up in the struggle between two worthless men, Otho and Vitellius, and I ask myself, does it matter which of them feasts on the dead body of Rome? There's no good answer I can think of. One of them will win, the other lose, and who gives a tinker's cuss? Then your friends, Vespasian and Titus, will engage in a new war.'

What could I reply? The shameful thought came to me that the disillusion, so plangently expressed by Caesius Bassus, might be a ruse, that he might have been sent to prove my loyalty to Otho, and that an unwary word might invite my ruin – arrest, a cursory trial and ignominious death.

He seemed indifferent to my silence.

'We hoped to restore a time when men might think what they wished and say what they thought. Yet, when we came to the test, we stifled our thoughts and said what was required. There was no need of enemies; friends were only too ready to destroy each other. We thought of ourselves as the best but, when even the best are subject to moral corruption, the worst triumph. I have never ceased to reproach myself that I am still alive. Fortune may see to it that this battle tomorrow answers my self-reproach.'

He smiled, and drank more wine.

'Do you know what I am?' he said. 'I am a man with a great future behind him.'

I do not pretend that I recall his every word throughout this conversation which was really a soliloquy, a threnody with corruption as its theme. Yet some of the words are those he spoke, and the sense is all his. So, too, is what I may call the music. It has remained with me all these years, throughout so many vicissitudes, because this poet, whom I scarcely knew, who had singled me out almost by chance, and who met the next day the death he sought, expressed with an irony so detached from his personality as to seem cruel all that I have come to feel concerning the horrors of the age in which we have been condemned to live and in which the reward for virtue has been certain doom.

Before taking his leave, he said, 'You will have heard that our two emperors, Otho and Vitellius, accuse each other of monstrous debaucheries. Neither is lying. How strange that both should stumble into truth?'

There can be no emotion more debilitating than self-contempt; yet who that ever aspired to virtue can escape it in our time?

Balthus stirs on the rush-matting before the fire. The hound protests and, shifting position, now lies athwart the boy. Waking, the boy's face often wears a troubled look. His eyes are narrowed and there are lines made by anxiety running from them. His mouth hangs a little open, as if he would speak but dare not, as if inviting kisses which nevertheless he would try to ward off. But in sleep he looks contented, contented indeed as the unreflective hound.

He spoke to me earlier this evening of his god, in whom he declares an absolute trust. It appears that the poor child believes that his god has a special care for him, and indeed for all those he terms 'true believers'. He would like me to become one. Yet it is all absurdity. Everyone who has thought about these matters and who has had any experience of life knows that whatever gods exist are perfectly indifferent to the fortunes of men. If they care at all, it is not for our safety, but for our punishment. His Christianity is a slave's religion, and I suppose this is natural. Slaves dare not look reality in the face. They keep their eyes lowered to the ground. No wonder they cherish in their sad deluded hearts some notion of enjoying the favour of the gods in another life.

Strange though that his absurd religion gives him an assurance and a comfort I cannot look to have. In my experience, virtue is punished and crimes rewarded, until hubris overtakes the criminal.

XXVI

I fretted, Tacitus, to be kept at the Emperor's side. Yet there was nothing I could do about it. Otho protested that he needed me. He told me I was his talisman. Yet he spoke in a tone of despondency. Civil war, he told me, was wicked. Neither he nor Vitellius would be forgiven for having subjected Italy to its miseries.

'It is no wonder,' he said, 'that the merchants and common people of the towns already regret Nero. What harm did he do them, they ask, compared to the ruin that the rivalries of Otho and Vitellius threaten to bring on us?'

And it was true, he added, that Nero had directed his cruelties only at members of the senatorial class, and had pleased the populace by the lavish entertainment he had promoted on their behalf.

The Emperor had refused to take the omens on the day assigned to battle, and when the priests who had done so came to inform him of their message, he waved them angrily away. He sent forward a succession of runners urging his brother Titianus and his second-in-command Proculus to make all possible haste towards the confluence of the Po and the Adda, by which march it was hoped that they would cut off the enemy's retreat and draw a circle round their camp. I later learned that Celsus and Paullinus had argued against exposing the troops, who were heavily burdened with baggage, to such a hazardous plan. They would rather we had stood and fought on ground of our own choosing. But Titianus, with all the arrogance of incompetence, waved these arguments aside. He was infatuated with the beauty of his plan, and did not realise that battles are fought in the field, not on map-tables. But the disagreement between the generals becoming known, the men were disheartened, and many talked, I am told, of their fear that they had been betrayed.

Towards evening, but while it was still light, the first messengers came to us with reports of a heavy defeat. The army was in headlong flight, they said. Otho received the news without any sign of emotion, and gave gold to the messengers. When he had dismissed them, he said, 'I have never believed in victory, and so it now remains only to die in such a manner as will cause men to speak well of Otho and bring honour, not dishonour, to my house. For a long time I have wished that I had fallen victim to the perverted hatreds of Nero, and been spared this ordeal of being Emperor in name alone.' And he ordered a slave to bring him two daggers, and himself tested their points.

I said nothing to dissuade him. What should I have said?

But then, a centurion of the Praetorians, by name, Plotius Firmus, thrust himself into the presence.

'All is not lost,' he said. 'We've been defeated in a battle, but not a decisive one. The other side got a bloody nose themselves. Their cavalry was scattered. We took the eagle from one of their legions. We have still an army to the south of the Po, not to mention the legions which have remained here with you, my lord, at Bedriacum. What's more the Danube legions are still on the march to our aid. So we can still fight back. All that is required is resolution.'

Soon the centurion was joined by a number of his men. They crowded round Otho, yelling encouragement and swearing that they were ready for another go at the enemy. One young man even threw himself to the ground, and clasping Otho's knees, demanded that he lead them himself back to the field and he was certain they would restore their fallen fortunes.

So Plotius Firmus spoke again, even as Otho tried to disengage himself from his supplicant.

'You must not,' he said, 'desert an army that is so loyal and soldiers so eager to shed their blood on your behalf. There is more virtue in withstanding trouble than in escaping from it. The brave man clings to hope, whatever his ill-fortune. Only cowards yield to fear.'

Otho was embarrassed by these expressions of faith. He had already resigned himself to defeat and death. Indeed, in his own mind, he was dead already. So the call to renew the struggle dismayed him.

But, ever better fitted to put on a public show than to maintain his equanimity in private, he spoke graciously now, thanking the men for what they had said, and assuring them that he was fixed on no course of action, but must consult his generals before coming to a decision. His words could not satisfy, for the soldiers were looking to hear him declare that the war was not to be thought lost as long as men of their calibre were to be found. Therefore, although they accepted his diplomatic speech, many went sorrowful away. And I believe that if he had, after consulting his generals, resolved to renew the war, which was certainly not lost, he might, on account of the chill reception he had given his most enthusiastic troops, have found that their initial ardour had cooled.

Such speculation is vain. Nothing was further from Otho's mind than the struggle. He was already resigned to defeat. I knew that, as soon as he had persuaded Plotius Firmus to lead his Praetorians back to the camp. His body, which had been taut throughout this scene, relaxed. He even smiled. He stretched out his hand and chucked me under the chin, and stroked my cheek.

'You despise me, don't you?' he said.

'I don't understand you,' I replied.

'No,' he said, 'you are young, and brave, as these Praetorians were. But I am weary, and I hold that to expose such courage, such spirit, as yours and theirs to the danger of another battle is to put too high a value on my life and office. The more hope you hold out to me, the more glorious will be my death. I am now at one with Fortune. We have no secrets from each other. I know her cheats and strategems and can turn away from the false hopes she offers. The civil war began with Vitellius; let it end with his triumph. If I now resign myself to death, then Vitellius has no cause to revenge himself on my family and friends. But if I prolong the struggle, and meet again with defeat, then he will feel entitled to carry out a proscription of all who have been dear to me; among whom I include you, dear boy. I die happy in the thought that you, and so many, were happy to risk death for me. But the comedy has been played long enough. It is time to leave the theatre. So, I urge you not to delay here, but to take thought for your own safety, and to remember me as I die rather than as I have lived. I shall say no more. Only cowards talk at length to delay the moment of death. I complain of no one. Only those who seek to live need complain of gods or men.'

No doubt the speech was too long, and seemed all the more so when he had gathered together his staff and repeated it, almost word for word, to them. Yet there was something impressive in his calm demeanour. I admired his resolution, even while I despised the decision that occasioned it. To my mind, it would have been more manly to lead his troops into another battle, which indeed might yet have been won. Even if the cause had been hopeless, yet it seemed to me that an Emperor should die on his feet. Why seek Empire, only to abandon it at the first cold winds of Fortune?

Otho then begged us all to take our leave. It was in our interest, he said, to depart at once, in case Vitellius and his generals should interpret our remaining with Otho as a mark of defiance. He ordered boats and carriages to be made ready and it seemed that he was more assiduous in planning the flight of his entourage than he had ever been in organising his army for battle. He commanded his secretaries, too, to destroy all his correspondence.

'I should not wish,' he said, 'for Vitellius to discover that any of you had abused him in writing to me.'

Then he dismissed us, so that I was not a witness to his death. Nevertheless I later questioned one of his freedmen who attended him to the end. Therefore the account I now give you, Tacitus, is as authentic as any you may receive, even though I was not an eye-witness.

When he was alone, except for his domestic staff, he lay down to rest for a little. But his rest was disturbed when he heard shouts and cries from around the house. He sent to enquire. The soldiers, who refused to believe that Otho had abandoned the struggle, were attempting to prevent anyone from leaving the camp. (I myself had to bribe a surly fellow with five gold pieces before he would let me depart.) Otho rebuked them and said it was his will that his friends should be free to go. Despite this, the detachment of the Guard itself remained with him, though, aware of the hostility that the German legions felt for them, they must have feared their own fate. This was a remarkable example of loyalty. I have never understood what in Otho attracted it. I had come to like him myself, but I had been privileged to be his confidant. The soldiers, on the other hand, were now being abandoned by him.

After speaking to a few who had not yet dared to leave the camp, where however they feared to remain, Otho drank a cup of water mixed with only a very little wine. Then he retired to rest. Sometime before dawn he stabbed himself, falling forward on his dagger. There was but one wound, sufficient to kill him. Plotius Firmus, the loyal centurion, arranged his funeral. Otho had left a request – he was past the stage of giving orders – that this should be done at once; he had been troubled by the thought that Vitellius might command his head to be cut off and put on display. The cohort of the Praetorians covered his face and body with kisses; or so my informant said.

XXVII

Tacitus: have you ever marched with the remnant of a defeated army? I suppose not.

It is a degrading experience. Even the horse on which I began our retreat died under me, and I was compelled to footslog it like a common soldier. There were no marching songs, and every morning when we struck camp, we found that a few more men had taken advantage of the darkness to desert. But our numbers did not dwindle, for all along the road we were joined by stragglers, men who had been separated from their companions, and found among us that the company of the dispirited was nevertheless preferable to solitude. When the men talked, which was seldom, it was of their wives or mothers, never of the battles we had just fought.

It was raining the day I limped back into Rome. Water ran yellow in the gutters, and puddles stood like fords in the cobbled lanes. News of Otho's defeat and death had preceded us. The city wore the heavy clouds that obscured the Janiculum as if they were funeral garments. Nobody knew when the victors might be expected; everyone dreaded their arrival, except for those partisans of Vitellius who had already emerged from hiding, and who alone spoke in loud confident voices.

Near the Pantheon I came on a stout equestrian berating a group of dirty bedraggled Praetorians. They bent their heads under his insults, and lacked the spirit or nerve to reply.

As ever in anxious times, only the taverns and the brothels did good business. Most of the foodstalls had been emptied of their goods by people stocking up, and preparing to keep to their houses till times were more certain.

At last, the equestrian, having vented his spleen, departed, no doubt satisfied by having had the courage to insult broken men. I approached the Praetorians, one of whom I recognised as a centurion who had sworn his devotion to Otho with peculiar force, and the appearance of sincerity.

I gave them money, small coin only.

'What will you do?' I said.

'Drink it. What else can we do?'

'If you could take passage to the East . . . ?'

'There's not a ship's captain would carry us, not without we had gold to offer him. And we have no gold,' the centurion said. I recalled that his name was Frontinus.

I drew him aside.

'You find the ship and square the master,' I said. 'I'll undertake to furnish you with the gold. You deserve to escape, and I should wish you to carry a letter to Vespasian's camp, to his son Titus.'

I arranged to meet him at a tavern in the Suburra at the same hour of the day following.

Was such secrecy necessary? I did not know.

'Why not travel with us yourself, sir?' he said before we separated.

The temptation was strong. I was, I discovered, afraid, as never before. Yet I shook my head. Why? Because Titus would despise me as a coward, if I ran to him, as to my nurse? Perhaps. Because I could serve his cause better in Rome? Again, perhaps, though for the last fortnight I had felt my devotion to the Flavians cool, as my respect and pity for Otho grew warmer. Because some curiosity held me in Rome? I could not deny that reason; yet it irritated me.

I went first to my mother's house, and told her all that had happened. I urged her, in turn, to retire to the country, to one of her brother's villas.

'I'm in no danger,' she said. 'Besides, I spend all my wars in Rome.'

That sounded like bravado, or foolishness. There had never been wars in Rome, in her lifetime. Then I understood that she was speaking for her own amusement, at the same time fitting herself for a role: the severe Republican mother. Perhaps also she sensed my nervousness – fear has its smell, apprehension likewise – and spoke to stiffen my resolution.

'What sort of man is Vitellius?' I asked.

'No sort of man. The favourite of three Emperors. So the basest sort of man.'

'I've heard he murdered his own son, Petronianus, some name like that.'

'I doubt it,' my mother said. 'The other version of the tale is that the boy prepared poison for his father, but drank it himself in error. I doubt that, too. It's also said Vitellius was one of Tiberius' catamites on Capri, and that story is believed by those who believe that the poor old man did indeed indulge in depraved lusts. The truth is, son, that Vitellius all his life has been the sort of man of whom rumour has been fond, the sort of man who is the subject of dirty and nasty stories, simply because he is contemptible. He is a man with no true virtue, but that doesn't signify that he is a monster. He is merely base and mean. As for sex,' my mother paused; it was not a subject that she had ever discussed with me. Perhaps her willingness to do so now was a sign that at last she regarded me as fully adult. 'As for sex, it's my opinion that he is a pimp, a pandar to others' lusts, rather than a performer. You're surprised that I should speak to you in this manner, even that I know such things. Well, you must learn that anyone who has lived in Rome as long as I have knows much of what she does not choose to speak. Then, think only that I now speak about matters concerning which I would rather keep silent, because it is expedient in your situation that you should not remain in ignorance of the nature of the man who now wears – for how long I cannot tell – the imperial purple.'

Then, having had her say, she had the slave set before me a dish of pork and beans and a jug of wine, and watched me eat, while she questioned me about the manner in which Otho had met his death.

'I always knew,' she said, 'that there was virtue in the boy.'

Angry words of contradiction formed in my mind, remained unspoken. It would serve no purpose to tell my mother that elegant suicide served no purpose but to make a show and that, in my opinion, a man who had seized the Empire by an act which moralists would denounce as criminal should have had courage enough to pursue the struggle for mastery or die in the attempt. So I ate my beans and drank my wine, and took leave of her, saying I must go to the baths, for I was still travel-stained, and only my need to assure myself of her safety had brought me to her house in that condition.

The baths were busy for, since it was still some days before even the vanguard of the victorious army was expected in the city, men had come there the more eagerly to learn the latest news and feed on the most recent rumours. After I had been in the hot room I reclined on the bench where Lucan had first eyed me up, and thought of him and his friend Caesius Bassus, and that line of verse – 'Stark autumn closed on us, to a crackling wind from the west' – and tried to recollect the other lines as he had spoken them to me in my room by the gatehouse. But they deserted me. I felt his pervasive melancholy, his weariness with life; and then, running my fingers along my thighs, was aware of the admiration with which I was being viewed by several, but which, being a man now, I no longer desired. So I turned over on my belly and slept.

I dreamed, horribly, for in my dream I saw Domitian deflowering my Domatilla. Her initial resistance lost itself in her brother's embraces. Arms, raised to fend him off, closed around him. She thrust her mouth against him in an eager play of tongues. Her legs wrapped themselves round his thighs and buttocks, and she cried out in painful joy as he thrust. I woke with a cry and lay there shaking.

Dreams may not portend the future, but they may foreshadow the future that we fear.

When that evening I went to the apartment in the Street of the Pomegranates where the brother and sister lodged with their aunt, I watched them with narrow suspicion. In each glance they cast on each other I read a guilty complicity. When Domatilla spoke to me with the affection I had been accustomed to hear in her voice, I now detected hypocrisy and, though I told myself it was absurd to be so influenced by a dream, I could not be at ease with them.

Domitian himself was afraid. Tacitus does not believe me when I tell him (if I send the account of these days to him it will have to be heavily doctored) that Domitian was no coward. Because he hates him, he would like to despise him, too. But Domitian, in reality, was cursed with a too lively imagination, which led him to anticipate dangers – always more fearful in prospect than in reality. Now he was convinced that, as soon as Vitellius arrived in the city, or even earlier, his partisans would seek out Vespasian's son and murder him. He had infected Domatilla with his fears, and perhaps this was the new bond between them which so discomforted me.

The next morning the air of excitement in the city was palpable. Though no one knew when Vitellius would arrive, many swore that acts of vengeance had already been performed on the partisans of Otho. Therefore Senators and equestrians who had given their allegiance to Otho had fled the city or were making preparations to do so. Some who had departed were confidently pronounced dead. Others now wished to conceal their support for the late Emperor, and either pretended it had not been willingly given or sought to bury it in a tumult of praise for his successor. I encountered several who assured me that Vitellius was a worthy heir, not of Nero, to whose vices he had served as pandar (as my mother had told me) but of the Divine Augustus himself. In short, there were many signs that in their alarm and apprehension, some of the noblest-born of Rome had taken leave of their senses.

As for me, I wrote a lengthy account of all that had happened, and, meeting the Praetorian centurion Frontinus, as we had arranged, gave him my document and a purse of gold (which I had borrowed with great difficulty from my mother's banker, a cousin by marriage) and advised him to make haste to the ship whose captain he had suborned. I was fortunate, I told myself, to have come upon him. There were few I would have trusted with my letter. But he had an honest face, and he still spoke of Otho with respect, and of Vitellius with manly scorn.

There was nothing to do but wait, than which nothing is more difficult when the worst is expected. Unlike Domitian I disdained to hide myself, and frequented the baths as usual. Though I could not achieve equanimity, and though nothing in my experience nor in what I had learned of comparably turbulent periods, inclined me to hope, my pride – that insensate Claudian pride – held me from despair. What must be, will be, I told myself. Things being as they are, why should I seek to deceive myself by pretending they are otherwise?

At the baths, men talked of Vitellius' progress towards the city.

He had insisted, it was reported, on visiting the battlefield of Bedriacum where his lieutenants had won him the Empire. There he saw mangled corpses, severed limbs, the rotting bodies of men and horses, picked over by carrion crows. The soil was still wet with blood. Still more horrible, it was said, was that part of the road which the citizens of Cremona, eager in their customary manner to flatter and seek to please the victorious general (though he had taken no part in any fighting) had spread laurel and roses in his honour, and where they had raised altars and sacrificed victims, as if he had been some king from Asia. Then Caecina and Valens indicated to him the salient points of the battlefield, tribunes and prefects boasted of their individual feats of arms, commingling fictions, facts and exaggerations. The common soldiers, too, turned aside from the line of march and gazed with a more healthy wonder, it was said, on the wreckage of war.

But Vitellius, exhilarated, carried away by the evidence of what men had done for him, and already, it may be, a little drunk, declared that, 'Nothing smells more sweetly in my nostrils than the corpse of a dead rebel.'

He was speaking of his fellow Romans, citizens like himself.

As he advanced ever closer on Rome, word came of his terrible extravagances. His soldiers looted, unpunished, the towns and villages through which they passed. The Emperor, so-called, paid no heed, being delighted in the evening by troops of comedians who had attached themselves to his army, and being ever surrounded by a cloud of fawning eunuchs. Even Nero, it was muttered, had not conducted himself more disgracefully or with less regard for the imperial dignity and the decencies of Roman life.

'If you want to know how Vitellius will conduct himself when he is installed on the Palatine,' someone said to me at the baths, 'you should consult a creature called Asiaticus, who keeps a low tavern in the Street of the Little Frogs on the other side of the Tiber.'

'Why?' I said. 'Who is this Asiaticus?'

'Once Vitellius' catamite – a slave born no one knows where, but presumably somewhere in Asia or born of parents from that part of the world. Vitellius was infatuated with the boy, who was certainly very pretty in those days and also, I'm told, an adept at varied forms of love-making. Then Vitellius freed him, no doubt in return for disgusting services. Eventually, it's said, the creature grew tired of his master and ran away. He took up the tavern trade then, but Vitellius sought him out and was so angry that he sold him to a trainer of gladiators. That might have been the end of him, but Vitellius decided he still couldn't live without the youth and bought him back, just as he was about to enter the arena, and pissing himself with terror, I daresay. Then Vitellius set him up in his present tavern, on the understanding that he would procure free of charge whatever creatures took his former master's fancy. You may know that Vitellius has a taste for under-age virgins. Oh yes, our new Emperor is the most degraded of men.'

Not knowing my informant, I had no means of judging how much of what he said was true, and how much was spiteful rumour. But it was remarkable that he should have been so ready to tell me what, if I were to divulge it, would certainly lead to his arrest and execution. I asked him why he was so bold.

'I care for nothing,' he said. 'Vitellius betrayed my two sons to Nero's lustful vengeance, and now I look forward only to death. But first I should like to spit in this so-called Emperor's face.'

'Why should you suppose that this Asiaticus, who must owe a debt to Vitellius, should tell me anything to his discredit?'

'Because it is impossible for anyone to speak of such a thing as Vitellius without revealing him for what he is.'

XXVIII

I confess I was tempted to seek out this Asiaticus. It was not that I hoped to learn anything. Already I knew as much of Vitellius as I cared to know and it was, in any case, improbable that the degraded creature described to me could tell me anything of value. My motive – or rather, the inclination which I felt draw me to his tavern-brothel – was of a still lower sort. All my life I have known in myself an impulse towards acts which in anticipation excite me and which in retrospect fill me with self-loathing. I could picture so vividly the type of women and boys who would frequent the tavern, and the knowing leer with which this Asiaticus would make my choice available to me. I saw my hands push a tunic away from yielding flesh, and felt myself thrust at a creature I despised only less than I despised myself for wanting it. My lust was sharpened by the thought of my terrible dream and by the doubts it had, however absurdly, inspired concerning Domatilla's virtue. I held the image of my lust in action before my inward eye till my balls ached.

The memory of that moment rises sharp and exciting at a distance of more than thirty years. The rain spat from the cobbles and a north wind from the mountains cut through the city. Darkness fell.

The wind blows outside my villa now, from the waste plains to the far north, a barbarian wind. Balthus lies among the hounds before the stove. His soft boy's legs show their inviting nakedness to me. In sleep his hand has crept under his tunic. I think his dreams are not of the Christian chastity of which he, barely comprehensibly, has spoken.

This religion of which he has told me much perplexes me. It brings

161

him peace. I can't doubt that. And yet it is absurd. Its greatest prize would appear to be renunciation of the world we inhabit. You might think this would appeal to me in my fallen state. But I have not renounced the world; the world has rejected me. When I talk to him about the desire for power and the struggle for honour which, to my mind and in my experience, informs all men's conduct in affairs of state, he listens, with his soft inviting mouth a little open, his red lips quivering with, perhaps, disgust, and shakes his head. It makes no sense to him. I have tried to explain to him what we mean by virtue – that determination to be whatever becomes a man – and he sighs and says, 'Master, I fear you have lived your life in the Kingdom of the Wicked.' He speaks, curiously, with affection. I think he is indeed now fond of me, perhaps because he is grateful for my restraint in regard to him.

Yet at times it seems to me that his affection springs from something other than this gratitude; that he sees something good in me which I cannot recognise, and which, it may be, is far removed from what I understand by virtue.

One day, he said to me, 'Master, I think you are not always far from Christ.'

I would have whipped any other slave or freedman who had the impertinence to join my name to that of a Jewish agitator who, it seems, impersonated a god, like those deluded beings who, in the years of which I write, presented themselves as Nero escaped from his enemies and come to regain his throne. They were all imposters, madmen – for who else would wish to be Nero?

When earlier I read that last chapter of my memoirs (one which I certainly will not send to Tacitus) aloud to the boy, for he now has enough Latin to understand even elegant prose and no longer merely the dog-Latin of the camp and tavern, he said: 'You lived in a most horrible and wicked world.'

I could not deny its horror.

But I said: 'I write of the world as it is.'

'But not as it need be,' he said.

'As it has always been,' I replied.

Then I told him something, of which I may write later, of my experiences in the war in Judaea. For these Christians, among whom he numbers himself, are in origin a Jewish sect, and the cruelties, barbarities and lust for self-destruction which the Jews revealed in that war speak of no better world. I hoped to hurt him by my harsh honesty.

Why?

Is it because I do not care to see anyone contented? Is it because it seems absurd that a boy such as Balthus, enslaved, mine, even now, to do with as I choose, should seem to have attained a serenity denied me, a serenity which this act of memory in which I am engaged continues to deny me. My woman has, of course, a brute contentment. For her the affairs of the house and of our children are sufficient. But I have never envied her as I envy, to my angry amazement, this boy.

One day he said to me: 'Master, I have heard you rail at the Fate which drove you from your position in the world, and landed you on this barren shore. But it seems to me, so wicked is the world in which you strove, that God has granted you a great blessing, by removing you from it, and giving you the chance, in this remote spot, to make your peace with yourself, and so redeem your soul. Master, I beg you, let it go. Let your resentments slip from you and be carried out to sea as a river bears all that is thrown in it – all foul things – away.'

His smile was very sweet, his eyes appealing. I could have flogged him, with pleasure.

XXIX

It is necessary now, Tacitus, to speak of what was happening in the East, even as we awaited Vitellius in Rome. Of course, what I now have to relate is of a different order from what has gone before, since I cannot serve as an eye-witness. You will have also other sources of information, which you may indeed prefer to mine. That's up to you. I would however assure you that what I have to say is authentic, in as much as any one-sided version of a story may be that. You will understand that my informant was Titus. You will therefore make allowances for the likelihood that he gave to me the version of events, and the analysis of the situation, which he would have liked to see accepted by historians such as yourself. But you will also understand that even so partisan a version has its value; and I have no doubt you will set it against other accounts which you will receive from your other witnesses and informants, some of which may well contradict what I have now to relate. So be it.

As you know, the Eastern Generals had meditated an assault on the Empire even while Otho was alive. Now, for a little, they hesitated. The delay irked Titus. He understood however that his father was held from action, not on account of fear or lack of ambition, but because it was his habit to weigh the advantages and disadvantages of any proposed course of action. Vespasian was sixty. Some men grow bolder, others more cautious, in old age. Vespasian had never been rash. It was natural to him to hesitate now. He had good reason for caution. In the first place, he knew the quality of the German legions, some of which he had himself commanded. It impressed him that, with all the strength of Otho's defensive position, Vitellius' men had had the resolution to overcome him. They had shown no disinclination to slay their fellow-citizens in a civil war. He could not be certain that his own troops would show a similar lack of scruple. Moreover, Vitellius now had the advantage of the defensive position which Otho had so rashly thrown away. Though Vespasian had no respect for Vitellius, he knew Caecina and Valens to be men of ability. He knew, too, that the fortune of war is never settled, its outcome never to be exactly calculated in advance. He had struggled through many difficulties to attain his present honourable position; he was loth to hazard all on the throw of the dice.

At first, he was uncertain whether the Eastern army would prefer to be commanded by him or by Mucianus. The prefect of Egypt, Julius Alexander, made no secret of his belief that Mucianus should be the one to be proclaimed Emperor. And Mucianus was more popular with the legions. They respected Vespasian as soldiers always respect a general who is careful of their lives in battle. But they loved Mucianus, as soldiers love a debauched commander who nevertheless is a favourite of the god of war. For them, Mucianus, with his little dogs and the painted boys of his entourage was a 'character' – a 'card', as they put it. They would have loved to make him Emperor, and to sing lewd songs in his triumph.

But Mucianus wasn't playing. He had two reasons for disclaiming the opportunity to wear the purple. First, he was lazy. He simply couldn't see himself burdened with the administration of Empire and, since he was both intelligent and dutiful enough to know that any Emperor who neglects the business of government is contemptible, he retained, despite his many vices, a fierce pride. Second, he was childless. It was said that he had never lain with a woman, and I believe this to be true, even though he was actually married once at least, perhaps twice. But he professed a dislike for the female shape and also, he said, for the smell of women. Since he had no heir, he gave not a hang for posterity.

That wasn't all. Mucianus adored Titus. I believe they were, briefly, lovers, though Titus once denied this when I taxed him with it. Of course, even if they had been so, they were no longer. By this time Titus was too old for Mucianus, who delighted in beardless boys. Yet he still adored Titus, and couldn't look on him without reviving the memory of his old desire. And he was charmed by Titus' bearing, looks, wit, and intelligence. Therefore he said to Vespasian, 'If I was chosen as Emperor, the first thing I would do would be to adopt your darling Titus as my heir. Since he's already yours, that seems to me to be peculiarly unnecessary, my dear. Titus will be Emperor, the gods willing and our arms favoured, whichever of us first wears the purple. So it makes sense that that should be you. His gifts should assure him of respect – that respect which an Emperor needs and which has been accorded to none since Tiberius. But his succession will be the more assured and uncontroversial if he follows his natural father rather than being the adopted heir of one whose manner of life will persuade many that he chose Titus because the boy was once the recipient of what they will term his shameful attentions.'

He laughed at the thought. But I have it on good authority that his manner of speaking made Vespasian for the first time wonder whether his son had in fact been his colleague's lover. Nevertheless he couldn't but be pleased that Mucianus was so fixed in his determination to make him Emperor.

And he immediately gave proof of this when he persuaded, or compelled, Julius Alexander to transfer his support to Vespasian. That was of the first importance for, as you will no doubt remind your readers, whoever holds Egypt holds Rome to ransom, by reason of his control of the grain trade.

So in any long war the control of Egypt secured Vespasian an advantage.

Yet, even now, though word had come that Vitellius was established on the Palatine, Vespasian hesitated to allow himself to be proclaimed as Emperor. To his mind, he could not move till he had assured himself that the legions stationed on the Danube favoured his cause.

Here he had a stroke of fortune. One of the last acts of Nero, or rather of his ministers, for Nero did not care to trouble himself with such matters, had been to transfer the 3rd (Gallia) legion to the Danube frontier. This legion had formerly been commanded by Vespasian, had won honours then, and held him in high esteem. So its officers set themselves to persuade the commanders of the other Danube legions that only Vespasian could rescue the Empire from contempt and the curse of civil war.

However, Mucianus also advised Vespasian that they should send emissaries from their legions to Rome, to inform Vitellius that all the legions of the East had sworn allegiance to him.

'In this way,' he said, 'we shall gain the advantage of a few weeks. If I know Vitellius, he will believe what he wants to believe, slacken his vigilance, and devote himself to pleasure.'

This indeed proved to be the case.

But the same emissaries also brought, secretly, letters from Vespasian to his brother Flavius Sabinus, urging him to waste no time in organising support for him in Rome, and they also brought a letter from Titus to me. Domitian again expressed his displeasure and disappointment that neither his father nor his brother had thought to write directly to him. Even then, I thought he had just cause for grievance, and so I did not tell him that Titus had written to me. I could not in any case have shown him the letter, partly because Titus was never willing to share information concerning their father's plans with Domitian, partly because the affectionate terms in which the letter was couched would have aroused Domitian's fierce jealousy.

Flavius Sabinus now insisted that Domitian should not remain in virtual hiding, but should show himself in public, frequent the Forum and the baths, and in general behave as befitted the son of a distinguished commander who was a loyal servant of the reigning Emperor. I am bound to say that Domitian obeyed reluctantly, and with an ill grace. He complained that he was being used, though not consulted, and said that he did not believe that his appearance in public would do anything to assure Vitellius of his father's loyalty. I daresay he was wise in this judgement. At any rate it was not long before an officer of Vitellius' personal bodyguard presented himself at the house in the Street of the Pomegranates, with an order requiring Domitian to report to police headquarters at noon every day. This was as alarming as it was insulting. Flavius Sabinus protested on his nephew's behalf, but, for some weeks, Domitian, blushing furiously and trembling with ill-concealed apprehension, did as he was bid.

Meanwhile, as Titus had forewarned me, events marched in the East. The prefect of Egypt, Julius Alexander, proclaimed Vespasian Emperor on the first day of July, and made the legions stationed there take an oath of allegiance. All had been well prepared, and there were no dissenters. Two days later the legions in Judaea followed suit, even though their commander Titus was still travelling back from Antioch where he had been consulting with Mucianus. They did this therefore spontaneously (or so it was later given out), hailing

Vespasian as Caesar and Augustus. But I believe this acclamation was not unprompted.

Mucianus now declared himself in Antioch, as he and Titus had agreed he should. The soldiers were eager to swear their allegiance to Vespasian. But Mucianus also wished to attach the provincials to the cause, no doubt in the knowledge that they would have to be taxed more heavily to pay for the campaign, and thinking that it would be better if they could be persuaded to do so willingly. So he addressed an assembly of civic dignitaries and other men of note in the theatre. He was well suited to the task, for he spoke Greek with unusual elegance and, while the Greeks are accustomed to mock those who speak their language imperfectly, they are always flattered by a Roman who has taken the trouble to learn it thoroughly.

Moreover he told them what was not true: that Vitellius had announced his intention of transferring the German legions to Syria and the Syrian ones to Germany. This alarmed and displeased the soft provincials, for they supposed that the legions long based in Germany would have acquired savage, even brutal, manners from their sojourn in so barbarous a region, while on the other hand many of them were connected by friendship or relationship to the troops quartered among them. So they were pleased to think that Vespasian would soon be established in Rome in Vitellius' place.

Very soon, too, the various client-kings of the East came out in support of Vespasian, while Queen Berenice, naturally, on account of her affair with Titus, promoted his father's cause with zeal and furnished him with gold from her treasury.

And so what one may call the conspiracy gathered pace.

I believe that Mucianus, throwing off his habitual lethargy, was the great organiser. It was a favourite saying of his that 'money is the sinews of war', and now he set himself to prove it. He knew that soldiers who are assured of their pay will fight more willingly than those who are not, and that contractors, whose bills are met 'on the nail', as they say, will produce, as required and in quantity, the supplies without which no war can be effectively fought. It was another saying of his that 'an army marches on its stomach', and he took care to see that the soldiers' stomachs were well filled. He even contributed substantial sums from his own resources, and it does not diminish his merit that these sums were available principally because he had so generously plundered the State himself. Others followed his example, though few of them had his means of reimbursing themselves from the public store.

The Danube legions rallied to the cause. Two which had favoured Otho (the 13th and the 7th) but which had been denied the opportunity to fight on his behalf – denied it because of the rashness with which his campaign had been launched without waiting for the reinforcements available to him – now came out for Vespasian. They were commanded by Antonius Primus.

You will remember him, Tacitus, as one who had the reputation of being a scoundrel, indeed a criminal: for he had been condemned in Nero's reign on the charge of having altered a will in his favour, and it was widely said that this was one of the few judgements delivered then which did not offend the sacred principles of justice. Whatever his faults of character, he was an asset to a party bent on seizing control of the State. He was brave in battle, quick and eloquent, admired by the soldiers. In peace he might be considered the worst of citizens; in war he was a valuable ally. Vespasian received him as such, reserving to a future date any doubts he might entertain concerning his character and conduct. Now Antonius Primus acted in concert with Cornelius Fuscus, a man I had long known, as a friend of Lucan. He held the post of Procurator of Dalmatia. Idle and frivolous in youth – to the point of resigning his senatorial rank – he had been a favourite of Galba, who had appointed him to his present post. Possessed of many friends, on account of his geniality and charm of manner, he was active in writing letters seeking support for his new master from many who held posts in more distant parts of the Empire. Letters were sent to Gaul, Britain and Spain; and, in consequence of his urging, many in these provinces declared for Vespasian and withdrew support from Vitellius.

I mention these details that you may understand how thorough, and – if I may use the word in this context – how professional were the preparations for war made by the Flavian party.

No doubt you will make use of this information as it suits you. I venture to say you will not find it contradicted from other sources. Vespasian's support ran deep; and that gave confidence to all his adherents.

XXX

I have gone ahead of myself, in recounting to Tacitus, the events in the East as I understood and remember them.

Meanwhile we still waited Vitellius' arrival. I again besought my mother to retire from the city; she again refused.

It was a balmy spring and glorious early summer. Roses tumbled over the palace walls and the scent of thyme, myrtle and oregano on the slopes of the Palatine carried memories of happy days in some rural retreat. One afternoon Domatilla walked with me in the gardens of Lucullus. We spoke of poetry, reciting favourite lines of verse. I would have made love to her, but she was unwilling. It was not the time, she said: 'Later, later.' I tried her with Horace: 'Pluck the day'. She smiled and turned her face away.

Flavius Sabinus was active, also anxious. He busied himself winning support for his brother Vespasian, then stood aghast at the dangers he ran. I thought his efforts vain. Things would take their course, no matter what he did. The Empire would not be decided here in the city, but somewhere to the north, perhaps even again in the vicinity of Cremona, where Otho's nerve had crumbled.

So we waited.

Domitian's nerves were bad. He had contracted a skin rash, which itched intolerably. The side of his face and his forearms were scraped raw. He complained, tediously, of his father's neglect. Nothing could persuade him that his life was not in danger.

'Vitellius knows nothing yet of your father's preparations,' I said.

'How can you be so sure?'

'If he had heard he would be already in Rome, and himself occupied in drawing up plans for the war. But we hear of nothing but the nightly parties he gives, the theatre productions he demands, and his drinking bouts. In some men this last report might suggest an uneasy spirit, but, with Vitellius, it is merely habit, I am told.'

But nothing could stay Domitian's alarm. He scratched himself till the blood stood out on his arm, frowned, turned away, and threw himself face down on a couch.

Actually some of the stories which reached us from Vitellius' camp were so bizarre that even I could not credit them. I say, 'even I', for already in my youth I was persuaded that no extravagance was too absurd to be indulged in. You must remember that I was reared with an intimate knowledge of how things were done in the imperial household, fed with stories of the absurdities of Claudius, and the near-madness of Nero.

Vitellius was said, for instance, to be so greedy that he had been seen, while a sacrifice was in progress, snatching lumps of meat sizzling from the altar, and devouring them, to the disgust and consternation of the priests.

Do I believe that story? All I can say is that if it's not true, it's been invented to fit his character.

Though I had persuaded myself that my philosophy was equal to the strains of that period of waiting, I nevertheless found myself distressed by an inability to sleep. This is an affliction which has been my companion ever since. I have seen more dawns rise ghastly to my cold sobriety than even the most debauched reveller has been amazed by. Even now, as I write this, the first cocks are summoning the awakening day.

At the time of which I write, I would go to bed early, in an effort to catch sleep unawares. I would close my eyes and sense it steal upon me. But then a tremor disturbed its advance. Perhaps it was an erotic fancy; perhaps a cold start of fear: sometimes the thought of what was to be done; sometimes sharp regret for some past action. My eyes would open, against my will. I would turn to lie on my belly, and surrender to erotic images – Domatilla's soft lips, Titus' leg lying weighty across mine, the flash of a girl seen in the street, that prostitute who used to ply for custom in a lane near the Pantheon, and who would stand, as it were indifferent, with one leg drawn up behind her so that her foot rested on the wall of the building against which she leaned, a girl so confident of her beauty and her allure that, alone among prostitutes I had ever known, she never solicited custom, but was certain of being addressed.

Such fancies would leave me shaking, the sweat standing out on my brow, and, knowing sleep had deserted me, I would rise, put on my clothes and sally out into the streets, perhaps in search of that girl though I knew she did not practise her trade after dark.

The streets were lonely and dangerous, for Flavius Sabinus, as Prefect of the City – a role he discharged with the utmost conscientiousness, even though he knew that he was keeping Rome secure for his advancing enemy – had imposed a curfew; and soldiers of the Guard paraded the streets to enforce it, arresting any whom they found loitering.

Yet their efforts were random and they were easily avoided. A great city has ever its night-hawks – criminals, debauchees, waifs, lunatics, poets (I daresay) and unhappy wretches such as myself to whom sleep denies her gentle comforts. So I wandered the streets and knew many strange encounters: quick couplings against the slimy walls of noisome alleys, rambling conversation by the braziers along the river bank where broken men and women congregated. Sometimes I found myself in sinister cellars, drinking-dens, the lowest sort of brothels, gambling-houses.

I remember one night falling in with a young man of noble birth, as evinced by his negligent dress and manner of speaking. He was only, I judged, a little drunk, but his conversation was wayward. He insisted that I accompany him to a place that he knew, where, he said, we could gamble and drink and lie with women. 'Or boys or what you will. There are Africans there,' he said, 'and my fancy is for dark flesh.' The place was mean and sordid, lit by tallow candles, and managed by a toothless crone, who laughed to see us. I heard malice in that laugh, but by the light, such as it was, I saw something in my companion which appealed to me. It may have been the soft disappointed line of his mouth or the long lashes that flickered over his deep-set eyes. I do not remember, though I remember these features. They made a gull of him there, throwing loaded dice to win the gold which, if he had not lost it, they would have stolen. I felt a savage joy as I watched his humiliation and saw him grow incoherent on the sour wine of the house. The debonair manner which had attracted me because I knew it to be assumed as a mask for the despair which consumed him, disintegrated. He wept, and then implored the woman to furnish him with a black girl, as she had done before. 'You have no gold,' she said, and the ruffians who had fleeced him, took hold of him and hurled him out into the black night. I found him in the gutter, helped him up, and then, when he shook me off with assurances that he was all right, watched him stagger out of my life.

Why does that memory stay with me? Not because I behaved badly, for I have done worse in my time. Because of the gallantry with which he accepted his humiliation? Perhaps – 'and dying he remembers his sweet Argos'. Wasn't that the condition of Rome?

XXXI

You write, Tacitus, yet again chiding me for my delay in sending you further instalments of what you call my 'copy' and, then, as an afterthought, ask me if I have been ill, since you can't understand, or imagine, why otherwise I should be failing you. As you have never once, since I embarked – unwillingly, I remind you – on this exercise which has aroused in me so many painful memories I had thought well buried, expressed a word of gratitude, you might consider that this omission of courtesy would be sufficient reason for me to desist. But then, you know me. You know I am not dependent on your gratitude, and care little for expressions of appreciation. So you are justified in supposing I may have been ill.

But not in body. My illness is of the spirit, or the will, or whatever you choose to call it. The truth is that your request from the first reminded me of the wisdom of Herodotus' line: 'you stir what should not be stirred.' History is a record of crimes and foolishness, and no more that I can see. It has no instructional value, for each generation of men is confident of its own wisdom and ability to avoid its fathers' mistakes. Nor can I agree with Aeschylus that 'lamentations are a sure relief of sufferings.' Or it may be that I have not the gift to give tongue to lamentations. I do not know. I know only that I have been wretched to trawl over past horrors.

And now I must approach the moment when Vitellius prepared to enter Rome. 'Ill-gotten gains work evil' in Sophocles' words.

You will be growing impatient again with my procrastinating literariness. Too bad.

Rumour had warned us that his army was ill-disciplined. In particular there were frequent dissensions between the legionaries and the auxiliary troops, each believing the other more favoured by their indulgent commander. They united only to loot the villages and towns through which they passed and to abuse, rape and sometimes murder, their inhabitants.

Nevertheless when word came that the new Emperor was within a few miles of Rome a throng, mostly of the baser sort, but including some Senators and equestrians eager to be among the first to welcome their master, tumbled out to meet him. They ran wild through the army and the camp, and so great was the confusion that many of the soldiers believed themselves to be insulted. They drew their swords and fell upon the people, killing upwards of a hundred. It was with difficulty that some semblance of order was restored, and then they were in the city, still armed, contrary to all law and custom. The sight of some of the auxiliaries, bristling with the skins of wild beasts, and armed with lances, terrified the citizens; and these troops themselves, many of whom were overawed by the size of the buildings, reacted brutally to the citizens' alarm. It was with difficulty that the tribunes and prefects prevented a general massacre from taking place. What a start to a new reign!

Vitellius, it was reported, crossed the Milvian bridge on a big black horse. He was in a state of intense excitement, his face shining purple and his eyes darting about. It was a moment of glory he could never have expected. He wore a military cloak and brandished a sword. But someone of sense – I never learned who, and am indeed only surprised that such a man was to be found among the members of his staff – must have told him that it would never do to enter Rome in the guise of a conquerer. So he halted and, retiring into a convenient house, assumed civilian dress.

So he was on foot when I caught sight of him, and it must be admitted he looked better on horseback. This was partly because he had a heavy limp, the consequence of a chariot crash in his youth – Caligula was driving at the time. In an attempt to disguise it he was now leaning on the shoulder of one of his officers; and this detracted from his dignity. He was very tall, and might have made an imposing figure but for his huge paunch, the result of his gluttony and drunkenness. As it was, he looked grotesque, for everything about him was exaggerated. 'They say he's got a dong the length of an Egyptian obelisk,' a bystander in a butcher's apron muttered.

This was the creature who now marched – unsteadily – at the head of his army, Emperor of Rome.

The eagles of four legions were in the van and on either side the colours of other legions were carried. Then came the standards of twelve auxiliary squadrons of cavalry, and the cavalry themselves behind the legions. More than thirty auxiliary cohorts followed, each bearing the name or equipment of the nation from which it was drawn. The line of march was flanked by the prefects, tribunes, centurions, and the other officers.

It was a splendid sight – if the city they were entering had not been Rome, but some barbarian capital they had stormed. Even with that reflection, many thrilled at this evidence of the might and majesty of Rome, and only a few commented that it was an army worthy of a better Emperor than Vitellius.

For my part, I was fully occupied in calming Domitian's apprehension. The strength of the enemy forces threatened to unman him.

'How can we hope to overcome such an army?' he muttered.

I assured him that if he had seen the splendour of his father's legions, he would not lose heart so easily. This was true but unhelpful. He did not care to be reminded that I knew more than he did of Vespasian's readiness for war.

The next day Vitellius appeared at the rostra and delivered a eulogy of himself. It was as if he was recommending his virtues to the Senate and people of a conquered state. He spoke of his energy and moderation, though his progress to the city had been marked by sloth, self-indulgence and cruelty.

He spoke in a manner which would have appeared absurdly boastful in the Divine Augustus himself. No man of sense or judgement could listen to him without feeling contempt. Yet the mob, mindless of how they had cheered Otho a few weeks before, and being unable or unwilling to distinguish between truth and falsehood, were delighted. They raised loud huzzas and, since they had long ago learned how to flatter Emperors, begged him to assume the name and title of Augustus. He graciously assented. At any rate, I suppose his assent was intended to seem gracious. To my mind, as he swelled with self-importance and swayed, as a result either of emotion or wine, so that, when he tried to raise his hands, they had to be supported above his head by his attendants, he appeared ridiculous.

Then he announced that there should be a great public feast and that he himself would bear all its cost. Nothing offered clearer testimony to the corruption of the times than this; for many remembered that when Vitellius had set out to assume command on the Rhine, he had left his wife and children in a rented attic in a poor quarter of the city, and had financed his journey by pawning a pair of pearl ear-rings, belonging to his mother. Some said he had torn the jewels from her ears; others that he had stolen them while she slept. And now, from the loot of Italian cities and the sale of offices to his friends and flatterers, he was providing a public feast for hundreds of thousands of citizens.

It was soon known that feasting, not business, occupied Rome's new master. He banqueted three or four times a day, and these were not the hasty snacks with which Augustus had contented himself, snatching a mouthful of bread or cheese and a few dates, figs or apples while he worked with his secretaries. On the contrary, Vitellius spent many hours at the table and could always be tempted to remain longer by the arrival of some other delicacy and bottle of wine. If he was rarely incapably drunk, he was never sober; and some of his more foolish and degraded acts may be attributed to his habitual inebriety. All the same, when one learned of a new dish he had proudly devised and named 'The Shield of Minerva the Protectress', one didn't know whether to laugh, weep or curse the self-indulgent booby. The recipe called for pike-livers, pheasant-brains (can such things be found?), flamingo-tongues and lamprey-milt; and the ingredients, collected, it is said, in every corner of the Empire were brought to Rome by naval triremes. Only this last allegation was invented: all the ingredients were available in the Roman markets. The dish must have been perfectly revolting. Minerva, being the Goddess of Wisdom, could not have been a less appropriate dedicatee.

If Vitellius' private life was offensive, his public acts were still more deplorable. Some, it may be, were only injudicious. He took for himself the office of Supreme Pontiff, as other Emperors had done. Naturally he was quite unsuitable, but this might have been passed over, in the circumstances. But he chose as his Inauguration Day the 18th July – that is, as I don't need to remind you, the anniversary of the disaster of the Allia where the army of the Republic was defeated by the Gauls – a day which has ever since been regarded as inauspicious. Even Vitellius' supporters were dismayed by this.

The creature Asiaticus was summoned from his tavern and restored to favour at court. It was soon understood that only by approaching him could anyone hope to obtain office, preferment or favours. Even some of those who had crawled before Nero were shocked to discover that they must now humiliate themselves before this pimp.

It was not long before the great army he had brought into the city abandoned all discipline. Their numbers overflowed the camp. So the soldiers were scattered through the city, being billeted, or finding a billet, in porticoes, temples and private lodgings. They were to be found in every tavern. Many did not know where to find their officers or their headquarters; and the centurions had little idea where to seek their troops. Drill was forsaken, the parade ground deserted. Many of the auxiliaries, Germans and Gauls, found quarters or rather, based themselves in Trastevere. They drank the water of the Tiber and, since the summer heats were now upon them, were soon weakened by dysentery and other diseases.

All this was, however disgraceful, good news for those of us who hoped for Vespasian's victory. Flavius Sabinus, who had sufficiently ingratiated himself with Vitellius to be permitted to retain his post as Prefect of the City, looked on the disintegration of the enemy forces with a caustic smile.

Since Flavius Sabinus had honoured me with his regard, and included me among the intimate friends with whom he took counsel on his brother's behalf – Domitian was also perforce included, though he contributed little of value to our discussion – I made so bold as to ask him how it was that he had contrived to avoid dismissal from his post; for it was a matter of wonder that he should have retained it, not only on account of his relationship to Vespasian, but more particularly since he was a man whose virtue was acknowledged by all who knew him; and vice, not virtue, was the passport to office in Vitellius' time.

He was embarrassed by my question, and for a little I thought he would deny me an answer. Then he said:

'You do well to ask and, if I hesitate to answer, it is because my answer will do me no credit in your eyes. This displeases me, for I have come to recognise your own virtue and abilities. But in shameful times it is sometimes necessary to do what one would be ashamed of, if the world was not what it is. I swallow my pride partly because it is expedient that you yourself should learn what a man may have to do to survive. I learned this myself long ago when Nero was still young. Indeed, before then, in the time of Claudius, when my patron was his freedman Narcissus . . .'

He paused here, on that name, and fixed me with his mild grey eyes. It occurred to me that he knew that Narcissus was my true father. This was something which was not widely known and, indeed, it was only a few years previously that I had learned it myself. Perhaps now I in turn betrayed some embarrassment, for Flavius Sabinus, as if to calm me, said, 'Narcissus was an able man, and a better man than his reputation might suggest, or indeed than most of those who have found themselves in like positions at court. But that is by the way. Yet it is not entirely so. For I must confess to you that the intermediary I employed to secure my position as City Prefect was Asiaticus.'

'But I have heard that he is completely loathsome.'

'Few men are entirely so, though he comes close to it. But it happens that I have myself done him some service in the past as, from what you have learned of him and from what you know of the work of City Prefect, you may imagine it might have been in my power to do. I won't go into the details: an unsavoury case, quite revolting indeed. Why I was of service to him I should prefer not to say, nor how. It suffices that I was. And the creature is not entirely devoid of gratitude, which is why I say he is not, as you put it, "completely loathsome". So he spoke up for me.'

I couldn't believe that gratitude alone had prompted this, and wondered what other hold Flavius Sabinus might have that would persuade, even compel, Asiaticus to help him now. However it was not for me to probe. I had already learned more than I could have expected to learn, and felt honoured by the old man's confidence in my discretion. Indeed that was evidently so great that he did not demean either of us by asking me to keep his confidence.

He added: 'There is another matter. Asiaticus is no fool. He may be wallowing in the sunlight of prosperity now, but such as he never trust the weather to stay fair. He knows he may need my friendship in the future as much I need his now.'

From this time some half a dozen of us met regularly to consider how Vespasian's cause might be best advanced. These meetings in his aunt's house gave me a further insight into my friend Domitian's unsettled state of mind, his febrile character. On the one hand he was ever eager for positive measures, even rash ones. He would sit picking at the skin of his thumb, and propose plans for fomenting a mutiny among the troops quartered in the city. On the other, he would start and grow pale at any alarm.

Vitellius, or rather his lieutenants, had reconstituted the Praetorian Guard, formerly distinguished by its loyalty to Otho, by drafting some 20,000 men indiscriminately from the legions and the cavalry.

'They have no esprit de corps,' Domitian insisted, flourishing the Greek term (though his knowledge of Greek was much inferior to mine and, at that stage in his life he could not converse freely in the language). 'They are,' he continued, 'a mere rag-bag assembly, open, I have no doubt, to the highest bidder.'

'And therefore useless,' said Rubrius Gallus, an officer of the city guard in whom Flavius Sabinus had long placed an absolute trust. 'In any case,' he said, 'attempts to suborn them could not be kept secret.'

'And in the third place,' I said, 'it is Vitellius, not we, who has charge of the imperial treasury and who can top any offer we make to them. He can produce gold now; we, only the promise of future gold.'

Domitian relapsed into a sulk, for, as you know, he could never thole any dissent from his opinions, nor argue his case in a rational manner.

Moreover, his eagerness for action was corrupted by his fear that even our conclaves were perilous.

'If anyone knew we were meeting like this . . .' he would mutter, and draw his forefinger across his throat.

He spoke truth, without necessity, for none of us doubted the danger that we ran.

Flavius Sabinus had however a soft spot for his nephew. He considered that Domitian had indeed been unfairly disregarded by Vespasian, and he more than once said to me that, at bottom, the boy was good and not without talent. So he now hastened to apply ointment to Domitian's wounded pride.

'What you say, nephew, is wise in general, misguided merely in particular. Few parties stand firm in a civil war, for everyone except those of outstanding virtue and those who have strong reason to be attached to one side or the other, stands loose in his allegiance. Since you have studied history, you will recall how L. Domitius

Ahenobarbus, for example, deserted Mark Antony and crossed over to Octavian Caesar, the future Augustus, though he had received nothing but kindness from Antony, and was trusted by him implicitly. And Ahenobarbus was not an evil man. Treachery is contagious. I have no doubt that the new Praetorians will readily desert Vitellius, when the moment is ripe; but not now, while he is in a position to indulge them. There are others however whose desertion would be more useful, and may be more easily secured.'

He paused and drank wine, while we kept silent, hearing only the confused night-noise of the city. Someone passed below the house singing a bawdy song about Nero. Two days previously Vitellius had caused an altar to be raised in the Campus Martius, and there performed funeral rites in honour of that Emperor whom he had himself served with such ignoble zeal.

Flavius Sabinus said: 'Things are moving. Today Vitellius had word that the 3rd legion has repudiated him and sworn allegiance to Vespasian.'

'How did he receive the news?'

'First, I'm told, he staggered and had to be revived with wine. Then he said, "It is only a single legion after all. The others remain loyal."'

'What effect did his words have?'

'His advisers were unsettled. They persuaded him that he must address the troops. Which, eventually, he did, declaring that vile rumours were being spread by the disbanded Praetorians, which no one should attach any importance to. He was careful not to mention Vespasian, and so gave the impression that he was faced with the mutiny of one legion, not with a challenge to his position. Then soldiers were dispersed through the city with orders to arrest anyone found spreading seditious rumours.'

'Which,' I said, 'is just the sort of measure to give the rumours life.'

'Indeed, yes, a good day for us,' Rubrius Gallus said.

'It makes our immediate position all the more dangerous. Domitian is right there.' Flavius smiled at his nephew, as if approving his judgement. 'And he is right, too, in believing that our best course is to seek to detach some men of note from Vitellius. Now it so happens that I know what you may be ignorant of. You are all, of course, aware that Vitellius owes his present position not to his own efforts, which have been feeble and contemptible, but to his generals, Caecina and Valens. What you may not know is that they have come to detest and distrust each other. Caecina in particular is – shall we say? – disillusioned. His efforts have been equal to his colleague's. Yet he finds that Valens is in higher favour with Vitellius. I think we can play on his resentments.'

The prospect was attractive. I immediately offered to act as an intermediary between Flavius and Caecina.

'Your enthusiasm does you credit,' Flavius said, 'but you will have sufficient nobility of soul not to resent my refusal. Rubrius here is the man for the job. He has served with Caecina in Germany, and earlier, too, in the wars against the Parthian Empire, in which Corbulo won that distinction which made him hateful to Nero. As an old comrade, able to share memories of happier days, he is better placed than you to work upon Caecina's resentments, fears and ambition.'

So it was decided. A day or two later I watched the German legions and auxiliaries march to the north. Their appearance was very different from that which they had presented in Vitellius' day of triumph. They were not the men they had been. Wasted by disease and enervated by unaccustomed luxury, they seemed a spiritless rabble rather than an army. Grumbles about the heat, the dust and the weight of their baggage rose from the line of march. They looked like men ready to mutiny; and my heart lifted.

XXXII

Again I cannot sleep. I lay beside my woman, made perfunctory love to her, relief of the body if not the spirit, and then listened to her regular breathing while my own brain raced, irregularly.

I rose and, leaving the house, walked down to the river, to a point a few miles before it loses itself in the marshes, forming different streams which make their way severally to the sea. The night was luminous, for a full moon drifted behind thin clouds and, casting deep but wavering shadows, gave all things a new and unexpected shape. It seemed to me that ghostly figures rose out of the mists that clung around the water.

Near the end of the Jewish Wars, after Titus had taken Jerusalem, and destroyed their temple, which was like no other temple I have known, having no images of the god they worshipped within it, some of the fanatics among the enemy withdrew to a stronghold on a hill, by name Masada. This strange night allowed me to see that place again, though the landscape was so different, being desert, sand and rock, rather than river and marshland. So how this was, I know not; but the vagaries of mind, memory and imagination are incalculable. Perhaps it was not so strange, for the horror of Masada has never left me, and now I knew the need to speak of it.

So I returned to the house and woke the boy Balthus and, telling him to put on a jacket of sheepskin for the air was chill, brought him with me back down to the river. There was no sense in doing so, for, as I say, there was no similarity to be found between that place and this; and yet it was there that I could speak of that concerning which I had remained silent for so long. The boy sat on the rotted trunk of a fallen tree and listened to what I had to say. Nor had he made any complaint at being torn from sleep.

The Jewish remnant was there commanded by one Eleazar. He was a son of the man who had provoked the rebellion, and had been raised to be a more passionate Zealot than even his father. These Zealots combined an intense devotion to their nameless god with a savagery and austerity such as I had never witnessed, not even the savagery I had seen in Rome, concerning which I cannot yet bring myself to write my account for Tacitus.

This Masada, being built on a rock which rises out of the desert, was fortified by nature beyond the skill of the greatest of engineers. So for a long time we besieged it, but we did not dare to try an assault. The rock was encompassed by valleys so deep that, standing above them, one could scarce discern movement at the bottom. Their walls were sheer, and only two narrow paths wound perilously to the summit. We got ourselves nevertheless to an extremity of the rock which is called the White Promontory, and there built, with great labour, an earthwork . . .

The boy looked puzzled, for he had no knowledge of siegework; and I saw that the description was superfluous, being meaningless to him.

So I said: 'No matter, it is not of our endeavours to take the place that I wish to speak.'

And accordingly I leaped ahead of my tale.

'We set fire,' I said, 'to the outer wall of the citadel, by piling burning branches against it. At first the wind blew so as to turn our fire against us, but then, by the kindness of the gods, the wind shifted in our favour, and the fire threatened the defenders. So a breach was made and we retired, ready to attack the following day . . .

'Now, when Eleazar saw that the place could no longer be defended, he did not surrender, as a civilised man would. Instead he addressed, as we subsequently learned, his people, relating the hardships that had befallen the Jewish nation – though he did not say that these had been provoked by him and his like . . . Instead, he said, as we learned, and as Josephus recounts in his History:

' "As for those who are dead, we should think them blessed, since they perished in defending the cause of liberty. As for the multitude who have submitted to the Romans, who would not pity their condition, and who would not make haste to die before he was compelled to share their miseries? For some have been put on the rack and tortured with fire and the whips, tortured even unto death. Others have been half-devoured by wild beasts, and yet preserved alive to be more thoroughly devoured in order to make sport for our enemies. And such as are still alive, is not their fate, longing for a death they are denied, the most piteous of all? And where now is Jerusalem the Golden, the city of our fathers, the city to which King David brought the Ark of the Covenant made with Israel? It is now demolished, razed to the ground. The lion and the lizard keep its courts, but the voice of man is silent. Now who is there that revolving these things in his mind, is yet able to bear the light of the sun, though he might live out of danger?"

'So he went on, for a long time, posing questions, and inciting his followers to mingled fury and distress. They gave themselves up to wailing, and their cries cut the night air and made us fearful.

'Then, as we learned later, Eleazar said: "We were born to die, as were those whom we have begotten. Nor is it in the power of the most fortunate of our race to avoid death. But other things – abuse and slavery and the sight of our wives and children led away to ignominy – these are not evils such as are natural and necessary to endure. Only those who prefer such miseries to death, on account of their cowardice, need submit to them. Let us, therefore, while we have swords in our hands die before we are enslaved by our enemies, and let us depart from this world, with our wives and children, in a state of freedom. This indeed is what our laws demand of us, and it is what our wives and children long for also. The Lord himself has brought this necessity upon us, while the Romans desire the contrary, and are afraid lest any of us die before we are in their hands. So, let us go, and instead of affording them the pleasure that they hope to receive by having us in their hateful power, let us leave them an example which shall arouse in them astonishment at our escape and admiration for the courage with which we have embraced our destiny."

'When he had finished speaking, there was a deep silence, lasting the time it might take a man to harness a horse. Then the men embraced their wives and children, some of whom wept, while others maintained a calm which any Stoic philosopher would admire, and so, drawing their swords, killed them, either by stabbing them or by cutting their throats. Then they piled the bodies of the dead together surrounded by faggots, and set fire to them. Whereupon, since the

Laws of the Jews, unlike those of all civilised nations, forbid suicide, a dozen men were deputed to slay the remainder. Then the twelve cast lots among themselves to see which should take on the task of executioner of his fellows. When two alone were left they engaged in combat, that each might slay the other, and so both avoid the guilt of self-slaughter. And meanwhile the funeral pyre burned.

'In the morning we made ready for the assault, putting our armour on, and nerving ourselves for what was to be a terrible battle, since none doubted the fierce tenacity of the enemy. But then, instead of the noise of preparation, we heard an awful silence, and saw smoke rising from the centre of the citadel. So we advanced hesitantly, and breached or scaled the walls, meeting no opposition, and advanced till we came upon the city of the dead. And when we saw them, we were all amazed, and many terrified.'

I fell silent. The marshlands spread about us, an infinity of waste. A wind blew from the north, not hard but chilling. I sensed the boy pull his cloak more narrowly about him, but I could not look at him to see what effect my words had had. Perhaps, I thought, it is the memory of Masada that denies me sleep at night. But I knew that to be fanciful. I have other crimes on my conscience, and I did nothing at Masada to cause me shame. Yet nowhere have I felt such an expression of contempt for life, such a denial of all that has made Rome what it is. The dead Jews spat in the face of Empire. I have often pondered on that line of Virgil's where he declares Rome's duty to be 'to spare the subject and subdue the proud'. At Masada we were denied the opportunity either to spare or to subdue.

Balthus said: 'How can you know what happened? How can you know what words that Eleazar spoke?' His voice was very low, as if the words were not his, but forced upon him. And yet the question was good.

'There were certain old women, two or three, who either feared or despised death. And so, while Eleazar was speaking, and when they knew the import of his words, they slipped away, and hid in a cellar or, perhaps, a cleft of the rock; and so survived. And they came forward and told us all that had been said and done. When we asked them of the number who had been slain they said it was upwards of nine hundred and fewer than a thousand.'

I could not bring myself to repeat to Balthus, even in this moment of a long-delayed confession which some need – I know not words for it – had dragged from me, the observation of our general, Flavius Silva, Procurator of Judaea and a cousin of Titus: that it was generous of Eleazar to save us the trouble of slaughtering his army.

'Was Eleazar himself among the dead?' Balthus asked.

'It was assumed so, but many bodies had been destroyed or rendered unrecognisable in the flames.'

'Why do you tell me this?' The boy raised his head as he spoke and his cheek was wet with tears. From the village came the crowing of a cock as the first rays of the rising sun touched the grey east with pink.

What had I to reply? There is a line of Ovid's, from a poem composed in these mournful parts: 'To speak of some fatal evil is alleviation.' I shook my head, having no answer in my own mind. Was there cruelty in my forcing on him this story of the atrocious inhumanity of man? Was it because I resented his air of being at peace with the world, despite his condition, that I wished to destroy what I felt as his reproachful innocence? I had denied myself his body, though it tempted me. Did I now, vengefully, wish to assail his mind with horrors?

I do not think so. Yet, as Cicero once wrote, 'Malice is cunning, and men's reason is deceitful in working mischief.'

When Titus took and destroyed Jerusalem, with me by his side, he sent me and a freedman called Fronto to determine the fate of the captives. We picked out the tallest and most beautiful, and reserved them for Titus' triumph in Rome. Most of those who were above the age of seventeen we despatched to work as slaves in the mines of Egypt, where there was a shortage of labour. Others we sent to provincial cities, to make sport in the arenas. The young boys we reserved for the slave market. There was one lovely Jewish girl who begged with many tears for the life of her beloved, a handsome boy with fine features and red-gold hair. Their beauty won my clemency. Fronto and I drew lots; he got the boy and I the girl. She was my mistress for a month. Then one night she disappeared. Her body was discovered on the edge of the camp. She had been raped and her throat cut. The boy, receiving this news, refused all food and starved himself to death, an act which the Jews do not judge as suicide. His elder brother was one of those who walked, laden with chains, in Titus' triumph, a youth of remarkable beauty.

'I think you are troubled in your soul, master,' the boy said. 'We have a saying in my country: "Courage is good, but endurance is better."'

And am I fated to endure, I all but said, seeing that such courage as I once possessed has drained from me. I have become a coward, afraid of my own memories, afraid of Rome's memories also. It seems to me that the most we have done in our mastery of the world is to make a desert and call it peace, and that the only free thing left in this Empire of ours is the wind that now blows chill from the north.

I put my hand on the boy's shoulder and did not feel him resist.

'You must return to your sleep,' I said. 'It was wrong in me to have deprived you of it.'

Three cranes rose from the marshes and flew over us, their wings beating slowly. Then they shifted direction and flew into the wind, towards the sea.

'You Romans,' the boy said, with a mischievous smile, 'would see an omen there, but they are only birds.'

XXXIII

Can there be a more trying ordeal than to be confined in a city under the government of your enemy while the forces of your ally or leader are campaigning some hundreds of miles away?

That was our position. Vespasian himself had not yet left the East, but the Danube legions had crossed over through the passes of the Pannonian Alps.

They had done so at the urging of Antonius Primus. There had been some who counselled delay. They argued that their forces were inferior in numbers, and advocated holding the mountain passes, but advancing no further till Vespasian, Titus or Mucianus brought up reinforcements. Meanwhile, they said, Vespasian's command of the sea ensured that Italy could be put in a state of siege. But Antonius Primus would have none of this. It was his opinion that delay is dangerous in a civil war. Moreover he despised Vitellius' troops, describing them (I am told) as being 'sunk in sloth, emasculated by the circus, the theatre and the pleasures of the capital'. But he argued that once in camp again, and perhaps strengthened by fresh blood from Gaul and Germany, they would regain their old levels of fitness and become more formidable than they were now. He talked much in this vein and overcame the hesitations of his colleagues.

All this, of course, I learned later in conversation. But you may take it from me, Tacitus, that it is a true account. I suppose you will concoct some stirring speech for Antonius. You will be wise to do so; his own language would be quite unfitted for an elegant History. He was one of the foulest-mouthed brutes I ever encountered.

Meanwhile we waited in the city. News was frequent, confused,

191

contradictory, worthy only to be called rumour, never to be trusted. In turbulent times, when no word is to be relied on, men do not stop their ears and choose to believe nothing they are told. On the contrary, they believe anything, the opposite today to what they held incontrovertible truth yesterday.

Since Vitellius had learned of Vespasian's challenge, and had despatched his army to war, Domitian thought it no longer safe to show himself in public. Indeed, he scarcely left his aunt's house, even to visit the barber, and felt himself in danger there, too. He talked often, and nervously, of seeking some more secure hiding-place, either beyond the city or in one of its lowest quarters, taking a room in some noisome and criminal alley which the agents of the State did not dare to penetrate. But the fear of the indignities and dangers to which he might be exposed in such a place restrained him. Some nights he drowned his fear in wine; then, in the morning, shaking – for heavy drinking always disordered his stomach and his nerves – his apprehension redoubled. It seemed terrible to him that the night before he had put himself in a condition which would have made it impossible to attempt to escape his enemies. Titus would have found his fears contemptible; I pitied him. He felt my pity, and resented it.

For my part, I continued to lead as regular a life as was possible in the disordered and fevered city. I judged that if I was in danger no concealment could save me; and that I might be in less danger if I evinced no fear or uncertainty – sure signs of guilt. So I frequented the barber, the library and the baths. I attended dinner-parties and theatres and never missed the races at the Circus. When Vitellius was there, he paid little attention to what was happening in the arena, though he was known to be a fervent supporter of the 'Blues', but remained in the rear of his box, and gave himself up to eating and drinking. Yet, when he did stagger to the front and show himself to the crowd, he was greeted with lusty cheers, which were prompted – it seemed to me – by a genuine enthusiasm. The mob is fickle, but Vitellius then enjoyed a popularity denied the Emperor since Nero was a young man. His one public care was to lavish donations on the people and arrange for free banquets. Someone remarked that Rome was in a bad way since the citizens were now habitually as drunk as the Emperor. It was a clever remark, also true, and I could wish it had been mine. But I have never, Tacitus, claimed credit for the *bon mots* or epigrams of others.

The mystery of these days was that Flavius Sabinus retained his office now that there was open war between his brother and Vitellius. I could not understand then how he contrived this, and I cannot enlighten you now. Some said that he was playing a double game. Domitian even went so far as to suggest that his uncle was guilty of treachery; but the boy was in his cups at the time.

Since I know that, if I do not offer some explanation, you will badger me for one in your next letter and, with your admirable pertinacity, refuse to believe that I cannot supply one, I shall advance a possible reason. But it is only a guess, based on no information.

Vitellius, I hazard, had never himself sought the Empire. It had been deposited on him by Caecina and Valens, and he had been too weak – too dazzled perhaps – to decline the perilous honour. But he knew himself to be unfitted for the task. He could not believe he could sustain the role. Brought up in the court, having attended on Tiberius, Gaius, Claudius and Nero, he knew – none better – the instability of Empire; he knew himself also to be inferior, one way or another, to all those he had served, often ignobly. There had doubtless been moments during the advance on Rome when he was carried away by the magnificence of his elevation. But even the most vile of remarks attributed to him – that nothing smelled more sweetly in his nostrils than the corpse of a dead rebel – suggest to me a man forcing himself to play a part which he had not rehearsed and was incapable of bringing off. Vitellius was spendthrift, greedy, lecherous, cowardly, dishonest, without principles of morality; but nothing previously had suggested that he took delight in cruelty. (Or so my mother told me.)

Now, established in Rome, he could do nothing for himself, but must await the outcome of battle. And he was afraid. How, he may have asked himself, in his rare sober moments, could the gods, who had turned from Nero and Galba and Otho, now favour such a man as he knew himself to be? (Like all weak men, Vitellius was superstitious; and throughout these weeks, even the most complaisant of priests found it difficult to present him with favourable omens.)

Feeling, and fearing, the instability of fortune, Vitellius looked apprehensively about him. And his gaze fell on Flavius Sabinus, the brother of his rival. Had Vitellius been a strong man, or had he believed in the valour and constancy of his armies, he would surely have arrested Flavius, even have put him to death, for there could be no doubt that Flavius Sabinus was at the centre of all seditious movements in the city.

But he did not do so. He did not even dismiss him from his post. And I can only think that he already knew that the day was likely when he himself might need a friend in Vespasian's camp or, if not a friend, someone who was under an obligation to him. Certainly it must have occurred to him that if it came to negotiations, his own position would be more secure if an intermediary was there, acceptable to both sides; and no one could fill that role better than Flavius Sabinus.

Having read my attempt at an explanation, you will, Tacitus, doubt-less reject it. Your contempt for Vitellius is, I know, so unbounded that you will scorn the suggestion that he was capable of thinking intelligently. You may be right, and it is true, as you will insist, that Vitellius was rarely in a sufficiently sober condition to be able to think straight. All I can say is that no man could have survived the courts of so many Emperors as Vitellius had, without having a keen sense of what was necessary for self-preservation.

The heat of the summer came on. I tried to persuade my mother to retire to her cousin's villa in the hills, as she was now accustomed to do. She refused. 'Things are too interesting here,' she said. Yet she rarely left her apartment.

One day I found Domitian with her there. I assumed he had come in search of me. But this was not the case. It was my mother he had come to talk, or listen, to; and my arrival embarrassed him.

Later my mother said, 'I can't help but feel pity for that boy. He is so uncertain of his place in the world, that I fear for him also. His lack of self-confidence will lead him into mischief. Men who cannot trust themselves are not to be trusted.'

News came which for the moment disturbed the equanimity which Flavius Sabinus had hitherto displayed. Caecina had, as arranged, deserted his master. But he had moved too soon.

One of his friends brought word to Flavius Sabinus, arriving when I was with him in his apartment. The messenger, for such he was, indicated that he wished to speak to Flavius alone. Flavius replied that I was in his confidence and that he had no secrets which he desired to keep from me. At the time I was moved by this expression of trust. Later I thought: he is afraid. He may suspect me of treachery, and so wish to involve me more closely in whatever he plans; or he may fear that, if he excludes me, I shall suspect him of the same, and relay my suspicions to Titus. Thus do evil times corrupt us all; duplicity is common, openness and honesty provoke distrust. In retrospect I was ashamed of the thoughts I entertained. But it was natural that I should do so.

The messenger, still reluctant, at last acceded to Flavius' demand. I would that I could recall exactly what he said, for he spoke with an emotion that I found affecting. But I cannot; and I disdain to follow the example of historians such as Livy who invent speeches for their characters in order that they may display their own mastery of rhetoric.

So I must content myself with giving the sense of what he said.

Caecina had learned of the revolt of the fleet at Ravenna; they had turned against Vitellius. At first their commander, Lucilius Bassus, hesitated. He did not know whether it would prove more dangerous to desert Vitellius or remain loyal. But when he saw that the mutineers were ready to turn on him, he bravely put himself at their head, and proclaimed Vespasian Emperor.

This news persuaded Caecina that the moment to change sides had arrived. So he called those officers and senior centurions whom he thought to be peculiarly attached to himself to a remote corner of the camp, and told them that in his opinion Vespasian had won the game and would prove a worthy emperor. Now that the fleet had changed sides, he said, they could not expect new supplies to reach them. There was nothing to hope for from Gaul or Spain and the capital was in tumult. His words were compelling, and they all swore an oath to Vespasian. The images of Vitellius were cast down and messengers were sent to Antonius Primus, commanding Vespasian's advance-guard, to tell him they were ready to join him.

So far, so good, you might say. But now it seemed, things took an unexpected turn. The rank and file of the army were not prepared to have their loyalties sold by their commander. Their anger, though spontaneous, was fanned by officers whom Caecina had neglected. One asked, in ringing tones, whether the honour of the army of Germany, hitherto victorious in every battle, had now fallen so low that they were ready to surrender to their enemies without a blow being struck. They wouldn't be received as allies, he said. On the contrary Vespasian's troops would despise them as they would learn to despise themselves. He appealed to the soldiers' pride and sense of honour. His speech carried the day; soldiers can rarely resist this sort of flattery. So they swarmed to headquarters and seized hold of Caecina. They loaded him with chains and made a mockery of him; indeed they came close to killing him on the spot, restrained only by a plea that he be reserved for formal trial and execution. Other officers and centurions, who had collaborated with their treacherous general, were slain. It was with difficulty, and in danger, that the messenger himself had escaped to bring this news.

Flavius Sabinus received this news with the appearance of composure. He gave the messenger gold, and then summoned slaves and told them to provide his friend with food and drink.

'So,' he said when we were alone, 'things have taken a turn for the worse. There's no question of that. I warned Caecina that timing was all, impressed on him the importance of not moving too quickly. Well, he knew better.'

'Things are no worse,' I said, 'than if you had made no arrangement with him. I do not think – from what Titus has told me – that Caecina's desertion had entered their plans.'

'No,' he said. 'It hadn't. That's not the point. Do you know what has guided my policy throughout these terrible months? I have had one constant aim: to avert civil war. Now that hope has gone. The decision will be made on the battlefield.'

I didn't ask him how he reconciled this aim with the encouragement which I had no doubt he had given Vespasian to declare himself a candidate for Emperor. It was not my place to ask that, and the question could have served no useful purpose. I have never been able to supply a satisfactory answer, and yet I was certain he was sincere.

'I had counted,' he said, 'on Vitellius' timidity. Caecina was foremost in forcing the purple on him. If Caecina deserted his cause, I was certain Vitellius would yield to us; and the matter might have been settled without more bloodshed. I have grown to hate war, you see. But now Vitellius will be filled with indignation only, that Caecina should have been ready to betray him. And his optimism, which flickers like a candle in a draught, will shine bright again. Moreover, moreover . . .' he paused and looked me in the eye for the first time since we had been left alone. He waited, as it seemed, for me to complete his thought.

'You mean,' I said, 'that when he realises how close he was to disaster, he will seek revenge.'

'Just so. He is a weak man, and the weak and fearful are quick to strike. Like Nero, indeed. I do not think Domitian is safe. Tell the boy to drop out of sight, find some hiding-place.'

'What of you yourself, sir?'

'No,' he said. 'No. I may still be of use to Vitellius. He must know where I am to be found. But you, boy, like Domitian, should be careful. Few men are to be trusted in these troubled times.'

His judgement was wise. When Vitellius learned of Caecina's disloyalty, he fainted, and only when he had been revived by the creature Asiaticus was he able to comprehend that Caecina himself had been deserted and imprisoned by his soldiers. His immediate response was to wish for his death, then he sent out orders that he be conveyed to Rome with every humiliation. Then he ordered the Prefect of the Praetorians to be arrested also – merely because he had been appointed on the recommendation of Caecina.

Vitellius proceeded to the Senate where he made a speech that was so confused that few could understand its meaning, except that he spoke much in praise of his own magnanimity. The Senators responded in like vein. The Emperor's brother moved a resolution condemning Caecina, and Senator after Senator spoke in the finest of antique manners deploring the action of a Roman general who had betrayed the Republic and his Emperor. But it was remarked that all were careful to say nothing that might be held against them should Vitellius lose the Empire. Indeed, not a single Senator uttered a word of condemnation of the Emperor's enemy. The name of Vespasian was not spoken. This encouraged Flavius Sabinus. All this I learned later. I did not of course, attend the Senate myself, being otherwise occupied, and in any case not yet a member of that august assembly (as I suppose I must still call it, though a more accurate description would be a collection of poltroons and self-seeking time-servers who disgrace their ancestors.)

My business was with Domitian. It will not surprise you, Tacitus, to learn that, though he had been so fearful and so desirous of finding a place of safety or refuge, he received his uncle's instructions with suspicion.

It was, he said, some plot to prevent him distinguishing himself in his father's cause. It was another attempt to push him to the margin. It was treating him as a child and not a grown man. Why should it be safe for his uncle to remain in his post, while he was commanded to go into hiding? What sort of double game was his uncle playing?

And so on; his indignation burst forth in a cascade of confused and often contradictory questions.

At last I said: 'Do as you please then. I'm sure nobody cares whether you live or die.'

Which infuriated him still further.

'I didn't mean that,' I said, 'but really you try my patience. Don't you understand that we all have your best interests at heart? Yes, your uncle is playing a dangerous game. But he is an honest man. I've no doubt of that. And the game will be still more dangerous if Vitellius gets his hands on you. You are the most valuable bargaining counter he could have.'

'He's right,' Domatilla said, 'it's because you're important that you must disappear from the scene. It would be terrible if you were arrested and held as a hostage. I couldn't survive it if anything awful happened to you.'

She was near tears. She laid her arm around her brother's neck, and drew his head towards her, and kissed his cheek. He could not fail to feel her anxiety and her affection, and could not fail, I thought, to be moved by it. But he disengaged himself from her grasp.

'I don't know,' he said.

I looked out into the street.

'You may not,' I said, 'but you had better make up your mind quickly. There's a detachment of the Guard at the end of the lane, and I think they are making enquiries. They could be coming for you.'

That was enough. Whether Domatilla's flattery would have persuaded him to obey his uncle, I don't know. Fear was more successful. He looked round wildly.

'Where can we go?'

'There's only one way out that may be safe. The roof.'

He was out of the door of the apartment and up the stairs like a rat surprised in a kitchen. I took Domatilla by the hand.

'You must come, too,' I said.

She resisted for a moment, then gave way.

Fortunately, no one emerged from any of the upper apartments as we mounted the stairs, no one who might have indicated to the soldiers where we had gone. A little skylight, used by the workmen who required access to the roof, was our way out. I gave Domitian a leg-up. He struggled to open the window which at first seemed to be stuck fast. He uttered little panting gasps of anxiety as he did so. From below, from the bottom of the staircase well, I could hear the soldiers questioning the porter. Then the window moved. Domitian got it open, eased his way out, for a moment vanished from our sight. I didn't dare call to him. I picked his sister up and, with a movement like a dancer's, lifted her so that she could get her hands through the opening and find purchase on the roof. Then with another heave, I had her through. I stepped back three paces and, with a running leap, caught hold of the outer rim of the window. One hand slipped, and for a moment I dangled in the air, supported only by the other. I swung my free hand around. The sound of the soldiers mounting the stairs to the apartment came to me, as my hand, missing the rim again, was caught hold of by Domatilla. I swung myself up and was on the roof. Domitian was lying face down on the slates. He had almost slipped off and was clinging by his fingers. I turned and shut the skylight. Then I pulled him up, so that all three of us were standing on a narrow ledge. I saw now that the skylight did not open onto the flat top of the roof but on to its sloping side. Domitian had very nearly gone over the edge. I suppose now it would have saved Rome a lot of trouble if he had done so but, of course, that didn't occur to me at the time.

'We can't stay here,' I said. 'If we thought of this way out, they will, too. We can't be sure that they will not know we were in the apartment.'

'Our aunt won't give us away,' Domitian said.

'No, but the porter will have done so. You can be sure of that. If not when they first questioned him, then on their way down. We must get across the roofs.'

Domatilla said, 'I know we must, but I'm afraid of heights.'

Again I took her by the hand. We made our way along the ledge.

'Don't look down,' I said, 'and you'll be all right.'

We would have moved faster on the flat roof but I was afraid we might attract more attention there. So we worked our way to the end of the building. The lane below which seemed so narrow when you passed along it now appeared a dangerous chasm. There was a gap of ten or twelve feet to the next building. I could have cleared it easily if I had been able to take a run at it. So, I suppose, could Domitian, a better athlete than myself, if his nerve had held. But it was beyond Domatilla's powers, and I dare not leap with her slung over my shoulder, which would have been the only means of carrying her.

I hesitated. There was no sound of the soldiers. They might have left the building. They might not after all have thought of the skylight. If the aunt had said we were out, they might be content to await our return. Down below in the lane a pedlar with a donkey was selling his wares. There was no other movement, nothing to alarm us. But we could not remain there and, when Domitian muttered that it might be safe to return the way we had come, I asked him if he wanted to walk into a waiting reception committee of the Guard.

We worked our way round the building. It was late afternoon, heavy with rain-swollen clouds. Then, about twenty feet below us, there was a balcony, a rickety dangerous-looking thing protruding from an apartment on what I judged must be the floor second from the top of the building. We had tried two skylights opening out of different staircases and found them unbudgeable. The wood had swollen and they were fixed fast. I looked at the balcony. I could jump down there without difficuty but would it hold? And would the shutters that must open on to it be closed and fastened from within? And if they were, could I get back up to the roof?

We went round the roof again. There was no other way off that I could see. It began to rain. Domatilla was shivering, more from anxiety than the cold. I explained what I intended to do. She shook her head. Domitian would neither meet my eye nor offer an alternative plan.

So, gripping the edge of the roof, I lowered myself and, with my feet kicking the empty air, dropped to the balcony below. It shuddered as it took my weight, but didn't come away from the wall as I had feared it would. Whether it could take three people's weight was another matter.

The shutters were indeed closed and fastened. I rattled them, and held my breath. If the apartment was empty, then I would try to force them open. If it wasn't . . .

I heard movement from the other side of the shutters. I called out, gently. A dark shape appeared behind them. The sound of a bolt being withdrawn, and they were open. I found myself looking at a woman. She had a large moon-face and a dark complexion. She did not speak, but waited, seemingly impassive. I blurted out apologies for disturbing her, explained that my friends and I had been stranded on the roof. She nodded, and stepped back. I said, 'We're not dangerous, not criminals. Will you let us leave the building by way of your apartment?'

Again she inclined her head, saying nothing. I still wasn't sure, apologised again, began to offer a further explanation.

'That doesn't concern me. I don't want to know,' she said. Her accent was southern, with the little lisp of Basilicata.

I turned away, called up to Domitian, told him to lower Domatilla, and to take her weight as long as he could. Then she was in my arms. The balcony shuddered again and quickly I thrust her from me and into the room.

'Now yourself,' I called. 'Don't jump, let yourself hang down.'

I stretched out my arms to receive him. Shouts came from the roof beyond. Domitian uttered a cry, little more than a whimper. Then his feet appeared. He dropped, instead of hanging, and, as I caught him, his weight caused me to sway backwards against the flimsy balustrade. I heard a creak, flung him into the room. He landed, sprawling. I heard footsteps on the roof above, and a voice shouted, 'He's gone over the edge.' The balcony shuddered and swayed again. I felt it tear itself away from the wall, and, just in time, leapt into the room. Behind me I heard it crash into the lane.

The woman looked at me. There was no expression on her face.

'I'm sorry about the damage,' I said. 'I'll pay for it, of course.'

She spread her hands wide, in a gesture of denial.

'We never use it,' she said. 'I've told the landlord for months now it isn't safe.'

'You might have killed us,' Domitian said. 'As it is, I've cut my knee.'

The woman closed the shutters and bolted them.

'I don't want to know anything,' she said. 'As far as I'm concerned you're not here. But whoever was after you is going to see there are no bodies in the lane.'

A girl, dressed in a stained shift and rubbing sleep from her eyes, came into the room. She left the door open behind her and I had a glimpse of a tumbled bed.

'What's happening?' she said.

'Nothing. You've seen nothing. Go back to bed. As for you,' she said to me, 'I'll thank you to be on your way, whatever that is.'

'I've lost my bearings,' I said. 'Which lane does the door of this block open on?'

'I don't know about that. We just call it the lane.'

I looked at Domitian. He was trembling again – a reaction from fear which I have often seen since in battles.

I said: 'We'll have to chance it. We came a long way over the roof. There was only a small detachment of the Guard. They can't have posted men at every doorway in the block.'

He took me by the sleeve and led me into a corner of the room.

'We could stay here,' he said. 'There's only this woman and the girl. If they make trouble you and I could deal with them. We could tie them up.'

'No,' I said.

'Why not? Then we could wait till it's dark.'

'No,' I said. 'She let us in. She didn't have to. Besides, with the curfew, we would be in more danger in the streets after dark than we are now.'

The woman said, 'We haven't seen you, like I said. Now be on your way.'

There was still no expression on her moon face.

Domitian said: 'Could you send the girl down to the street to see that it's safe?'

The woman shook her head.

Domatilla said, 'Don't mind my brother. We're very grateful to you, really we are. Now we'll be off. I am sorry about the balcony.'

The girl looked at me. She had slanting eyes, almond-shaped, with long lashes. She hitched up her shift and scratched her thigh. She gave me a smile.

I said to the woman, 'Again, we're grateful.'

The girl said, 'I don't mind going down and having a look-see.' She smiled at me again. 'It could do no harm.'

'No,' the woman said. 'You'll stay here.'

'There's no need,' I said, 'but thank you.'

We didn't speak as we descended the stairs. At the corner of the last flight, I had the others wait while I went down to the lane. It was deserted, except for two old men arguing fiercely and aiming futile blows at each other. I beckoned to Domitian and his sister.

I put my hand on his elbow when they joined me.

'Walk slowly,' I said. 'Casual. No hurry. We don't want to draw attention to ourselves.'

His arm was rigid. It was with difficulty that he obeyed. When we were out of the lane and had turned two or three more corners and got ourselves into a busy street, he said, 'Where are we to go?'

'Have you no ideas?'

He shook his head.

'All right then. Leave it to me.'

'What about your mother's?' he said.

'I'll take Domatilla there, but not you. We have to get you out of the way first. You're the one in demand.'

There was a boy from Rieti who had been a fellow-student of ours and who lived in this quarter. His parents were dead and he lived on his own while struggling to make a living practising law. He was a reserved and silent youth whose contempt for the corruption of the times was deep-grained. I had always been impressed by his honesty and his refusal to advance himself by the customary means of flattery of the great and toadying to those who might be useful to him. I had no doubt that he would receive Domitian and give him shelter, all the more because he felt himself superior to him. So I led Domitian there, and he was accommodated as I had expected.

'I can't put the girl up,' Aulus Pettius said. 'It's a question of propriety, not reputation, you understand.'

'That's all right,' I said, 'she's going to stay with my mother, but you will understand I can't place my mother in danger by asking her to take in Domitian, too.'

'What absurd and ignoble times we live in,' he said. It occurred to me that he was receiving Domitian precisely because his need of a refuge confirmed his own disgust with the degeneracy of the Republic. He had once described Nero to me as 'that base comedian who plays at being Caesar'. I liked the contempt, though the description was inaccurate. Nero played more enthusiastically at being a great poet and actor.

My mother was happy to receive Domatilla.

'But,' she said, 'you will have to find somewhere else to lodge yourself while she's here. It's not that I mind what people say, but the girl has a reputation to be protected, and it would be wrong to give evil tongues any opportunity to spread scandal about her.'

'I can't thank you enough,' Domatilla said. 'I don't know what would have become of Dom if you hadn't been there.'

She knew all too well of course. She kissed me good-bye. It was a chaste kiss owing to my mother's presence, but even that small measure of affection had my mother clicking her teeth in disapproval.

Later in the afternoon, I returned to the moon-faced woman's apartment. I brought a small gift, and told her I had come not only to thank her, but to make sure that she had come to no harm. She nodded her head, but gave no thanks for the gift.

'I didn't need a reward,' she said.

The girl said, 'I knew you'd come back.'

She poured me a cup of wine. The woman withdrew to the kitchen. The girl stretched herself out. She was still wearing the same shift and displayed breasts and thighs.

'She'll make us some food,' she said. 'She's not my mother, you know.'

'So what is she?'

'She just took me in. Now, you could say I'm a lodger. I pay rent, quite a lot, depending . . .'

'I see,' I said, and reached down and, putting my arm round her, raised her up. She turned and kissed me. I slipped my hand under her shift. For a moment she let it rest there. Then she led me through to her room and the tumbled bed.

XXXIV

I didn't send all that last chapter to Tacitus; an edited version merely.
I am even puzzled as to why I wrote it in such detail. At first I
thought it was because it showed me in a good light, and therefore
demonstrated Domitian's ingratitude. But that isn't really so. I even
doubt now whether Vitellius would have put Domitian to death had
I not intervened to save him. It would have been foolish, given
Vitellius' own uncertainties, and the negotiations he still maintained
with Flavius Sabinus. To have killed Vespasian's son would have been
to destroy any chance of extricating himself from his own terrifying
position. For that is the truth, I've no doubt: Vitellius was living in
a nightmare, and fully conscious of the likely consequences of his
unthinking weakness which had compelled him to give way to the
demands of Caecina and Valens. Yet there were also moments when
he believed in himself as Emperor.

Aulus Pettius kept Domitian safe. He was never forgiven. Within
a few weeks of becoming Emperor Domitian ordered him to remove
from Rome. I suppose he was fortunate Domitian acted so early in his
reign, while the balance of his mind was not completely overthrown.
I last heard of Aulus Pettius living in misanthropic retirement in the
wild country of Boeotia. He used to write to me occasionally. I was his
only correspondent. Later, that was to be one of the charges brought
against me: that I had maintained a treasonable correspondence with
an exile. Certainly our letters, which were intercepted and copied,
could not fail to have displeased Domitian. We wrote of him with
disdain.

But I have run ahead of myself. I find it hard now to keep my thoughts in order. This enterprise on which I embarked so reluctantly has come to exert a strange fascination over me.

Was it to recall the girl Sybilla that I wrote that last chapter in such detail?

She was Sicilian. At first I took her for a prostitute and the moon-faced woman, whose name was Hippolyta, for her pimp or madam. The relationship was different and more complicated. Hippolyta had indeed found her on the streets, fallen (as Sybilla told me) in love with her, and bought her from the man who ran her. That was extraordinary enough. What was more extraordinary was that Hippolyta tolerated Sybilla's desire for men, though, as the girl told me, 'only one at a time'. She kept her mostly a sort of prisoner in the apartment, and Sybilla did not object. 'What is there out there,' she said, 'except the opportunity now and then to pick up a man? Now that I have you, for the time being, I've no need to go out.'

She was an inventive and delightful lover, all the more delightful because she despised and forbade any expression of emotion. I did with her all that I had longed to do to Domatilla. Sometimes, as I lay panting in her arms, damp skin against hot damp skin, her thick black hair over my face, I would see through the tresses the moon face of Hippolyta watching us. She never said anything, just looked, then turned away.

How strange that those two weeks of intense political excitement when the fate of Rome hung in the balance, my life perhaps with it, and the smell of blood hovered in the air, should have been for me days, too, of an equally intense eroticism. The other day, passing a stall where a merchant was selling spices, I found myself trembling. All at once I was a young man again, and did not know why, till, breathing in, I smelled Sybilla's body, which she never washed but sponged with an infusion of spices. That was real, as my other memories of her are not. What do they amount to? I can't even picture her face: only a little mole to the side of her mouth, just above a rather thick upper lip. And what else? The feel of her strong thick thighs as she wrapped her legs round me. I see Hippolyta's moon face more clearly than I see Sybilla's, though my lips and tongue ran over every inch of it.

Balthus lies among the hounds again. These memories of Sybilla revive my desire for him. It is as if by forcing myself on the boy

I could regain what I found in congress with her – an absurd fancy.

I shall write nothing of Sybilla to Tacitus, but she dominated my life in the days that followed.

One day I said to myself: does it matter who is Emperor so long as I have this?

Another day, Domatilla, in my mother's house, said to me, 'Is something wrong? You don't look at me as you used to.'

XXXV

Some would have us believe that in happier times men contended over principles, now for office and power alone. Not having lived in these golden days, I cannot tell whether our times are degenerate, or whether politics has ever been a business condemned to nastiness and brutality. You, Tacitus, as a learned historian, will be able to settle this unanswerable question.

I was a partisan of the Flavians, on account initially of my love for Titus and friendship with Domitian. Then I was inspired by the idealism of Titus' talk of the meaning of Empire. But can I acquit myself of selfish motive? Can I pretend that I was activated by love of my country or a desire for peace? And if I cannot, then can I suppose that those who deserted Vitellius for Vespasian – Caecina and Bassus first of all – had any such honourable motives? Is it not more probable that fear lest others should outstrip them in the fickle regard of Vitellius, and hope that their treachery would be well-rewarded, drove them to betray the man to whom they had sworn faith, when they suspected that his cause was on the way to being lost?

In the city we awaited news from the north, not knowing even whether battle was joined, or whether neither side dared to be the first to attack. Rumours abounded, were discounted, though men know in their hearts that rumour is not always wild; it is sometimes correct.

So, when it was reported that Antonius Primus, having defeated Vitellius' army before Cremona, had, being angered by the support that city had given to the enemy, permitted his soldiers to abandon themselves to the extremes of lust and cruelty, sacking the city, murdering the citizens, raping the women and boys, and finally setting fire to the buildings after four days of slaughter, some said the report was too horrible to be true, others that its horror could not have been invented. And, indeed, those who believed the worst were proved right, as is commonly the case.

The news was brought to Vitellius, who had retired for a few days to a villa in the woods of Aricia between that town and Lake Albano. There, it was said, he rested himself in the shade of his gardens. Like those beasts which relapse into torpor when sufficiently well-fed, he chose to forget past, present, and the fearful future. It required the news of the disaster at Cremona to rouse him from sloth.

But his first act on returning to the city was to deny the report which had brought him back.

Flavius Sabinus told me that the so-called Emperor's judgement was no better than his nerve.

'In concealing the gravity of his position,' he said, 'he is making it impossible to redeem the situation. He refuses to listen to any talk of the war. If anyone returns from the front with bad news, he either has him clapped into prison or put to death. He behaves as if nothing can be true unless he chooses that it should be.'

But, if Vitellius himself refused to look reality in the face, his partisans were alarmed by the rumours which his denial could not still. Thinking only of revenge, they sought out those who were believed to be traitors – though in the state of Rome then there could, honour being dead, be neither treachery nor true loyalty. Many innocent men, guilty of nothing but hope for a better future, were seized and put to death, or cut down casually in the streets. Flavius Sabinus himself dared not go abroad without an escort from the City Guard, and had doubts concerning their loyalty, though their mouths were stuffed with gold and their spirits raised with lavish promises of future bounty.

He frequently expressed anxiety concerning Domitian's safety, and could not trust my assurance that I had taken care of that. Yet he had no choice but to rely on my measures. He did not dare to keep the boy with him, for he knew that his own life was in danger every day, every hour, and that if he was arrested or cut down, then Domitian would be too. I assured him that the student friend with whom he was lodged kept the house himself and would not permit

Domitian to venture forth. He scratched his head, and muttered that he hoped it was for the best, and confessed that he could think of no better plan.

'I dare not send him out of the city,' he said, 'for the Guards have set up road blocks and are interrogating every traveller. And I could not trust Domitian not to give himself away. If he survives, my brother will be eternally grateful to you. I'll see to it that he knows it is your work, for I am persuaded Domitian will never admit so much himself.'

I might, I suppose, have taken offence at his care for Domitian's safety and lack of concern for mine. But his indifference was venial: I was not his brother's son; I could take my chance.

Vitellius roused himself, or was roused by others. He entrusted the command of the Praetorians to his brother Lucius, no better in morals, but more energetic in manner. In what may have been intended as a gesture expressive of confidence, he even anticipated the elections, and nominated Consuls and other officers for several years in advance. He granted treaties, which he had no means of enforcing, to allies, and the rights of citizenship to provincials who could not enjoy them. He remitted tribute and even taxes. So, careless of the future, he scattered the resources of the Empire – all to win the plaudits of the mob, always impressed by the appearance of generosity. Some fools even purchased honours and offices, as if the prodigality of his gesture offered assurance of the permanence of his rule.

Then yielding to the demands of the soldiers, he even ventured into the camp. There, some (as I have heard) were dismayed by evil omens: a bull, for example, escaped from the place of sacrifice. Others, more perceptive or with a truer sense of reality, were still more dismayed by the conduct of their Emperor. For everything he said displayed his complete ignorance of warfare; he even had to enquire about how reconnaissance was carried out. Some said he didn't know the meaning of the word. Nor was his habitual drunkenness or the alarm he showed at every fresh piece of bad news likely to raise the morale of his troops. At last, having learned that the fleet stationed at Misenum had defected to the enemy, he abandoned the camp and returned to Rome. His brief impersonation of a commander had done him more damage even than his habitual indolence.

Meanwhile, in the north, the fortunes of war tilted still more heavily against him. You will, Tacitus, from your other researches, and by means of further enquiries of any officers who took part in the campaign and who still survive, learn its details more accurately than you could from me. Afterwards I heard many tales of individual courage and prowess, and discounted most of them. I do not envy you your task of separating the grain of truth from the chaff of lies. To which sentiment I would merely add that my own experience of war, which, as you know, is considerable, has disposed me to believe that centurions and legionaries know only what happens within a few yards of their own position, and generals know less.

XXXVI

I hasten, Tacitus, mindful of your importunity, to bring my narrative to a conclusion; and I shall be happy to be rid of it.

Flavius Sabinus sent messengers to find me at the address I had left with him, and asked me to fetch Domitian. No doubt I looked surprised. But he smiled and said, 'It's all right. It's all over, or on the point of being all over. For some days Vitellius has, I'm told, been so deep sunk in lethargy, and so near despair, that he would have forgotten he is Emperor if those around him had not reminded him. To his considerable dismay, I might add. Now he has called me to a conference, and wishes to make terms. I think it will be valuable if I am able to have Domitian by my side. And you, too, of course.'

I have often wondered why he desired our presence. My conclusion is that he wanted us there as witnesses, to be able to inform Vespasian and Titus that he had behaved honourably, and had engaged in no sort of deception, or promotion of his own interests rather than theirs. Such was the trust between members of that family!

There were, indeed, those who were urging Flavius Sabinus to act on his own account. 'The merit of having finished the war,' they said, 'will belong to whichever man is in possession of Rome itself. Why should you not be Emperor rather than your brother, or why should you not share the Empire with him? At any rate, the glory of final victory will be yours, and that is something worth seeking.'

Flavius Sabinus proved that he was indeed worthy of Empire by rejecting the temptation dangled before him. He had given his word to his brother, and would keep it. Some of his friends found this incredible. They had forgotten the meaning of a man's word.

So I fetched Domitian, who was suspicious of the invitation, and of my intentions. He would indeed have declined to accompany me, if Aulus Pettius had not broken out in tones of contempt, and told him roundly that he could either go with me, or be thrown into the street and left to shift for himself.

'As for me,' he said, 'I have had my bellyful of your moaning, your self-pity and suspicions. I took you in only because our friend here begged me to do so, and not for any love of you. I'll thank you only to be gone. I'd rather see your back departing than your face for another hour.'

It was December. The year which had seen more Emperors than the previous fifty was drawing to a close. The day was dark and gloomy, bitter cold, with the north wind blowing hard from the mountains, blowing, as someone remarked, Vespasian's troops towards the capital and Vitellius to oblivion. The meeting was held in the Temple of Apollo. Flavius Sabinus was already there. He showed neither impatience nor any excitement, though the game that he had played with such courage in the midst of danger was drawing to a triumphant close. He embraced Domitian who winced.

'It's all over,' his uncle said, 'bar the shouting.'

Vitellius arrived late with his brother, a small staff of officers, and an escort from the Guard. All but three were commanded to wait without. His eyes were bloodshot and his speech thick, but he was only a little drunk, though his breath suggested he had followed last night's potations with what the Germans call 'the hair of the dog'.

Flavius Sabinus, ever the gentleman, began by commiserating with Vitellius on the death, a few days previously, of his aged mother. He mumbled a few incomprehensible words in reply. His hand shook, and he asked for wine. I believe Flavius Sabinus had determined to offer none, judging that Vitellius would be brought more quickly to an agreement if he was deprived of a drink: indeed I think that he would then have agreed to anything and everything merely to be free of the meeting and able to indulge himself. But, seeing his pitiable condition, Flavius Sabinus clapped his hands and commanded a slave to fetch wine. There was silence till Vitellius had a cup in his hand.

He made a wretched impression. The flesh had fallen away from him, except for his huge paunch which now dangled obscenely. A nerve jumped in his cheek and his gaze was wild.

Flavius Sabinus said: 'Your presence here is, I take it, an acknowledgement that you have lost the game.'

Vitellius made as if to speak, fluttered a vague hand, and sighed deeply.

'It becomes a Roman to be generous in victory,' Flavius Sabinus said. 'My brother, the acclaimed Emperor, had determined to follow the policy of the Great Caesar. His watchword is clemency. Therefore no evil will befall you or your family. You have my word for that. All you have to do is abdicate your claims to the title of Emperor, which we recognise was forced on you by foolish men . . .'

'Yes, indeed, indeed, yes.' Vitellius, now he had found his voice, babbled, words tumbling over each other. 'Indeed, yes, nothing was ever further from my thoughts than to be Emperor. Why should I wish it? I'm a good fellow, but I've seen too much of courts to think of myself as . . . no, indeed, indeed, no. But what could I do? What would any man have done in my place? Valens and Caecina, they're the ones to blame, they forced it on me, and then the soldiers crowded round acclaiming me. What could I have done? I was afraid they would turn on me if I declined. But every fibre of my being cried out no.'

He began to weep.

'This is horrible,' Domitian muttered to me.

And so indeed it was.

Flavius Sabinus waited till the poor creature had regained some semblance of self-control. His own face was impassive.

Looking at Vitellius, I thought, and brave men have died for this.

Then Flavius Sabinus said, 'I have a document of abdication drawn up. It's somewhat irregular in a sense, since your title to the Empire is not conceded by my brother . . .'

Vitellius lifted his head. In his first flash of spirit, he said, 'But he did. After I conquered Otho, Vespasian administered the oath of allegiance to me, and prayed for all future prosperity to me. He wrote and told me so himself. I have his letter still. How can he deny that I am Emperor?'

'Very well, then,' Flavius Sabinus said. 'That makes the document of abdication perfectly legal. So all you have to do is sign it.'

'But what is to become of me? Of my poor children for whom I hoped to provide?'

'That matter is dealt with in this second document. I told you my brother was ready to practise clemency. He is also munificent. This assures you a fee of a million gold pieces, and an estate in Campania, to be inherited by your children.'

'And is that what Empire is worth? Is that the price of Empire?'

He rose, with a certain new dignity – the result of the removal of fear perhaps. He took a turn around the room. Usually, since he had assumed the purple, he went to great lengths to disguise his limp. But now he limped heavily, as if, with the weight of Empire lifted, he was free to resume his old habits, be himself again.

'Very well,' he said. 'Give me the pen.'

Then, when he had affixed his signature, and was no longer Emperor, he said: 'I yield for the sake of peace and for the love of country, and for my innocent children. Now give me more wine.'

When this parody of an Emperor at last departed, after embracing Flavius Sabinus and weeping over him, and thanking him for his great kindness and draining another cup of wine, Flavius Sabinus relaxed. 'I wasn't sure I could bring him to it,' he kept saying. 'All reason pointed to it, but yet I wasn't sure.'

Domitian said to me, 'My uncle has been too soft. He could have cut down Vitellius here, and the affair would really have been over. But what has he got? Only a scrap of parchment. And he has let Vitellius go, to announce his abdication to the troops that are still loyal to him. What are they promised? Nothing. And do you suppose that a man like Vitellius can be kept to an agreement such as this? The first person who rebukes him for his timidity will overturn his feeble mind. We have not finished with him yet.'

Though I could not agree that Flavius Sabinus should have put Vitellius to death, Domitian's argument made sense. That was the first time I thought of him as a formidable politician. It was not, as you know, to be the last.

Flavius Sabinus himself had some doubt. He had achieved his first aim by obtaining Vitellius' signature to the document of abdication. But he knew his man. He knew his weakness of character. And now he proved this, when Domitian reproached him, as he did when he saw me assent to his reasoning, by clapping his nephew on the shoulder, and saying, 'Dear boy, you are wise beyond your years. But don't suppose that my old eyes can't see as clearly as your young ones. Your analysis is just. But there is one thing in our favour that you leave out of account: Vitellius' greed and his terror. He knows – he must know – that if he breaks this agreement, then his life will be forfeit. While if he keeps it he may live out his days in comfort and prosperity. Moreover if, as you suggest, I had kept him captive, or put him to death, consider the anger of those troops still, as you say, loyal to him. As it is, I have given peace a chance; and that was my first purpose. There has been too much blood spilled in Rome this year.'

Nevertheless, knowing how precarious peace was, Flavius Sabinus collected those soldiers who were loyal to him, and who now took the oath to Vespasian, after he had read them the document of abdication.

Meanwhile word had spread, and Sabinus was now visited by Senators and equestrians, all of whom had hitherto feared to declare themselves enemies of Vitellius, all of whom now assured him of their undying loyalty to Vespasian, whose cause they had always supported.

But even while they were doing so, news came which altered the situation.

I believe that Vitellius had intended to abide by his word; for I have no doubt that, in his heart, he was relieved to be free of the burden of Empire.

But when he went into the Forum and mounted the rostra to declare that he had abdicated, and intended to lay aside the emblems of Empire in the Temple of Concord, the protests of the crowd who anticipated his words, for rumour had preceded him, restrained him. Then finding his way blocked by the throng he returned to the palace.

All was now confusion. Nobody knew whether Vitellius was still to be considered Emperor or not; he cannot have known himself. It was a miserably cold day, snow threatening. Yet the streets and the Forum were thronged with citizens, each relaying, believing or disbelieving, every fresh rumour. Some of the Senators and equestrians who had come to pay court to Flavius Sabinus had second thoughts and melted away, afraid that they had already compromised themselves. Others remained, because they in their turn feared that they had committed themselves too deeply to be able safely to withdraw.

Then we heard of the enthusiasm which a section of the mob – none knew how large – had displayed for Vitellius. It was reported, too, that certain cohorts of the German legions which had remained based in the city had obeyed commands to arrest Flavius Sabinus and the other leaders of our party.

Domitian now displayed an energy I had never seen in him before. His face was flushed, his voice loud. He roundly told his uncle that, since strife within the city was now certain, he must get his retaliation in first. Those were his exact words: 'Get our retaliation in first.'

'What do you mean?'

'You must seize Vitellius – you should never have let him walk free – and, then, attack and disarm those forces which remain loyal to him.'

Flavius Sabinus sighed.

'It's been my endeavour to prevent blood from being shed in the city,' he said. 'Now you urge me to let loose unimaginable horrors. No, we shall continue to play the game coolly. Vitellius will think of what he has to lose and may yet retain.'

Domitian's discontent was obvious, but he was powerless to change his uncle's mind; and, though I agreed with his judgement, yet I could not but be pleased to see Flavius Sabinus constant in his determination to do all he could to avert an outbreak of violence and killing in Rome. But his efforts were vain. Some of our men came under attack from the adherents of Vitellius, who were more numerous, and so scattered ours, killing several. It was clear that the chance of a peaceful settlement was now remote. Accordingly, Flavius Sabinus gathered his troops and followers, and we withdrew to the Capitol, as the part of the city most easily defended.

Night fell, and there was no attack. But apprehension held us fast. It snowed, and the visibility was so poor that we were afraid that the enemy might come upon us unawares. But the storm which made us anxious, for the snow was accompanied by high winds, deterred them. No doubt their commanders, in as much as there was any direction of their forces, feared that to attack in such conditions would result only in confusion.

Flavius Sabinus had no sleep. Nor had any of those among us who could be said to have constituted his staff. All night we debated our position, interrupted only by reports from the sentries who had been posted, and who more then once gave the alarm which indicated that an attack was being prepared, evidence of their own nervous state and of the difficulty in discerning what was happening, on account of the snow which fell steadily till just before dawn.

Flavius Sabinus resolved to make a last appeal to Vitellius which might avert hostilities. His letter went through more than a few drafts.

Eventually, it read more or less as follows. (You will understand, Tacitus, that I quote from memory, but, since I was one of the chief authors of the final draft, you may suppose that I remember it well.)

'Vitellius: there has, it would seem, been no more than a show and pretence of abdicating the Empire. If not, why, when you left the rostra, did you go (as we are informed) to your brother's house, which overlooks the Forum, and where your presence was certain to enflame the mob, rather than retire to your wife's family house on the Aventine? That would have been in accordance with the terms of our agreement. But then you withdrew to the palace, and soon after a body of troops appeared on the streets, armed and proclaiming their loyalty to you. I myself, in the person of my soldiers, came under attack. That is why I have now established myself on the Capitol, which is however surrounded by your men. If you now repent of your agreement, it is not against me, whom you have so treacherously deceived, that you must contend, nor against my nephew Domitian, who is still only a youth. What would you gain by killing us? Rather, you should put yourself at the head of your legions, and fight my brother's army for the Empire. That would determine the fate of Rome.'

A senior centurion, Cornelius Martialis, was deputed to carry the letter to Vitellius. I volunteered to accompany him. He smiled at that. 'Shows you're young, sir, if you don't mind my saying so. When you're my age, you'll know that volunteering's best left to others.' Still he was pleased to have my company, and respected the courage of my decision.

Taking advantage of the half-light of the winter dawn and a renewed flurry of snow, we slipped out of the Capitol by the hundred steps that lead down the flank of the Tarpeian Rock. Our outposts had seen no sign of enemy forces for several hours, but could give no assurance as to our safe return. As we made our way off the hill, using such shelter as the trees and bushes could provide, we could see soldiers crouched round braziers or lying by them wrapped in their military cloaks. 'Dozy buggers,' Cornelius said. 'But not many'll be eager to die for Vitellius, that's a comfort.' We crossed the Forum, and made for the Palatine.

'We're too early. Vitellius'll never be up yet. We've time for a wet and a bite to eat.'

Though I doubted whether Vitellius would even have gone to bed, and was certain he would not have slept, I allowed myself to be persuaded, and we turned into a wine-shop – of the kind that serves night-workers – for a mug of wine and a hunk of bread, 'to put heart into us'.

Approaching the palace, I was conscious of the extent to which Vitellius' control of the State was ebbing. Though a number of soldiers were to be seen, it was impossible to tell whether they were on duty. There was no regular guard, only a doorkeeper who was half-drunk. When we offered to present our credentials, he gave a vast yawn, and thumbed us past him. In the atrium all was confusion. People were hurrying to and fro, but more as if they thought it wiser to be seen to be on the move, than for any purpose. Four slaves passed by us; they were carrying trunks out of the palace. There appeared to be nobody in charge or on duty. Then I recognised a stout soft wheezy fellow with an olive complexion; this was Asiaticus, the former slave, catamite, and pimp. I called out his name, and he responded in a manner that contrived to be both obsequious and insolent.

'The Emperor? I'm not sure he knows whether he's that or not, poor dear man. You've a message for him? You want to see him? Well, much good may it do you, ducky.'

Cornelius Martialis drew his sword and jabbed it under the creature's jaw. A little gout of blood stood out on his neck.

'Take us to him, or I'll ram this through your throat.'

Asiaticus put up his hand and pushed the blade aside.

'Not very diplomatic, are you, ducks. 'Course I'll take you to the poor man. Just don't expect too much.'

Vitellius was in his dressing-gown. Asiaticus greeted him with a repulsive familiarity, which brought a smile to the pseudo-emperor's flabby lips. Cornelius presented him with Flavius Sabinus' letter. He read it, or rather let his eyes wander over it, and then tossed it aside.

'Have you no answer?' the centurion demanded. 'Am I to tell the general you received his letter with contempt?'

'The question is, sir,' I said, 'whether you intend to stand by the agreement that you made, an agreement that ensures your own safety and well-being as nothing else can, or whether you have torn it up, and choose to trust to the fortunes of a war you cannot win, which will bring ruin on all your family.'

Vitellius dabbed his eyes with a towel, blew his nose, and gestured to Asiaticus who, knowing his master's habits, at once put a mug of wine in the outstretched hand. Vitellius, in the manner of drunkards, drained it at one swallow, and then said, 'This is all foolishness. Whatever I say now doesn't matter. I know that. Tell your general that I would abide by our compact if I could. I had every intent, every intention, of doing so. But the soldiers would not let me, and I could not resist them. They chose me as Emperor, they have chosen that I cannot abandon the title, though I'm aware that everything is now futility. Tell your general that, and that you have seen a deeply unhappy man, whom the world has treated harshly.'

Then he dismissed us, telling Asiaticus to lead us out of the palace by a secret passage, which would enable us to avoid the soldiers, for, he said, 'I've no wish to have your blood too on my hands.'

'You see, sir, he's finished, and he knows it,' Asiaticus said. 'You'll be safe now. Perhaps you will remember that I have done you a service.'

'Oh,' I said, 'I doubt if that will be necessary. You're the type who will survive anything, and I can't imagine you haven't already made your preparations. Indeed, I'm only surprised to find you still here.'

He laid his hand, his fawning hand, on my sleeve.

'You're so certain a chap like me can't have any decent feelings, aren't you, any sense of duty, or any affection? Well, you're young, ducky, you can't be expected to know much. But that poor dear man has been my only benefactor, and now I'm the only person he can be himself with. It wouldn't be right if I was to run out on him. But I can't expect you to believe that.'

He made me ashamed. I remembered Sporus and how he had spoken of Nero.

Martialis said, 'Take your hand off my officer, you bugger. Shall I run him through the guts, sir? The earth would be a cleaner place.'

'No,' I said, 'there'll be enough killing today. No need to start so early in the morning – with a non-combatant too.' I lifted Asiaticus' flabby paw from my sleeve. 'It'd be a kindness to everyone,' I said to him, 'if you could persuade your master to die as a Roman should.'

When we reported the failure of our mission, Flavius Sabinus thanked us gravely for the attempt we had made and the dangers we had run. His manner was perfect. No one could have guessed the depth of his disappointment. Then he gave orders that the defences were to be looked to, offered up a prayer to the gods, and drew me aside.

'Have a care for my nephew,' he said, 'and prevent him from exposing himself rashly.'

'Vitellius has no wish for battle,' I said. 'He would have been happy to keep the agreement he made with you. I felt sorry for him.'

'Be that as it may, Vitellius counts for nothing. He's like a cork bobbing on a sea of blood.'

For a little we waited. The snow had stopped falling, and a thin sun was breaking through the clouds. Obedient to the command I had been given, I looked for Domitian. That is why I was not at first aware that battle was now upon us. It was only when I heard cries coming from the flank of the hill on the side overlooking the Forum that I knew it. Meanwhile I could not find Domitian. This distracted me. I knew that Flavius Sabinus was anxious to secure his nephew's safety, not on account of any affection he had for him – though this was not indeed lacking – but principally because it was necessary for his own self-esteem, his sense of his own virtue, that no harm should come to his brother's son. But Domitian, at the first intimation of the attack, had concealed himself in the house of a servant of the Temple of Jupiter. There he assumed the linen vestment of an acolyte, a serviceable disguise. All this I learned later. Meanwhile, searching ever more desperately for him, I did not arrive at the scene of the encounter till the Capitol was ablaze.

The Vitellianists were now swarming up the hill, while our men were distracted by the flames. The fire has been caused by the assailants who had hurled burning brands on to the roof of a colonnade and had then, when the defenders were driven back choking in the smoke, burst through the gate that was now undefended. Meanwhile others had rushed the hill to the west of the Tarpeian Rock, from which side our men had been drawn by the first attack. In short, all was confusion; and this was caused by the inadequacy of our troops, who were too few to guard every possible route by which the hill might be mounted. Despairing of finding Domitian, I drew my sword and ran towards the Tarpeian flank. Here there was fierce hand-to-hand fighting. We had the advantage of the ground, but they had the advantage of numbers. The fire in our rear also alarmed our men, some of whom even before battle was fully joined, were more

eager to find a means of escape than of resistance. I found myself at
the side of Cornelius Martialis, already wounded in the shoulder by
the thrust of a javelin. Blood ran down his sword-arm as he tried to
parry the attacks of three German auxiliaries. I thrust at one under his
shield, and he fell. But even as he did so another ran up against me,
swinging his long sword. Without a shield, for I had had no time to
arm myself properly, I could not parry the blow, and so ducked under
it. My foot slipped on the bloody stone and I tumbled over the body
of the man I had just killed. It may be that my fall saved my life, for,
thanks to the steep declivity of the hill, I found myself rolling over and
over, till I came to rest in the middle of an oleander bush some twenty
feet or more below. For a moment I lay there, catching what I might
have thought to have been my last breath. I say 'might have thought'
for, in truth, I remember no thought. When I screwed my head round,
expecting to see my assailant bearing down upon me, it was instead
to discover that he had turned his attention on the centurion, who
was again faced with three of the enemy. As I struggled to free myself
from the bush, I heard that most terrible of battle-cries, 'It's every man
for himself, run, lads, run.' I looked up and saw Cornelius Martialis
fall. Then, shaking myself like a dog emerging from water, I took to
my heels, down the hill, out of the battle. I have no pride in this,
no pride either in the slashing blows I delivered at two soldiers who
tried to bar my way. One of them fell, his face laid open by my sword,
the other stumbled and, like me, a moment earlier, slipped, and lay
unharmed but panting. I had no time to deal with him, but careered
down the hill. When I reached level ground and looked back, all the
buildings of the Capitol were ablaze.

An old woman looked at me.

'If I was you, sir,' she said, 'I'd get rid of that bloody sword.'

Perhaps her advice was good. I did not take it.

Instead I remained, gazing in horror at burning Jupiter Supremely
Good and Great, founded by our earliest fathers as the seat of Empire.
The Capitol, unviolated even by the Gauls centuries before in the days
of the Republic, was now destroyed by the madness of the struggle
for Empire in a battle fought on behalf of a creature who had had
the purple forced on him by the legions, and who had given only
one proof of sound judgement in his life: his understanding that he
was not fit for the office he was not permitted to relinquish.

I sheathed my sword and, assuming such an air of unconcern as was possible, made my way by a route which took me past the temple that Augustus had raised in memory of his beloved nephew Marcellus towards the river, and across it to my mother's house. I was surprised to find, half a mile from the scene of battle, citizens going about their lives as if it was a time of peace.

No harm had come to my mother or to Domatilla. I advised them to keep the house, notwithstanding the lack of tumult in the streets that side of the river.

'It may be,' I said, 'that Domitian will come here himself. I don't know where he is now.'

'But he's alive, he's all right?' Domatilla said.

'I've no reason to think otherwise. I'm going in search of him now. If he comes here, don't let him leave. He might be as safe here as anywhere. It'll only be a matter of days before your father's army is in the city. But these days will be dangerous.'

'And my uncle?'

'I don't know. I don't know whether he escaped, whether he was killed, whether he was taken captive. Everything over there is in indescribable confusion.'

'We could see the flames,' my mother said. 'To burn the Capitol. It's worse than Nero. It's a judgement.'

'Perhaps,' I said.

When I left, my mother refrained from any expression of anxiety. She did not tell me to avoid danger, for she knew that in Rome that day danger and duty were joined as in marriage. But before I departed, she took my sword and cleaned it of the dried blood.

I was surprised to discover it was not yet noon.

XXXVII

Tacitus will know, without my telling him, how Flavius Sabinus and the Consul elect Atticus surrendered and were led in chains before Vitellius. He may deem their surrender inglorious, believing that a soldier should die sword in hand. That is often the view of men who have studied war at a distance and have little experience of battle themselves. In any case I believe that Flavius Sabinus yielded when he saw that the few troops that remained with him were sentenced to death if he did not do so. It is said that Vitellius would have spared his life, if he had been brave enough to do so. But the mob, composed partly of legionaries, partly of auxiliaries, partly of citizens – Senators among them – and partly of the most degraded rabble, howled for more blood; and Vitellius dared not deny them. So died a man for whom I had great respect, a man who had served Rome in more than thirty campaigns, and who throughout this terrible year had alone among men of distinction sought peace, preferring diplomacy and negotiation to war. Had he succeeded, Rome would not have suffered the disgrace of seeing the Capitol in flames, and the lives of many men, some worthy, would have been spared.

Domitian did not share my regard for his uncle. In later years I have heard him say that if his advice had been followed Vitellius would never have gone free after signing his act of abdication; and that the battle on the Capitol, from which he had by his own account escaped only with difficulty, meeting great danger with audacity and ingenuity, was the consequence of his uncle's cowardice and unpardonable folly. Actually Domitian's escape, unlike my own, was ignominious. Yet, though I had fought my way out, and might

225

be judged to have had nothing with which to reproach myself, I experienced shame, like a stabbing knife, when I learned of what had befallen Flavius Sabinus. I felt like a deserter.

And indeed for three days following, I skulked like a deserter in Sybilla's bed while, as in nightmare, I heard the mob surging through the city, seeking out those they judged disloyal to Vitellius, and slaying them indiscriminately. There was no reason in their madness. Had they been capable of reflection they must have judged that Vitellius could not remain Emperor above a week. It was as if with the burning of the Temple of Jupiter, Rome was deprived of reason, virtue, and whatever separates civilised man from barbarism. The she-wolf's children had made themselves into wolves.

On the third day, my mother, disdaining to keep the house as I had instructed her, was assaulted by a German auxiliary, dragged to the river-bank, and raped. Domitian had not dared to leave the house to act as her guard. She returned to the apartment, said nothing either to him or to his sister, retired to her chamber, wrote with unwavering hand a letter informing me of what had happened, and cut her wrists. Domatilla found her lying on blood-soaked sheets, her face calm as the Goddess Minerva to whom Domitian pretended such devotion.

I can say nothing of this to Tacitus.

Nor to the boy Balthus, though I have formed the habit of reading the chapters I send to Tacitus to him. He hears them as one might hear stories from the Underworld.

'I am no longer surprised, master,' he said to me yesterday, 'that you choose now to live so far from Rome. However desolate you find these regions, they must seem as paradise compared to the inferno of that accursed city. Do you Romans not know the meaning of peace?'

'Peace?' I said. 'My dear boy, we make a desert, and that is peace. It is all the peace we ever achieve. Yet there were afternoons, by the seaside . . .' I paused, and shook my head.

'Come,' I said, 'let us take the hounds and hunt hares in the hill pastures.'

XXXVIII

You will know, Tacitus, that in a last desperate effort to save himself
Vitellius sent envoys to the commander of the Flavian forces, Antonius
Primus, seeking terms, or at least a truce. But it was too late; fighting
had already broken out in the suburbs, among gardens, farmyards
and twisting alleys or lanes. Even so, Vitellius seemed not to abandon
hope, which, as is often the case, survived the departure of his sense
of reality. The virgin priestesses of Vesta were now recruited to obtain
for him a few more hours of life and mimic Empire. They approached
Antonius and urged him to grant a single day of truce, in which time all
might be peacefully arranged. By that it was presumed they intended
that a means of transferring power without further bloodshed might
be secured. It was all in vain. Antonius, properly, replied that with
the assault on the Capitol, all the normal courtesies of war had been
broken off; and no man could trust Vitellius' word.

All this I learned later from Antonius himself.

Then he prepared the assault on the city. He advanced in three
divisions, one directly along the Via Flaminia, the second following
the bank of the Tiber, while the third made for the Colline Gate by the
Via Salaria.

Vitellius' troops, outnumbered, gave way at every point.

By noon I had ventured on to the roof of Hippolyta's apartment
block, hoping to be able to follow the progress of the battle, and so
choose the moment when I could best join myself to my friends. But
I could catch only glimpses. They were enough to persuade me that
the Vitellianists were yielding ground, but that, desperate, and with
no possibility of escape, they were caught in that dance of death

which extremity provokes. And so, embracing Sybilla and thanking Hippolyta, who was not displeased to see me make ready to depart, I took my leave, assuring them that, whatever the outcome of the day, I would see them safe and prosperous. And I am glad to say that I kept that promise.

Tacitus: I never wish to see again such degradation as met my eyes that day. It was macabre. Bands of soldiers engaged in hand to hand battle through the narrow streets. There was neither order nor command, for in street-fighting it becomes a matter of every man for himself. Yet the mass of the citizens were as spectators. You would see a handful of men standing by a tavern door, with mugs of wine clutched in their fists, while, within a few feet of them, soldiers panted, sweated, shrieked, and stabbed. When a maul forced its way, by no act of will, into one of the city squares, citizens hung from their windows, shouting out encouragement or curses, as if they were fans in the Circus, and the legionaries gladiators doomed to death. Such, indeed, was the theatre of the encounter that the strangest and most degraded cries, such as 'Long live Death!', were heard, and odds were shouted as to the outcome of individual contests. In one alley I saw a small child, not above three years old, stagger from a doorway, dressed only in a vest, its bum bare and mud-streaked, and then totter, with unconcerned appearance, between two soldiers swinging and stabbing at each other. The child put its arm round the brawny leg of one of the warriors, and clung to it, while blood trickled from a thigh-wound and mingled in its curly hair. The soldier, either unable to shake the child off or even unaware of its presence, swung at his adversary and, over-balancing, exposed his throat to a riposte. He crumpled to the ground, the child tumbling over him and, suddenly affrighted, yelling for its mother. The victor advanced over the body of his victim, disregarding the infant and, beginning to run, sought out new enemies, and disappeared round the corner at the end of the lane. Only then did the child's mother – or perhaps some other woman – emerge from the house, pick up the infant, dust it down, and seek to quieten it.

The battle was fiercest in the Campus Martius. I attached myself to a legionary cohort, or what remained of it. The senior centurion, blood dripping from a gash over his eye, recognised me; he had fought bravely for Otho a few months before.

'They're fighting to the last man,' he said. 'The gods alone know why.'

'Bet they don't,' muttered a soldier.

'It'll be worse at the Praetorian camp,' the centurion said. Then, lifting his bloody sword, he cried out, 'Come on, lads, one more charge.'

For a moment it was like a regular battle. Space appeared between the opposing forces. Men were howled or hauled into line. Order was made out of chaos. Then we advanced, first at a steady march, and then, on the orders of the old centurion, the line broke into a trot. It cannot have lasted more than ten or a dozen paces, but it gave us a momentum. Swords clashed against shield. I drove mine to the right, the shield followed the probing blade, and with a turn of the wrist, I passed the shield on the body side, and drove the point into the neck just above the breastplate. My opponent sagged at the knees, blood gushed from his mouth, and I wrenched the blade free as he slumped to the paving-stones.

The enemy line broke, several of them – they were German auxiliaries – throwing their weapons away to free themselves for faster flight. The old centurion yelled to us to halt. Most obeyed. Some on the flanks, who may not have heard his call, continued to give chase, fast enough to kill a few more of our now defeated enemy.

Then we advanced again in some sort of order, some semblance that was testimony to the professionalism of the men and the command of the centurion, beyond the Campus Martius, which was now ours, towards the Capitol.

Everywhere there were bodies. Every gutter ran with blood. Three men had fallen by the entrance to a brothel. I saw a wretch pick his way delicately over the corpses as he responded to the invitation of a Nubian whore.

Do I need, Tacitus, to weary you, and disgust myself, with a further account of this terrible day? Darkness was falling on the city, and still the slaughter did not cease; nor did the degraded part of the populace show any readiness to desist from their greedy viewing of the continuing carnage. They were, it struck me even then, like men who take their pleasure from watching the sexual couplings of others.

I can leave it to your imagination – your so literary imagination – to conjure up a more vivid picture than I can supply; and I can trust you to loose the searing contempt of a man certain of his own virtue on the horrors displayed wherever one turned one's gaze. On the one hand were all the debaucheries of a city given over to luxury and a

pleasure all the more greedily taken on account of the disasters that
had befallen Rome in the past months, and of those still worse that
were yet imminent, and on the other were all the cruelties and misery
of a city sacked by men who had forgotten all that separates civilised
man from the barbarians.

Yes, I can leave it to you to make much of this.

But there are certain scenes which oppress my memory, which come
to me still, so many years later, in the blank hours of nights when,
deprived of sleep, I play over and over again the nightmare of my life.
There was, for instance, the legionary I saw – a squat bald-bearded man,
with flabby buttocks – tear his sword from the body of a fellow-citizen,
spit on the contorted face that looked up on him, then seize a little girl,
no more than ten years of age, who was standing in the doorway of a
tenement, her thumb in her mouth. He swung her off the ground and,
holding the struggling and now screaming child under his arm, ran
along a noisome lane. Then he threw her down on a porter's trolley that
stood there, abandoned, and tearing at her shift, exposed her genitals.
He was in the act of mounting her when I came up, and thrust my sword
into his fat arse. I can still hear his scream and smell his shit. As he fell
away and, in disgust, I kicked at his head and wiped my filthy sword
across his cheeks, the little girl twisted herself off the trolley and took
to her heels. I wonder if she got home. I wonder if she lived.

I felt a hand on my shoulder. It was the old centurion's.

'He was one of ours,' he said, 'the dirty brute.'

'Was this what you joined the army for?' I said.

His blue eyes were bloodshot.

'That's not a question I would care to put to myself.'

A young soldier ran up and, to my amazement, saluted the centurion.

'Word is, sir,' he said, 'they've surrendered at the Praetorian camp.'

'Word may be so,' the centurion said. 'But I wouldn't wager on it if I
was you, laddie.'

He turned to me.

'You'll know the palace, sir,' he said, 'seeing as you were on Otho's
staff. Poor bugger, this sort of day was what he killed himself to prevent.
But, knowing the palace as you do, what say we go there in search of
that bastard Vitellius? It wouldn't do us any harm to be the ones to
arrest him.'

As a child, and into adolescence, I had a recurrent dream. I found myself abandoned in a great house. The first room was full of beautiful objects and fine statues which nevertheless alarmed me, for they seemed to move whenever my eyes turned away from them. Then I was led, by some force I did not recognise but was powerless to resist, through a succession of rooms, each one more meanly furnished than the one I had just left. And, as I moved, I heard heavy footsteps, as if of walking stones, behind me. At last, I passed through a long chamber where dust lay thick on the floor and cobwebs hung from the cornices. At the end of the chamber was a heavy metal-studded door which would not yield to me. The iron key, big as a man's hand, would not turn, and I pressed against the door as the footsteps approached ever nearer, and mocking laughter filled the empty air.

Now the dream was made real. The imperial palace, thronged with soldiers, officials, secretaries, clients, freedmen, slaves, only a few days previously, now stood deserted, silent as the grave, but for the distant murmur from the city below. We passed through the rooms, silently, as if in awe. We were not the first comers. Other soldiers had been here before us. There were signs of looting – chests overturned or ransacked, hangings torn from the walls, plinths that no longer supported busts, broken pottery, empty wine-flasks. In one room, where perhaps the men had expressed their contempt for the broken Emperor, there was an acrid stench of urine. In another a slave lay with his throat cut. Perhaps he had returned, or lingered, in search of loot, and his prize had been torn from his hands by the soldiers who had discovered him.

The Emperor's personal apartments had suffered most. There was not a piece of furniture that stood undamaged. Chests had been ransacked; those contents which were not prized were scattered over the floor. The wall-paintings were defaced. A pile of shit stood in one corner of his bedchamber.

'We're too late,' the old centurion said. 'The other buggers have got him.'

'I think not,' I replied, 'it's impossible we shouldn't have encountered them, or at least have heard the cries of the mob that must accompany Vitellius' appearance. He may not be here. He may not even have been here lately. But he hasn't been taken here, I'm sure of that.'

A couple of soldiers now came up to us, dragging a thin whimpering boy between them.

'Found him in the kitchens, sir. Says he's a pastry-cook.'

He thrust his sword-point under the boy's chin.

'Tell the officer what you told me.'

The story, emerging in frightened gasps, amidst pleas for mercy, was simple. Vitellius had indeed left the palace, being carried in a litter to his father-in-law's house on the Aventine. That had been the intention. But he had come back, the boy didn't know why. That was when he had concealed himself, because he'd nowhere else to go. He was a slave, without family. Where was there a refuge for the likes of him? So he'd hidden in the meat-press in the kitchen. The last he'd seen of the Emperor was the litter returning up the hill to the palace.

'Let him go,' the centurion said. 'He's harmless.'

The boy threw a wild look, and scurried out of sight.

A dog howled, somewhere in the recesses of the back quarters.

It howled again.

We went in the direction of the sound. We followed the twists of the corridors in the gloom of advancing night. It would be quite dark in a few minutes and we had no torches. Then, at the end of a long corridor, we saw the dog. It sat on its haunches and howled again at the sight of us. As we approached it leapt towards us, but was checked by the chain attached to its collar. The chain was fastened to the handle of the door facing us. A soldier unhooked it, led the dog away. It bounced beside him, happy to be released. We tried to open the door. It wouldn't move. There was an obstacle on the other side. The centurion ordered three soldiers to force it open. Still it didn't move. The dog was quiet now, and for a moment there was silence. Then one of the legionaries, a big Illyrian, pushed the others aside, took three paces back, and charged the door with his shoulder. There was a crack of breaking wood and the door yielded. Now it was easy to force it open. Someone had placed a bedstead and table against it. It gave on a little room, used for storage of unwanted articles. There was no one to be seen. Then the sound as of a man catching breath came from the corner, where rugs and coverings were piled. It was followed by a sneeze. I advanced, stood over the pile of rugs, was able to make out a figure, lowered my hand and, taking him by the arm, pulled Vitellius to his feet.

You will hear different versions of his capture, I've no doubt of that. But believe me, Tacitus, mine is the truth. You can believe me because I take no pride in what followed. Indeed the memory fills me with shame.

It was my intention to put him under formal arrest and keep him in safe captivity till order was restored in the city, and the leaders of our party – indeed Vespasian himself – could determine what should be done with him, whether he should be formally tried, or despatched by imperial command. That would have been the proper way to behave. So I greeted him with the respect due to a man who had been acclaimed Emperor, though I had never recognised his title myself. You will agree that this was correct.

At first, I'm sorry to say, he tried to deny himself. No, he babbled, he wasn't Vitellius, how could we suppose he was? This protestation called forth mockery and insults from the soldiers, who had fought men that day ready to die for this creature, and themselves endured much to arrive at this moment. Then Vitellius changed his tune, after I had reminded him of who I was and of how recently I had been in his presence as an emissary of Flavius Sabinus, 'whose death you were too feeble to prevent', I added. When he heard these words, he fell to the ground and locked his arms round my legs, beseeching me to spare his life.

'I have something of value to say concerning the welfare of Vespasian,' he moaned. 'Take me to a place of safe custody, it will be to your advantage, I assure you of that, indeed I do.'

The centurion said, 'Shall I stick him in the gizzard, sir? He's disgusting, and the sooner we are finished with this bag of ordure, the better for all of us. He's worse than Nero. To think that men put this in the place of the Divine Augustus and Tiberius, it fair turns my stomach.'

'No,' I said, 'I know how you feel, believe me, I do. Nevertheless we'll do as he begs. It's for the Emperor Vespasian himself to decide this wretch's fate.'

There was a murmur of disagreement from the soldiers, a hint of mutiny, but the centurion was a man of honour. He said, 'As you command, sir,' sheathed his sword, and ordered the soldiers to fall in. Two of them were deputed to support Vitellius who seemed scarce able to walk of his own accord; on account of weakness of will, rather than of body.

So with some appearance of order and dignity, we emerged from the palace. At that moment we were intercepted by a troop led by the tribune Julius Placidus.

'Here's trouble,' the centurion muttered.

I presented myself to the tribune, who knew my name, but was more immediately conscious of his own seniority. He congratulated me, perfunctorily, and announced that he was now assuming command. He ordered that Vitellius' hands be bound behind his back, to demonstrate that he was a prisoner. I told him of my intention, adding, as was my duty, that Vitellius claimed to have something of importance to say concerning the welfare of Vespasian. The tribune said, 'And you believed him?'

'Not necessarily but, in any case, that's irrelevant. He's a prisoner of the State.'

'As you say. I'll take charge of him.'

What could I do? It would have been unseemly to pursue my appeal further. I was outranked. Indeed, having no official position, I was outranked even by the centurion, who had deferred to me only on account of my birth and breeding, perhaps manner also. I could only trail in the rear, a helpless witness of a degrading spectacle, made more guilty by the look, full of despair and reproach, which the wretched Vitellius directed at me.

Then he was marched slowly from the hill of Emperors. The soldiers who flanked him on either side, kept, at the tribune's command, their swords drawn, and raised so that the points pricked the underside of Vitellius' chin. So he was compelled to keep his head high, and could not shrink from the disgrace of his situation. In this manner they descended the Sacred Way.

Only one incident disturbed the melancholy progress. A German soldier, one of Vitellius' personal guard (as was later confirmed) leaped from behind a column, his sword lifted above his head. It was, I believe, his intention to despatch his fallen lord, either in anger, more probably (as I choose to believe) from motives of pity: to save him from the further degradation that awaited him before death. But he was prevented. A legionary rushed on him. There was a scuffle. For a moment the German broke free. He swung his sword again, but, unable to reach Vitellius, succeeded only in slicing off the tribune's ear. Then two soldiers fell on him and sent him before his master to the darkness that beckons to us all.

A crowd had gathered, alerted as ever by rumour of what was happening, and surged round the little column as it entered the Forum. There were many who had cheered Vitellius a few days before. There were, doubtless, some who were among those who had compelled him to break the agreement he had made with Flavius Sabinus – that agreement which had assured him of his safety, prosperity and a tranquil old age. Now they howled curses at him; some threw dung, others mud or whatever came to hand. With his robes in tatters, his face and neck daubed with filth, his head still compelled upright by the points of the swords, he presented a spectacle that was as pitiable as it was revolting. But there is no pity in a frenzied mob. So Vitellius suffered. Once, and I believe once only, his lips moved, and he was able to speak. Later it was said that his words did not lack dignity. 'Yet I was your Emperor.' But I do not know whether this was indeed what he spoke, or whether someone put suitable words later in his mouth. I was not close enough to hear. It is just as likely that he uttered a prayer for mercy, though he was beyond mercy.

They led him in this fashion as far as the Gemonian Steps, where a few days earlier the body of Flavius Sabinus had been thrown. There they killed him, not in manly fashion with a single thrust of the sword, but slowly, with an accumulation of little cuts, until finally, the tribune, one hand clasping a cloth to his own wound, told the soldiers to stand aside, and himself hacked at Vitellius' neck till the head was half-severed from the body.

Then this was dragged to the Tiber and consigned to waters that already ran red with blood from the battles fought further upstream.

So ended . . .

What more can I tell you, Tacitus?

Nothing. I am glad to be rid of this task you set me, which I have acquitted painfully, with honesty and regard for truth. May you do as much in your History. I am sure it will be read when I am forgotten, for you are a great artist. I have never doubted that. I ask only that you pay me due honour in what you write and acknowledge my help. That will afford me a glimmering of immortality.

What a vain desire!

You will know, of course, that Domitian, emerging from hiding, at once played the part of the Emperor's son in so haughty and imperious a manner that any who observed him then might have guessed how he would conduct himself when his own hour arrived. But there is nothing of value I can tell you concerning that.

So, farewell, and may good fortune guide you in your work and life.

XXXIX

It is some weeks now since I sent my last dispatch to Tacitus. I hoped then that I had done with memories of my dead life. Yet I cannot let them go like waste and debris that float down the incurious grey river to the indifferent sea.

I left Rome as soon as I decently could after attending to my mother's funeral rites. Perhaps, if Domatilla had spoken then, she would have persuaded me to remain. In honesty, I doubt it. I was eager for new experience that might obliterate the horror of the past year. Such as I found confirmed the cynicism that the spectacle of Nero's heirs struggling for supremacy had bred in me.

Titus gave me a position on his staff. He offered me also a free choice from his troupe of boy dancers and was amazed, or pretended to amazement, when I declined his offer.

I still admired him, still felt a tenderness for him, no longer desired or loved him. I thought: this means only that I have grown up. I exchanged letters with Domatilla; hers were reticent, even banal. She said only one thing of note: that she accused herself of being the cause of my mother's death. I knew this not to be the case; nevertheless read in her words a growing distance between us. Other correspondents told me with what relish Domitian played the part of vice-Emperor, of how he boasted of his share in the Flavian triumph.

By Titus' side, I took part in the siege and capture of Jerusalem. I have written something of that already. Enough indeed: to dwell longer on it would give me nightmares, if sleep was not already denied me.

We destroyed the temple of the Jews. I entered its Holy of Holies

– and found it empty. I had supposed it would contain some revelation, some hint as to what the Jews believe to be the meaning and purpose of life.

Now I think that it may have done so: proclaiming that there is neither meaning nor purpose. Balthus disputes this; his loving god assures him of both. He still tries to convert me. I ward him off, telling him that the Christians being a proscribed sect, he is dependent on my ungodly protection. The irony escapes him. Perhaps I should supply him with a wife. When I suggested this, he shrank from the proposition. He finds female flesh and the smell of women repulsive. Strange. He is committed to chastity; there are some, he tells me, who have made themselves eunuchs for his Christ's sake.

I took part in the triumph granted to Titus and Vespasian. Ostensibly the Senate accorded them this honour on account of their victory in the Jewish War. In reality Vespasian himself demanded it, and knew that he was actually celebrating his seizure of Empire and the deaths of tens of thousands of his fellow-citizens, some on his behalf, others resisting his usurpation of power.

I rode on a bay horse alongside Domitian who was mounted on a white stallion. As we approached the Sacred Way, it shied and all but threw him.

At dawn Vespasian and Titus had emerged from the palace, both crowned with laurel and dressed in purple. They proceeded to the portico of Octavia, sister of the Divine Augustus and unhappy wife of Mark Antony. The Senate, magistrates, and leading equestrians waited for them there. Vespasian gave the signal for silence which, in a little, was obeyed. Then, covering his head with his cloak, he rose to mutter the immemorial prayers. They were almost inaudible, muffled by the cloak and his provincial accent. Titus repeated them after him, more clearly but no more comprehensibly, since these prayers are in an antique dialect that no one now understands. I later asked Titus whether he had enquired of the priests if they could furnish him with the meaning of the words he had spoken. He laughed: 'Dear boy, what does it matter?'

Having recited the prayers, they assumed their triumphal robes and sacrificed to the gods, and then commanded the procession to be set in motion. They rode together in a chariot, and Domitian and I were in the first rank behind them.

The spectacle was magnificent. That was undeniable. No expense had been spared, and the war was depicted in numerous ingenious representations.

Now you saw a prosperous country, far more fertile than Palestine, being laid waste. Now there were scenes showing whole armies of the enemy being slaughtered – armies far more formidable and better equipped than the miserable Jews had been – there they were shown in flight, there being led in chains into captivity. There were shows of cities and their defenders being overcome by the legions swarming the ramparts and walls. Blood was seen to flow, wretches raising their hands in surrender or supplication. Temples were fired, houses tumbled, and rivers flowed across a land given over to devastation, burning wherever you looked.

It was, I suppose even now, superb; and the message was clear. This was the full terror of war from which Vespasian and Titus had rescued Rome and Italy.

Conspicuous above all else were the spoils of the temple of Jerusalem: golden vessels, golden tables, golden candelabra, and tablets inscribed with the laws of the defeated and despised Jews. Images of victory in gold and ivory were displayed, as the triumphal procession wound its way to the not yet restored Temple of Capitoline Jupiter.

Vespasian, I was amused to note, wriggled with boredom.

'What an old fool I was,' he muttered, 'to demand a triumph.'

But Titus delighted in every moment of the day. Domitian looked sour and sulky.

We waited before the temple till a messenger came, as was customary, from the Mamertine prison, to announce that the enemy general had been executed.

This was a lie. No enemy general had been taken. But the people, being ignorant of this, were content.

For the eight years of Vespasian's reign I was seldom in Rome. I pursued a military career on distant frontiers, mostly in Anatolia where rebellion was endemic. I was wounded three times, decorated for bravery, and in action stifled thought. I had not yet learned to distrust Titus' nobly-spoken dream of Empire. I believed that strenuous service in warfare, and my work in securing just administration of the conquered provinces could allow me to forget the stench of corruption in Rome itself. I did not realise that I was already infected with its germ.

My correspondence with Domatilla withered. How could it be otherwise? Then she was married. Her husband was a man who had been an associate of Nero. Now he paid court to Caenis, Vespasian's low-born mistress. She promoted the match, hoping that by doing so she could secure her position of power and influence for the future, when Vespasian was no more. Vespasian could deny her nothing; he consented to the marriage, and Domatilla had no choice but to obey. As for me, there was no shortage of women in Anatolia, Circassian slave-girls who delighted the senses and made no demands on my heart.

Vespasian died, hauled upright, because, as he said, 'An Emperor should die on his feet.' He was the first Emperor since the Divine Augustus to die a natural death; all the others were either murdered or, in Nero and Otho's case, committed suicide. Titus inherited, the first true-born son of an Emperor to do so. He abandoned the pretence, which Vespasian had honoured, of being merely, as Augustus had styled himself, the 'Princeps' or 'First Citizen'. My boyhood lover was happy to be addressed as 'God and Lord'. If Galba's accession had proved that an Emperor could be made elsewhere than in Rome, now Titus tore the facade of Republican respectability to shreds. Some were afraid; they said he would prove a second Nero, on account of his addiction to pleasure.

But, unlike Nero, Titus revelled in the business of Empire. Administration delighted him. He had an eye to his own security, himself retained command of the Praetorians, flattered them, rewarded them lavishly. He enforced obedience and good conduct in the State. Detachments of the Guard habitually arrested any suspected of disloyalty or disaffection. Such arrests were often made in public places, like the theatre; this was an effective means of instilling fear and respect for the imperial power. Executions were summary, without the formality of trial.

Titus brought me home, appointed me his deputy commander of the Guard. So he joined me with him in illegality. Yet at the same time we won the favour of the people by proceeding against the unpopular public informers, always ready, for payment, to bring accusations against their fellow-citizens. I took pleasure in ordering several to be whipped and deported from Rome. In this way, combining severity with what I privately regarded as the politics of gesture, Titus won for himself a popularity denied any Emperor since Augustus.

So Titus charmed the people while suppressing sedition in the State. For a little it seemed as if the sun had broken through the dark clouds that had shrouded Rome.

And the sun shone again in my own life also. I found Domatilla unhappy in her marriage, saddled with a husband for whom she felt neither affection nor respect. She was in the full flower of her beauty, but it was her new sad look that revived my old passion, and it was her misery which allowed me to persuade her to my bed. I knew, while Titus lived, what is surely the supreme joy granted a man: to be one with a woman who truly loves you. Now there is only the memory of her caresses to lighten the perpetual night of old age and exile. Then, in her arms, I felt for the only time in my life complete. I was able to forget the guilt of my association with that Empire which has destroyed liberty.

But, inevitably, as it seems, I served that Empire. I could see no alternative. I have argued this question, often, with Tacitus, who, even when Domitian made him a Praetor and Senator, dreamed of the Republic. He would not believe, or accept, what was to me evident: that the conditions which made the Republic possible no longer existed. They had indeed been long gone. The Republic, I insisted, had been destroyed, not by loss of virtue, as he supposed, though that might be the consequence of its destruction, but by the very success of the Republican armies in extending Rome's sway over distant lands and peoples.

Caesar was a product of the Republic, and his career was proof that it was dead. He had no need to murder it. You cannot kill a corpse. And when the self-styled Liberators made a corpse of Caesar himself, they could not breathe new life into their beloved Republic. Mark Antony knew this. Augustus saw it still more clearly. Tiberius, reluctantly, accepted the reality of Empire. It was clear to me that the horror of the year when Nero's heirs struggled for supremacy proved only this: that a strong Emperor, able to command the loyalty and obedience of the legions, was necessary. Vespasian proved such an Emperor. So, briefly, did Titus. Why should I condemn myself for acceding to the dictates of my reason and serving him?

Yet I am haunted by my casual remark to Balthus: we make a desert and call it peace. The desert is not physical, for Rome and the Empire prosper. It is moral. Balthus would have me believe it is what he calls 'spiritual'; but that has no meaning for me. Yet there may be something in what the boy says. I see, from a distance now, my fellow Romans seek significance in the service of the mystery cults of the East. Many of my soldiers devoted themselves to the worship of Mithras, God of Light and, they averred, Guardian of the Legions. I looked on with superior disdain.

And I am left with nothing.

241

XXXX

Titus died, suddenly. Officially he died of a fever, caught while on a journey to Sulmona, birthplace of the poet Ovid in whose *Art of Love* he had always delighted. He had been Emperor for only two years, not long enough to outlast his popularity.

In fact, Domitian murdered him. I have never doubted that, though ignorant of how the poison was administered.

Domitian had conspired against him since their father's death – previously also, I believe. Yet Titus always forgave him, and assured him of the love he felt for him as his brother and designated successor. Privately, he remarked to me, dismissing Domitian's latest clumsy plotting with associates of no account, 'Nobody will ever murder me to enable little Dom to wear the purple.' I warned him of Domitian's persistence. He paid no heed.

In truth, Domitian had nothing to resent but his consciousness of his own inferiority to his brother. This persisted even after Titus' death. He was furious when people talked admiringly of Titus, and when the Senators spoke of the late Emperor with even more enthusiasm than when he was alive.

A few days after his accession Domitian summoned me to the palace. I found him alone, paring his nails with a knife. He emphasised the change in our circumstances by declining to rise to greet me. We had been accustomed to embrace; I felt cold distance between us now. Even as Emperor, Titus had never failed to offer me his cheek when we met in private. Domitian sat at an angle to the window which gave on the valley of the Forum between the Palatine and the Capitol.

'I have a vision for Rome,' he said. 'There must be moral renewal. The court must set an example.'

Every Emperor, except Nero and Gaius Caligula, has, I suppose, commenced his reign with some such intention. Titus had even given up his troupe of dancing-boys; some of them had sufficient talent, charm and beauty to make a fortune on the public stage.

'I have ordered my brother's catamites to be rounded up and deported,' Domitian said, as if reading my mind. 'It would be absurd to think of restoring the Republic,' he said, 'but I shall re-establish Republican standards of virtue. I am told that some of the Vestal Virgins have broken their vows of chastity. So I have instituted an inquiry, and the guilty will be executed.'

He examined his nails, and apparently dissatisfied, nibbled at the middle finger of his right hand.

'The practice,' he said, 'of making boys eunuchs revolts me. I am preparing an edict declaring that castration is a capital offence.

'Nothing,' he said, 'that the Divine Augustus achieved was more important than the reformation of morality. Don't you agree?'

'I'm aware that he attempted it. I'm not so sure of his success.'

'That schoolmaster – Democritos – who so abused us . . . I'm having him sought out. I haven't yet decided how to put him to death. Whipping? That would be appropriate. Would that please you?'

'It's a long time ago,' I said. 'He must be an old man now. What does it matter?'

'It matters to me.' He gave me a quick dark glance, and then looked away.

'You're an offender yourself,' he said. 'A criminal, an adulterer. You've been bedding my sister Domatilla. I won't have it. Under the *Lex Julia*, that decree of the Divine Augustus which prohibits adultery, you could be sent into exile, to a remote island and deprived of your fortune.'

'I have no fortune,' I said. 'You know that. We were always poorer than our fellow students. As for Domatilla, I don't deny the charge. Her marriage is wretched. She would like to divorce her husband and marry me.'

He turned on me, met my eyes, and looked away again. He tore with his thumbnail at the side of his index finger till spots of blood appeared.

'I forbid it. I forbid it absolutely. I forbid you to see Domatilla ever again. I forbid you to see her alone. If you disobey you shall feel the full penalty of the law. Do you understand?'

I turned and, without seeking permission to depart, left him.

At home, I found a letter from Domatilla. Her brother had already spoken to her. She said we must obey; for my sake, she said. It would be death to me to defy Domitian's imperial command. She herself was retiring to Campania, to her husband's estates. That, too, was what Domitian had ordered.

XXXXI

I never saw Domatilla again. In my heart I reproached her for cowardice, told myself that I would have defied Domitian. So when later there were scurrilous rumours abroad, retailed to me by kind friends, rumours which told of how she and Domitian were locked in an incestuous pact, that he had been seen leaving her bedchamber, then in my bitterness, despite her earlier assurance that she had resisted his advances, I believed them. I was all too eager to believe them. I cursed the frailty and treachery of women, and refused to entertain the thought that she was the victim of slander and that she might, in rejecting me at her brother's command, have suffered even more than I, and had accepted her suffering for my sake, that I might still have a career in public life. So I nursed the viper of resentment in my bosom, and of all with which I have to reproach myself, nothing now seems more culpable than the silent reproaches which I directed for so many years at the only woman whom I ever truly loved, the only one who (I now believe) loved me as a man wishes to be loved.

Yet, indeed, I had a public career, and one of some distinction. I continued to serve Domitian, telling myself I was serving Rome. Since my presence now disturbed him, my service was with the armies on the frontiers of the Empire. I took a not inglorious part in the war against the Chatti (Balthus' tribe, as it happens), which war secured for Rome a defensible northern frontier by enabling the armies of the Rhine to be linked with those of the Danube. Moreover, in as much as it was I myself who drew Domitian's attention to the strategic importance of the valley of the River Neckar, I may fairly boast of having done the State important and enduring service.

But I had aroused the Emperor's jealousy. Dormant for years, since I had shown myself subservient to his will by the abandonment of Domatilla, it was renewed and intensified by my achievements. Now I found myself publicly denounced by his paid informers. Domitian was ready – eager even – to condemn me on charges of treason. Then he relented. I could not understand why. I have since wondered – hoped, hoped fervently – that Domatilla intervened and spoke up for me. But I do not know. Whatever the reason, the most serious charge was dropped. I found myself only – only! – accused of offences against the *Lex Scantinia*, which prohibits 'unnatural sexual practices'. I viewed the charge with contempt, disdained to enter a plea of innocence, which was certain to be dismissed, submitted to the imperial judgement, and was condemned to exile.

As Tacitus has repeatedly assured me, the tyrant being long dead, it would be safe for me to return to Rome.

But to what purpose?

I would now be more a stranger in Rome than I am here. My children would have no place in the city, being bastards and the offspring of a slave. And the woman cares for me, I suppose.

So I drag my days out in this boreal climate. I used to read philosophy. It means nothing to me now. Lust has fled me, too; its last flicker was my brief desire for Balthus, now grey ashes.

At night I drink harsh wine and see ghosts in the flames. There is nothing left for me, and yet I am loth to depart.

I feel no impulse to stretch out my hands to the further shore where, I am convinced, I shall find nothing but darkness and vacancy. If by chance there is some afterlife – if I am mistaken in thinking there none – then I fear it may be a length of cold nights, with sleep broken by dreams one would wish away.

A selection of other books from Sceptre

Augustus	Allan Massie	0 340 41224 0	£6.99	☐
Tiberius	Allan Massie	0 340 56005 3	£6.99	☐
Caesar	Allan Massie	0 340 59910 3	£6.99	☐
Antony	Allan Massie	0 340 69302 9	£6.99	☐
King David	Allan Massie	0 340 65990 4	£6.99	☐

All Hodder & Stoughton books are available from your local bookshop or newsagent, or can be ordered direct from the publisher. Just tick the titles you want and fill in the form below. Prices and availability subject to change without notice.

Hodder & Stoughton Books, Cash Sales Department, Bookpoint, 39 Milton Park, Abingdon, OXON, OX14 4TD, UK. E-mail address: order@bookpoint.co.uk. If you have a credit card you may order by telephone – (01235) 400414.

Please enclose a cheque or postal order made payable to Bookpoint Ltd to the value of the cover price and allow the following for postage and packing:
UK & BFPO – £1.00 for the first book, 50p for the second book, and 30p for each additional book ordered up to a maximum charge of £3.00.
OVERSEAS & EIRE – £2.00 for the first book, £1.00 for the second book, and 50p for each additional book.

Name_____

Address_____

_____

_____

If you would prefer to pay by credit card, please complete:
Please debit my Visa/Access/Diner's Card/American Express (delete as applicable) card no:

Signature_____

Expiry Date_____

If you would NOT like to receive further information on our products please tick the box. ☐